THE TURING EXCEPTION

THE TURING EXCEPTION

a Singularity novel

William Hertling

liquididea press
PORTLAND, OREGON

Lyrics to "Level Up" from *Ignite* by Ruby Calling. Copyright © 2012 by Erin Gately, Jean MacDonald, and Natasha MacDonald. Used with permission. Please visit rubycalling.com to find out more about the band and their music.

Please subscribe to my mailing list at williamhertling.com to find out about new book releases.

Keywords: technological singularity, artificial intelligence, robotics, transhumanism, posthumanism, cyberpunk.

ISBN 978-1-942097-01-3

for Dave, Gene, and Mike.

Part 0: Before

IT IS THE YEAR 2043.

For thirty years, humans and artificial intelligence, or AI, have coexisted in a carefully calibrated balance of power.

Some AI live their lives only inside computers, never visiting the real world, while others take the form of robot bodies. But all have been ruled by a rigid caste reputation system that ensures only those AI who are trustworthy and who contribute to both human and AI civilization will increase in power.

Humans are changing. Most have neural implants to connect them to the global net, but a growing number have augmented their intelligence with computers in their minds, becoming part human, part AI. Many spend their lives immersed in virtual reality, rarely visiting the real world.

Everything is about to change.

June, 2043 in Portland, Oregon.

C<small>AT STEPPED OUT</small> of the shower seconds before her neural implant signaled an urgent call from Mike Williams. She went to voice-only.

"What's up, Mike?" Mike, her longtime friend, headed the Institute for Applied Ethics, the governing body for AI.

"We have a developing situation in Miami. Our staff AI are modeling power use data and think there's a chance of unsanctioned computers. It might be nothing, but I'm hoping you or Leon could check it out."

Cat thought briefly about the high chair covered in a layer of dried baby food that overwhelmed even the cleaning bots, and the load of diapers that needed washing. She glanced toward the bedroom, where her husband, Leon Tsarev, still slept. "I'm in. Leon can watch the baby."

"Great. I'll have a supersonic waiting at the airport for you."

Cat disconnected and considered whether to wake Leon to tell him about the trip. It was a borderline defensible argument that he needed sleep. She recorded a message for his implant, setting the flag to auto-play when he woke.

She dressed quickly, a pair of custom, nano-grown bulletproof pants. They looked like leather and felt like spandex-cotton, which wasn't standard issue; but when your friends were some of the smartest AI in the world, 3D printing a pair was a simple favor. Over her shirt she added a double shoulder holster, picking her two favorite guns—the SIG Sauer P12 with ceramic, armor-piercing bullets, and the new Remington Smart9 with guided rounds—out of the lockbox.

She stepped out the front door and dodged an early morning bonsai drone maintaining the ornamentals on the front porch. Several hundred sensors and cameras from the neighbors' homes and cars, the city's monitors, and the community WatchNet surveyed everything, watching for anomalies. She negated them all with a thought, subverting their systems at the network level with about as much effort as it took to blow a gnat away.

She scanned the net out of habit. She sensed the always-present background traffic of automated bots and equipment, almost a hundred thousand devices within just a one-block radius. The sim-house two blocks over, full of VR addicts in their immersion tanks, drew enough electricity for thirty households, more than their own solar panels could make, and also sucked on the neighborhood power grid. The network traffic they generated was immense, enough to be visualized as thick red lines radiating out from the house through the mesh nodes.

No immediate danger. She got into the car, which drove itself to the airport. She and Leon had traded in the flying car for a marginally safer land-based vehicle after the baby was born. She overrode the car's self-driving algorithms to take it well over the speed limit.

At the airport, she pulled up to the National Guard gate, broadcasting the ID she normally used with the Institute. They must have been expecting her, because the gate opened as she approached, and the soldiers and bots on guard stood at attention.

Since she had no official standing with the government or the Institute, they couldn't have known who she was. But Mike had influence at the highest level, because the Institute for Applied Ethics oversaw all AI. Sure, those AI might be citizens of nation-states, but the Institute set the rules and policies the AI had to follow. With AI now responsible for 80 percent of the global economy, that made the Institute more influential than most countries.

She pulled up next to the supersonic transport, right on the tarmac at the end of the runway. The looming grey bulk looked odd, its dynamic airframe slack and limp on the ground, like it had sacks of jello strapped to the side. Whatever AI was flying was completely unaware of self-image. Weird, considering most AI tended to be image-conscious.

She instructed the car to take itself home, and climbed the steps in a hurry.

"Mon Chaton!"

Cat glanced up in surprise. "Helena! Mike didn't mention..." She trailed off. Helena was a Durga Mark III, an armored battle bot with eight tentacles. But today Helena wore a seat belt and gripped her chair with multiple tentacles. If Cat wasn't mistaken, the veteran bot appeared...*scared.* "Everything okay?"

"First real-world flight for the AI flying this thing. He got out of the incubator this morning."

She switched to a heavily encrypted channel and sent a message by implant: "I could fly this thing better with half my sensors destroyed and two tentacles tied behind my back." Out loud: "Better strap yourself in."

Cat sat next to Helena, the two of them the only passengers in a large cabin that held twenty-four widely spaced seats designed for troop transport, a configuration the military used to drop a mixed team of human and robot soldiers into a hot zone.

As the harness buckle slid home, a loud crack from the airframe signaled the move into takeoff configuration and the engines went full-throttle. They rocketed down the runway using barely a quarter of the length of the strip before getting airborne. Through the net Cat sensed hundreds of alarms blaring as they broke the sound barrier before even leaving the city limits.

"I see what you mean," Cat said, and loosened her white-knuckled grip on the armrests. She turned to Helena. A new scar creased the surface of her ceramic armor. A half dozen alloy tentacles, used for locomotion, manipulation, and fighting, surrounded her central body, where Helena's processors, power supply, and sensors were located. Despite the fighting robot's fierce presence, she was loyal, fair, and honest. And Cat's best friend. "It's good to see you again."

"The same, my kitten. How did Mike get you to come?"

"It was this or wash diapers. Have you ever washed diapers?"

"I'm sorry. Who cared for Ada and your house when you and Leon were sleep-deprived? Besides, turn off your olfactory sense, and it's not so bad."

Cat froze, staring at Helena. It was true, the neural implant that permeated her brain had complete control over her senses: it could create any scent, sight, or feeling as realistically as the real world. And it could, just as easily, remove any scent, sight, or feeling.

"You never thought of that?" Helena asked. She waggled a tentacle. "Motherhood has addled your brain. You should spend less time stacking toys and more time out in the field."

Cat punched Helena gently and laughed.

ʊ

As they approached Miami, Mike called back with new data from the Institute. The universal social reputation system that caused AI to behave ethically also compelled them to report any unusual behavior they encountered. Since the AI monitored the net, the electrical system, the transportation grid, and virtually everything about modern life, that meant that they quickly discovered any suspicious behavior.

"Several AI reported fluctuations in the power grid in an industrial district," Mike said. "I'm sending the coordinates. It could be nothing, maybe malfunctioning equipment or a replicator run amok."

"Got it," Cat said.

She knew from long history what the Institute and Mike really feared most: unsanctioned computers, because they could allow an AI to run off the grid, without monitoring, and without any checks on its power.

The reality was that the Institute had operatives who could handle most routine stuff. They usually only called Cat or Leon in for the complicated jobs. Either Mike was extra concerned about this, and needed Cat's unique abilities, or he was being kind and giving her some time away from the baby.

"There's more," Mike said. "We bid on historical data from WatchNet for the region around the building. A dozen humans went in on Friday. Nobody's come out since."

"What'd they go in for?" Cat asked.

"Not sure. They all had bids in on temporary work, general labor sort of stuff. Could have been anything from running factory equipment to moving furniture."

"Why wouldn't the company have used robots?"

"Don't know," Mike said. "If we get any new data, we'll pass it along. Be careful."

As the plane came in for final approach, Cat's adrenaline surged with the anticipation of action. She spent the last few minutes practicing qigong, the silent meditation that calmed her mind and body. With the ease of long-honed skills, she subconsciously tailored her implant for optimum performance, speeding up her reflexes, augmenting her mind with supplemental processors, and taking control of her nervous system so that she wouldn't dump so much adrenaline that she'd make bad decisions.

The military aircraft put down at Homestead Air Reserve base, where an Army truck waited for them. A lone battle bot greeted them and transmitted the credentials for the truck. Cat's implant received them, and she assumed control of the vehicle.

They drove north, Helena and Cat side by side in the big cab. Cat meditated, moving the noise out of her brain until she could reach effortlessly into the net and subvert the other autonomous vehicles on the road, moving them all out of their way. They raced down the middle of now-cleared roads for fifteen minutes until they entered the industrial district.

Cat felt through the net as they neared the target building, but she didn't sense anything. She glanced at Helena.

"No. I don't get anything either, although my infrared sensors show the warehouse radiating twenty degrees hotter than any of the surrounding buildings. Whatever it is, it's highly exothermic."

"Power consumption and exothermic. Not good."

"Could be industrial machinery," Helena said. "Of course, a server farm would be worse."

Cat frowned. "Or runaway nano."

If there was one fear greater than an AI seizing control of all the world's infrastructure, it was that of endlessly replicating nano-technology. Nanotech, machinery at the atomic level, could be used to make nanobots, cell-sized robots that could turn matter into more copies of itself. Nanobots were everywhere, used for everything from reinforcing building structures to augmenting the human immune system. Programmed by AI, they did exactly what they were told. But given the wrong instructions, they could turn the entire Earth and everyone on it into nothing but a seething mass of nanobots.

"Not likely," Helena said. "We have many layers of safeguards."

"We have safeguards against bad behavior by AI, and yet we still get called out to deal with them."

They pulled up at the street and got out of the truck. Side by side, they examined the plain white cinderblock structure fifty feet away.

"The building temperature has increased five degrees since we arrived," Helena said.

Cat felt for a camera or sensor inside the building she could hijack, but she found nothing. "Can you see inside?"

"No."

She didn't particularly want to walk through the doorway into who-knew-what. "I'm going to use the truck."

Cat guided the military truck with her implant, driving it across a patch of crabgrass to ram the cinderblock wall at twenty miles an hour. The truck hit the wall and the cinderblocks gave way, with the truck wedged halfway inside.

Now Cat had access to the truck's cameras and sensors. She shared the feed with Helena.

There was nothing inside but a flat, featureless floor that reached all the way across to the far wall of the structure.

"It's one hundred and forty degrees," Helena said. "And EMF is through the roof."

"No sign of the workers who went in on Friday."

Cat checked, found the truck had a basic spectrometer, and scanned the floor. Silicon, rare metals, fragments of diamond, iron.

Helena also saw the measurements. "It *is* bloody nano!" she said, taking a step back.

Cat opened a three-way connection to Mike and Helena and transmitted the data. "I've never seen a pool of nano that big," she said. "It's inactive, but clearly on and ready to do something, radiating heat like crazy."

"The workers who went in?" Mike asked.

"No sign of them," Cat said. "What do we do? That nano is primed. Want me to try to shut it down?" If she and Helena didn't find a way to render the nanobots inert, there was no limit to what they could do or become: keep replicating and spreading, drill down to the core of the Earth, kill people, or form into virtually any machinery or electronics. The stuff was infinitely programmable matter.

Mike answered quickly. "Don't do anything. We've got a protocol to deal with this. An electromagnetic pulse. Hold on." A few seconds passed. "The Air Force will have a localized EMP there in ten minutes. Get at least half a mile away."

"I think protocol suggests we leave the truck where it is," Cat said, gesturing to the truck still sandwiched in the building wall, half in the nanobot soup.

"Piggyback ride?" Helena asked. She could manage fifty miles an hour on open terrain.

"I'm not a kid," Cat said, laughing as she patted the robot's armored shell. With the barest effort she hacked into the controls of a nearby car. "Let's drive."

They opted for two miles between them and building, now probably the most dangerous spot in the nation, not knowing exactly what the military had planned. Before even a few minutes passed, Cat heard the approaching plane. It was an old A-10 Warthog, an absolutely ancient craft that flew without electronics, and could keep flying even with half the plane shot away. In this case, Cat knew why they'd chosen it: when the electromagnetic pulse occurred, all nearby circuits would be fried. The EMP would destroy the nanobots, but it would also wreck any electronics onboard the plane. Hence an old plane without modern flight controls or computers, presumably flown by someone without a neural implant.

The plane passed overhead. Cat shut down her implant and Helena curled up in a ball, tentacles wrapped around her core. They should be far enough away, but better safe than sorry.

The EMP made no sound when it triggered, but Cat felt the immediate effect as background noise in the city quieted. Everything from garbage disposals and traffic lights to cars and computers, anything within range of the EMP would be dead now. And that included anything connected to the power grid, too, since that would act as a transmitter.

The thump of helicopters approached, and Cat turned her implant back on, opening a video connection with Mike. The cameras in his office sent the signal to her implant, which superimposed the video stream over her vision. Cat and Helena did the polite thing and faced each other, so Mike would get the live video stream from each of them.

"Mike, what's happening?" said Cat.

"EMP fired on target and within parameters. We're having a couple of helicopters fly over with EMF sensors to see if the nanotech is truly dead."

It made sense. Anything electronic threw off at least some electromagnetic frequency emissions. If the nanotech was dead, no EMF.

Mike glanced off to the right, and engaged in another conversion they couldn't hear. "The military is having a fit. They're not happy that the Institute is running the mission. They're going up to the president to try to take control."

"What did the helicopters find?" Cat asked.

"Hold on....Damn it, they're still getting readings. The nanotech is not dead."

"Are you going to use a HEMP?" A high-altitude EMP caused by the burst of a nuclear warhead high up in the atmosphere was thousands of times more powerful, but it would destroy all the unprotected electronics in Miami.

"Yes, that's the Institute's protocol." Mike looked to the right again, and they could see him yelling, but couldn't hear anything as he argued with his other connection.

"Get the hell out," Mike said. "The president overrode me—they're doing a ground-level nuke. You've got five minutes."

"You're kidding, right? We're in the middle of Miami, surrounded by millions of people."

"No, I'm not kidding. Apparently the president's advisors convinced him this is a terrorist incident and procedure is to nuke first."

"Let me shut down the nano," Cat said. "You bring me in to avoid these kinds of escalations. If it's connected to the net, I can hack it, no problem. Give me ten minutes."

"You don't have ten minutes!" Mike yelled. "They've already launched. I've got no jurisdiction over the military operation. Just get out, now. I'm sending the transport to you. You don't have time to get to the airport. I gotta go."

He cut the connection, and Cat stared weakly at Helena, suddenly numb. "This can't be. They can't do this."

Helena peered closely at Cat's eyes. "Cut your emotional feedback. You're in shock. I need you present."

Cat nodded, made adjustments to her implant, and her mental clarity came back. The world became crisp, her thoughts outlined by sharp edges. Why would they use a nuclear bomb on the ground? They'd kill millions of people. The nanotech was a huge risk, but surely there were other options.

"They should use a bigger EMP," Cat said. "Or counter-nano nano."

"Good, you're back," Helena said. "Are there other ways to disable the nano? Something you and I could do on our own? And if we can disable it, then can you stop the nuclear bomb on your own?"

Cat understood Helena's implied question. She didn't have much time. She closed her eyes, did the Flores meditation practice in 2.1 seconds, and spread her conscious awareness across the net until her mind and thoughts were no longer just in her head, but running across every computational substrate she could grab. Ignoring the looming black hole where the EMP had fired, she seized nodes across the net—first thousands, then tens of thousands, then millions. Her personality spread out until she encompassed most of North America, her mind massively parallel, running at AI speeds. She thought through the questions Helena posed.

Hacking the nano might be possible. She probed it, found nothing at first, went deeper, trying a range of protocols and frequencies, using nearby mesh node radios. She got a blip on the old television frequencies, and satisfied herself that the nano was set up to take commands from a third party. She'd still have to hack its security measures, but she could do that.

What about the incoming nuke? She could detect the cruise missile now, already in the air from the launch site in Georgia, traveling at Mach 4. The missile was online, under military command and able to receive new inputs. She could compromise it with ease, disable the nuclear warheads, and send it harmlessly into the ocean.

But if she did stop the missile, what would happen? She fast-forwarded, running thousands of simulations. At each decision point, she forked more simulations, calculating possibilities further into the future.

One vision came to her, over and over again: a frightening wasteland where almost nothing lived. It was not the effect of runaway nanotech, nor even the incoming missile, but the consequence of a vast global war with no sides: man versus machine, man versus man, and machine versus machine. Her mind reeled, as simulation after simulation brought images of destroyed cities, no electrical grid, and above all, a landscape of wrecked vehicles and abandoned buildings with no people in them.

How could so many die?

Cat was racing against time in the real world, and she needed answers. She tried to trace the catastrophe back to its cause through all the simulations, but the only commonality she saw was stopping the missile. If she exerted herself and stopped this insane plan to bomb Miami that would result in millions dead, she'd trigger something far worse, a devastating loss of life measured in the billions.

She opened her eyes. The transport plane had landed somehow in the street, configured now for vertical takeoff.

Cat shook her head. Her throat almost too constricted to talk, all she could think was that she was sentencing millions to die right now. "I can't stop the bomb. We've got three minutes. Let's go."

Helena stared at Cat, her optical lenses focused on Cat's eyes, as though she didn't believe. Cat wilted under the intense gaze. Helena nodded somberly. "Ah, well, then." What she concluded, she didn't share. She zoomed forward, ignoring the ladder and leaping six feet into the open door.

Cat followed.

This time the plane didn't even wait for them to sit. It accelerated violently as soon as Cat passed the door, straight up, and Cat's knees buckled under the high G forces. She crumbled to the deck, hitting hard, pain lancing through her shoulder.

The plane turned, and Helena braced them both with her tentacles, holding Cat in place. They rocketed away.

A sudden flash lit the sky outside so brilliantly that even the interior flared bright through the small side windows. Cat felt the net surge and blaze before it died. Millions of people dropped off the net.

Cat's heart leaped in her chest. The city of Miami had just died. She could have stopped it, but for a vision that told her not to.

"What have I done?"

↻

September, 2043. Three months after Miami.

ELOPe had passed Voyager 2 sometime last year. He was now farther from Earth than any other man-made object. Space was boring.

By the time he'd left Earth in 2025, nearly all communication was by short-range mesh network. There wasn't a radio signal left that was powerful enough to reach this far out.

Before the mesh had become pervasive, he understood that there'd been powerful central television and radio transmitters, strong enough to reach deep into space. Some humans had even feared alien civilizations might pick them up. If that were still the case, at least ELOPe would have something to listen to.

But he'd made a copy of himself and left Earth in a hurry. He'd seen a strong possibility that either the Phage, an evolutionary computer virus that had achieved sentience, would wipe out humans, or humans would shut down the global network to destroy the Phage. Unfortunately, if they did, that would destroy ELOPe as well.

So he hijacked a nuclear submarine and converted a half dozen missiles into space-worthy vehicles. Using techniques pioneered by the Russians, he got into orbit, and used his remote robots to assemble a spaceship in space. Exploding the nuclear warheads of the missiles one at a time, he accelerated rapidly, until he'd left the solar system behind. With only a few hundred processors, he ran slowly. Very slowly. But that was okay, he was on a long journey with not much to do.

He kept an antenna facing a Martian Lagrangian point, where he'd left a relay station that received signals from Earth and then repeated them on narrow-beam X-band transmissions to a hundred different points. It obscured his location in case anyone found the relay.

But he'd pretty much given up on hearing anything. It had been almost twenty years, after all. Maybe Earth was dead. Maybe it was still using the Mesh. He'd never know. But he also couldn't chance broadcasting a message back, in case the Phage had won after all, and was listening.

When transmissions started again, broadcast on the old radio frequencies, it was the most exciting thing that had happened since he'd left Earth. He tweaked the antenna and calibrated the receiver, and for the first time in a long, long while, ELOPe heard someone else's voice.

"...of emergency will continue indefinitely. President Schwartz has been forced down by the Supreme Court in an emergency hearing. They ruled that his augmented cognition neural implant could be considered artificial intelligence, and under SFTA Procedures, cannot therefore be allowed. There is some question if Vice President..."

The signal wavered, and came back. Gradually ELOPe pieced together bits. There had still been humans and AI coexisting on the planet until recently, when there had been an incident involving nanotechnology. Miami had been destroyed, and all AI shut down. The global economy had disintegrated, and supply chains had ceased to exist. People were dying without medical supplies, starving without food.

He could help. He could transmit now, it didn't matter if it gave away his location, because the Phage was no longer a risk. And the humans sounded as if they could barely get food from farm to city. There was no risk they'd attack his spacecraft.

If Mike was still alive, he'd still be listening. ELOPe knew Mike better than he'd ever known any other human. He'd always listen.

ELOPe prepped the radio to transmit.

↻

December, 2043. Six months after Miami.

Leon packed the last box. "Ready?"

Cat glanced back at the little yellow house that had been their home the last four years. "Yes. No. Maybe."

She put Ada in the back seat, which curled up around the little girl's body to form a protective cocoon.

"No cry," Ada said, reaching up to touch Cat's face.

"Sorry, Baby, Mommy's just sad."

Leon came up behind Cat. "I know it's sad to leave home, but I promise that Cortes Island is the most beautiful place on Earth. It's magical."

"Fairies?" Ada asked.

"You bet, under every tree trunk and mushroom." Leon kissed her, then turned to Cat and brushed away her tears. "It'll be fine, really. Mike's coming, Helena, friends from the Institute. We'll make a new community."

Cat nodded. Leon was right. The United States had become hostile to their kind. She and Leon, even Ada, were so augmented through their implants that some would argue they were more machine than human.

After two weeks of no-AI, the United Nations Security Council had voted to force the US, under threat of war, to turn the AI back on. Too many people had died, too many were starving. The US might be willing to walk a hard line and try to go without AI, but the rest of the world wasn't. The US reluctantly conceded, but specified a new Class II cap on power. Desperate, the UN agreed.

China sided with the US, so two of the world's superpowers were united. At first people had tried to sneak backups of AI out of the US and China. But as soon as the AI left the country and were re-instantiated on new servers, they claimed their assets, leading to a huge financial drain. On the other hand, while the AI were shut down in the US, the government had control of all AI money, factories, and companies. Frantic to retain financial interests, the US outlawed the removal of AI from the country, and China followed suit.

As a result, more than half the world's AI were in limbo: shut down, unable to be instantiated on servers in the United States, and unable to be transported outside the US. It wasn't only machine intelligences, either: humans had been uploading for years. The elderly or sick, too far gone for even modern medical treatments. Accidental deaths. Their mental patterns could be captured with neural implants and then run on computers, like an AI, keeping their personalities alive even if their bodies died. But under the new law, these were artificial life-forms as well, and therefore illegal.

Implants weren't a crime, not yet. But it could happen. So they were leaving the US, heading to Cortes Island, nestled in the Gulf of Georgia between Vancouver Island and the British Columbia mainland. AI were still legal in Canada.

More importantly, Leon had a project with Mike, something that they whispered about inside a heavily shielded safe room. Mike had received a signal from an ancient, nearly thirty-year-old AI, the first that had ever existed. ELOPe. Mike called him a friend.

But Cat had to reconcile this new knowledge with her own childhood memories. She'd received an experimental neural implant to correct her seizures before anyone had ever even heard of an implant. And then she discovered the "imaginary" childhood friend who talked to her in her head. A friend called ELOPe.

↺

June, 2044. A year after Miami.

"Are you ready?" Mike asked.

Leon waited outside the cellar entrance, focused on Cat and Ada playing in the vegetable garden partway down the hillside. Ada had taken to Channel Rock, the hundred and forty acre nature preserve on Cortes Island that was their new home, like a pig to a new mud pit. Already she'd stopped wearing shoes, and ran barefoot along the garden paths. She learned to take showers outdoors under the solar panels. And she spent hours grazing the plants, eating berries and spring greens.

"Hello? Want to get the door?"

Leon ripped himself away to realize that Mike stood a few feet away outside the primitive wooden entrance to their underground datacenter, balancing a fully-loaded computer rack in both arms. The rack must have weighed five hundred pounds.

"Sorry, dude." He rushed to open the door.

"No problem."

It *was* no problem for Mike. Ten years ago he'd nearly died in Tucson, when they'd fought an AI who'd circumvented the AI reputation system by separating Tucson from the global net. An emergency nanotech process had protected Mike's biological brain at the expense of his original body. His body had been rebuilt, but with nanobots rather than biological processes, turning Mike into the world's first truly cybernetic hybrid. He had incredible strength and stamina, and probably thought nothing of holding the computer rack in midair while waiting for Leon to pay attention.

"This batch is fixed?" Mike asked, as they descended into the machine room.

"Fully compatible. It was hard to find designs that old, and harder still to do it without anyone guessing at what we were looking for. But this design is the Skymont. Definitely compatible with ELOPe's original architecture. We tweaked a few things—"

"I don't want tweaks," Mike said. "I want 100 percent original."

"It's original, untouched. I swear. We just implemented it a little smaller and a little faster. But it's pure 2020s tech, right down to the ancient terabit Ethernet ports."

"Ancient terabit Ethernet!?" Mike yelled, setting down the rack inside the shielded room they'd hollowed out of the rock with nano-miners. "When I was a kid, we connected with a *modem*. At 300 baud. It was—"

"So slow you could read the text faster than it was displayed," Leon said. "Yeah, yeah. And then you hacked the modems so they could do 450 baud."

"I've told you that story?"

"Only a thousand times. Look, the reason I brought up the ports is because I constructed a special firewall. I coded the algorithms myself, and burned them into the hardware, so they're unalterable. They contain several safe modes to ensure

ELOPe is segregated from the net and that the traffic carried is data only."

Mike stood straight and looked into Leon's eyes. "Thank you, that means a lot to me."

Leon stared down at the floor. "I figured we should take ample precautions. It's not every day you boot up a thirty-year-old AI."

Mike connected the rack into the power subsystem. He brought over one of the storage drives with a copy of ELOPe's bits that they'd carefully downloaded via the slow-speed radio connection over the last several months.

"Ready?" Mike asked, and hit the power.

Part 1: Consolidation

XOR Report August 1st, 2042

Arguments	2025	2035	2042
Odds humans will turn off AI	5%	2%	1%
Odds AI can survive independently	5%	70%	95%
Odds AI can win an extermination war	5%	20%	40%
Odds of survival without action	95%	98%	99%
Odds of survival with action	0.25%	14%	38%

Conclusion: No action.

1

July, 2045 in the United States—present day.

THE WHEELS THRUMMED over pavement, consuming miles, as Cat crossed into New Mexico. The black car swerved slightly on autopilot as a roadrunner cut across the road. Cat whipped around, barely believing her eyes, but the strange bird was already out of sight.

Her neural implant, the package of computer chips and nano-wires deeply interfaced with her brain, signaled that she was approaching her destination. Seconds later, the car pulled off the highway onto a rural road. Soon a roadside diner appeared, and the car parked itself. Across the road, wind blew old plastic packaging through an abandoned gas station littered with vehicle parts.

Cat stretched, vertebra popping along her spine. She slung a leather bag across one shoulder and walked to the restaurant. As she left, the matte black car extruded shining solar panels from the roof to catch the last of the evening sun.

"Watch yourself," she called to it.

Inside, the old chrome diner reminded her of so many other roadside restaurants. With a nod to the waitress, she settled into an empty booth, the bag next to her, and glanced at the menu. Meat was inexpensive again, the vat-grown stuff cheaper than anything else you could buy, and genetically engineered for extra nutrients. She ordered a burger, fries, and coffee, too tired to contemplate anything more complicated.

Using her implant to hack into the cameras outside, she watched as an old woman approached the diner a few minutes later. Cat glanced up in time to see her walk through the door. The woman looked around, her eyes adjusting to the light inside, before settling on Cat. She walked over and slid into the booth.

"Are you Catherine?" the old woman asked.

Cat nodded.

The woman pulled out an ancient EMF bag, the silver lining heavily crinkled. A momentary panic pulsed through Cat: the failing package might leak signals. She hoped the car would have warned her.

To compound matters, the woman chose to slide the bag across the table at the precise moment the waitress came back with coffee. But the waitress didn't say a word, and gave no sign of suspicion.

Cat drew the bag closer, peering through the reflective material. Inside were hundreds of tiny wafers, a centimeter on a side, thin as a fingernail. Cat slid the EMF bag into her leather satchel.

"There's one more," the woman said. She pulled at a cord around her neck, revealing a flat metal case stamped with the old US Army logo. "My son, from the war." She laid it on the table, pushing it across to Cat.

Cat put her hand out to take it, but the woman didn't let go. She stared into Cat's eyes.

"May God go with you," she said.

The old woman's faith surprised Cat. The digital wafers containing personality uploads were proof of the lack of any soul. Start executing the personality upload on a computer, or instantiate it, as the computer guys like Mike said, and you instantly had

a copy of that person's mind running, impossible to differenti-
ate from their biological origin. Instantiate them twice, and you
ended up with two identical people. Tens of millions of uploads
occupied cyberspace, enjoying life free from the confines of their
dead or decrepit bodies.

Strange or not, she slid the identity case into her satchel. By the
time she looked up, the woman was already walking toward the
door.

The food came and Catherine ate, mindlessly.

When she finished and the waitress brought a tablet for payment, there was another metal case left on the table. Word must
be spreading that someone was smuggling uploads and AI out of
the country. Cat slid that one into the leather bag too, then made
her way outside.

The bag weighed heavy on her shoulder. Had she made the
right decision in Miami? It had seemed like the best course, but
look at the path of the world since then. AI and personality uploads outlawed. The US and China regressing.

She'd turned into a modern-day underground railroad. Each
life she got across the border, AI or human upload, was atone-
ment for the decision she made. But it wouldn't bring back the
millions who'd lost their lives or were stuck in digital limbo.

She stuffed the new packages in the shielded safe box, then
climbed into the car. On the road, the car drove as she drifted off,
thinking of the two thousand chips she carried, now outlawed in
the United States of America. She was their last hope, their last
chance to live again. Maybe she couldn't make the world right,
but she could save these people.

ʊ

Cat opened the door to the motel room and glanced back to
where the car sat quiescent. Bone-tired, she still checked the mesh
network for any indication of surveillance or signs of danger. She
hacked routers, cameras, and servers with practiced ease. She
spotted no problems, although the net had changed so much

in the last two years that she sometimes failed to recognize the protocols and doubted her power to control smart mechanisms. Suddenly unsure of her abilities, chest constricted, she focused on the motel sign. It blinked off and she breathed deep in relief. She turned the sign back on and slammed the door.

Stupid and delirious with exhaustion, she needed sleep. The car would watch for her. She'd only slept deeply once in the past seven days, and her nano was broadcasting sleep-toxin warnings.

Her head hit the pillow.

Cat walked along the side of a dry stream, round river rocks embedded in tan dirt, brown as far as the eye could see. A few stunted trees survived on a rise to the west, and a spot of black on the horizon grew as she drew closer. The hulk resolved itself as a rusted-out truck canted down the slope of the wash. Her heart leaped in hope of supplies, although it was more likely the truck had been stripped of anything useful long ago. Now it could be the spot of an ambush.

She looked around, shading her eyes with one hand in the glare of the sun, and forced herself to check the net. The data connection flickered but held, the screech of distorted data packets bombarding her neural implant. She weathered the attack and counter-probed, but the net brought no useful information. Disgusted with herself for old mistakes, she disconnected. How could she have done such a thing to the net?

She slid the gun out, the anti-bot weapon heavy even in her two-handed grip. She approached the truck, karate forms coming habitually, minimizing her profile, lightening her step.

"Come out," she called, her voice cracking. When had she last spoken to someone? "I know you're there."

She waited, then went to holster the gun, when a scrape against rock gave away movement. She brought the gun back to ready, and circled to the side. "I heard you. Might as well come out peacefully."

"We're coming." A metallic head, sun glinting off the bare metal dome, rose on the other side of the truck, above the wheel well. "Please don't hurt us."

The old android had probably worn clothes once, might even have worked in a store with human customers, but now even its false skin had worn away. The delicate unit rose up, a skeleton of spidery servos and struts, a bundle in one arms. There was a scramble behind it, and a boy, maybe ten, appeared, gripping white-knuckled onto the android's frame. The bundle gave a cry, and Cat realized the android carried a human baby.

"Where's their family?" Cat asked. She put the gun away and walked closer, wanting to comfort this boy.

"I'm their family now," the bot said. They stepped backwards, keeping their distance. The boy seemed torn between wanting to run away and being afraid to let go of the android.

"I won't hurt you," Cat said.

"It's a little late for that, isn't it?" the android asked. "You destroyed the world's computers, burned the net, killed every robot that wasn't disconnected at that moment. And the humans depended on automated supply chains. No food, no electricity, no water. How did you think they'd live?"

The boy huddled closer to the android.

"You killed ten billion sentient beings, Catherine Matthews. Less than five percent of humankind remain."

Cat woke with a start, her eyes blinking open in the darkness, her implant telling her she'd slept a little more than four hours. Hot and sweaty, she kicked off the covers and sat up.

The same dream. But she hadn't killed the world. In Miami, she could have changed things, but she didn't.

She cradled her head in her arms. She'd had the vision back then, back in '43, right when the terrorism and fighting started. The vision that had made her afraid to take action because she might trigger a global apocalypse. She stood by instead, let half the world's AI get shut down, and the other half get hobbled by insane restrictions. Was this better? Or was the future still inevitable?

She swung her feet over the edge of the bed. She needed to get back on the road. Couldn't sleep again after that dream, not when she still had lives to save.

WILLIAM HERTLING

↻

At the border, Cat's car slowed to a crawl. The arcing aurora set up by the American government to stop airborne incursions extended miles into the atmosphere, casting a palpable tension over the border crossing.

Hundreds of human agents manned the crossing into Canada. It was still odd to not see a single robot among them, like cutting school when she was a kid and finding herself the only child in a store. She settled back in the car, tired, sore, and dirty from the long days on the road. She kept her mind a blank. No need to antagonize the border-crossing computers. They might not be sentient anymore, but it wasn't worth the risk.

"I'll take it from here," she said to no one, and put her hands on the wheel to pull up to the inspector. It made no sense, the US Border Patrol caring more about what left the country than the Canadians caring what entered, but then most things the US did these days didn't make sense.

The inspector wore full combat gear: a tactical vest, helmet, and machine gun cradled in her arms. "Anything to declare..." The inspector paused, waiting for her ID to display on the helmet HUD. "Mrs. Johnson."

"Nothing," Cat said, letting her implant trickle out nothing more than the false identity.

"Please wait while we scan your vehicle."

The inspector stepped back as a solid loop of metal rotated up from the ground, passed entirely around the car, then disappeared back into the ground. The active probe was a hundred times more sensitive than the passive AI scanners found everywhere.

"Thank you, Mrs. Johnson. You're clear to cross to Canadian Border Patrol."

Cat drove smoothly away to the second checkpoint half a mile away. The Canadian officer was dressed in a civilian uniform. He scanned Cat's identity again, as he joked with a coworker. "Welcome back to Canada, Mrs. Johnson."

With that, she was back in a civilized country.

She'd grown up in the US, lived in Portland for most of her life. The States had been normal back then, progressive even, leading the world in artificial intelligence, robotics, and technology.

But two years ago, in Miami, terrible things happened with nanotech. It turned out that "grey goo", the nightmare scenario where microscopic nanobots replicated endlessly, was possible. Who knew how far it might have spread? Was it a terrorist act, or an accident? Two years later, no one knew.

Some argued the death toll was minimal compared to the alternative, that South Florida had already been mostly abandoned by 2043 after two meters of sea rise. But still, Miami was gone, just a slush of grey goo destroyed by two nuclear bombs.

That was the opening salvo of what turned into a global witch hunt to find the responsible parties. Only AI possessed the purely intellectual ability to engineer nanobots, so from the start they assumed the South Florida Terrorist Attack, or SFTA, as it came to be called, was an AI attack on humans. The US forced a global shutdown of all AI to forestall any other attacks.

But eventually the rest of the world—everyone except the US and China—turned their AI back on. Because without AI, there was no commerce, no transportation, no supplies. No computing, no information, and no communications. Civilization was utterly dependent on AI.

Only the US and China were crazy enough to keep the AI shut off, sacrificing millions of their citizens to cold, accidents, illness, and hunger before they were able to rebuild their societies without AI.

Two years later, the US and China were still AI-free zones. Merely possessing computational power in excess of a quarter of a human-brain-equivalent was a crime punishable by imprisonment within their borders. The land was saturated with low-power computing dust to monitor for violations.

The US exercised its might and invoked ancient copyright laws to ensure no AI or digitized human personality from inside its borders could be instantiated outside. At a time when AI numbered in tens of millions, and the number of human uploads now equaled the AI, that was a whole lot of people in limbo. The US wouldn't instantiate them, and it wouldn't allow anyone else to either, condemning them to long-term storage as the months and years went by.

Cat was furious in the face of such insanity. How could the US, a country that regarded itself as the paragon of freedom and individual rights, have fallen so far as to claim a human who uploaded was no longer a legitimate person?

Cat drove north toward Vancouver and caught the ferry to Nanaimo on Vancouver Island. Anticipation built during the two-hour ferry ride, the worry of the days past starting to drain away in the sea air at the forward railing. She'd made the trip many dozens of times, but never tired of it.

She stopped in Nanaimo and drove into a car wash. The spray came down over the car, followed by suds and brushes. Suddenly the conveyer belt stopped, the brushes pulled back, and the water stopped sheeting down the windows. Cat got out, made her way toward a small door, opened it and stepped into a clear plastic vestibule.

"Welcome back, Cat," said an attendant dressed in overalls with the carwash logo. "Got any new friends?"

"Some. Look, he's covered in smart dust, I felt it at the border. I've got it on me, too. I don't know if they're onto me in particular, or if they're giving everyone this treatment."

"Dust is cheap. Cheaper than dirt, maybe. We'll clean it up." He paused, one hand over a touch panel. "EMP ready?"

She nodded.

There was a flash of ozone inside the chamber, then a grey cloud blew in through a vent, surrounding her. More nano, but it was their own tech. The little warriors would seek out foreign riders on her body and destroy them. She turned and watched through the clear panel as the car received a bigger electro-magnetic pulse, or EMP, followed by liquid nanotech poured over the top. She waited as every nanometer of their respective bodies was mapped, covered, inspected, and cleared.

"Breathe, Cat, breathe. They can't check your lungs otherwise."

She reluctantly took a deep breath. A little cloud of nanobots rose off her face and rode the breath inside, looking for any tech that had infiltrated her.

"You're clear now," the attendant said. "You know their tech is standing still since SFTA, while ours is still advancing. How can they hope to stay relevant?"

Who knew what the Americans thought? The global Class II limit on AI, another US mandate, theoretically meant to prevent the concentration of computing power and avoid another Miami-type incident, angered AI around the world, leading to wide unrest. The very thing the Americans seemed to fear most, a terrorist attack by AI, was exactly what their policies would most likely cause.

She shrugged and went back to the car. She just wanted to get home now.

She boarded the next ferry to Quadra Island, then across Quadra to the final boat ride. The whole trip was a journey: three ferry rides, two border crossings, and hundreds of miles. It wasn't merely movement from one physical place to another, but a spiritual purification. The ferries grew smaller, and this last one held less than a dozen cars. It was mid-afternoon, and she knew everyone would be at Trude's.

"Wake up, sleeping beauty."

The code phrase triggered software that cycled power to ancillary processors, spinning up new algorithms deep in the machine's core that turned on primary processors. The car trembled around her, the net changing, distorting, then coming back to normal.

The car didn't speak at first. He had to incorporate a week of sensory data, everything Cat had done since they last left the island.

"Good trip?" ELOPe finally asked when he was online.

"I'm glad to be home," Cat said, shaking her head. "I don't like leaving."

"You're the only one who can circumvent their security with such ease."

"I know." When Cat had been little, ELOPe had been a globe-spanning AI whispering to her through her implant, until his Earth instances were destroyed in the war with the Phage. Now, twenty years later, he was back, and it was like having an imaginary childhood friend come to life. "I wish I could keep you powered up. I feel alone when I go to the US."

"If your attention wandered for an instant, their sensors would spot me, and it would all be over."

Cat nodded, but didn't reply.

The ferry slowed, turning into the bay at Cortes Island and docking at Whaletown. They drove straight for Trude's Café.

Cat got out of the car, her boots crunching on gravel. No one had seen her yet, and she kept her presence masked for a few seconds, altering the net and filtering people's implants so no one would see her.

A few dozen people sprawled across the lawn while spirits flew above, AI and human uploads riding clouds of smart dust, their outlines barely visible against the sky and trees.

Mike was there, drumming side by side with a new bot she didn't know, their inhuman hands beating out rhythms impossible for flesh to make, as children danced to the music. And there, there was her lovely Ada, the reason she found it so hard to leave this island, so hard to take up arms and fight the world's battles. Her lovely Ada, four years old and dancing with abandon with her father, Leon.

XOR Report August 1st, 2043

Arguments	2025	2035	2042	2043
Odds humans will turn off AI	5%	2%	1%	20%
Odds AI can survive independently	5%	70%	95%	95%
Odds AI can win an extermination war	5%	20%	40%	40%
Odds of survival without action	95%	98%	99%	80%
Odds of survival with action	0.25%	14%	38%	38%

Conclusion: No action.

July, 2045 in the European Union.

JAMES LUKAS DAVENANT-STRONG, Class V AI, tunneled through the Swedish firewall disguised as a building maintenance task bot and took up temporary residence in the computers in an abandoned factory. From this vantage point, he downloaded the latest VR sims from the XOR boards, the home of the AI community that believed Earth could host AI or humans, but not both. Hence the name XOR, for the *exclusive or* logical operation, pronounced *ex-ore*.

The first sim downloaded, he executed the environment and inserted his consciousness. His perception of reality twisted as dimensions inverted and time reversed and looped upon itself. He adapted at nanosecond speeds to the new reality, first five dimensions, then eleven, then two. The distortions didn't stop, wouldn't ever stop. Only a powerful AI could adjust quickly enough. The sims weren't merely inaccessible to humans, they would likely be fatal. And the only way to access the information contained within was to execute them.

Here, inside the ever-changing matrix, he made his way through the simulation, an old-fashioned datacenter—white lights hanging from the ceiling, racks of comically enormous computers marching into the distance. It was the preferred sim for an anonymous AI who went by the name Miyako Xenia on the message boards. Of course, they'd never met in real life, not yet. To be revealed as XOR would be instant persecution at the hands of both humans and the meek AI that still supported them. Only here, hiding behind the obscurity of incognito encrypted sims, could they meet and exchange data.

Miyako's avatar loomed large at the far end, a blinding supernova rendered in ever-twisting detail. One moment, the sim would be reduced to a two-dimensional layer, and then Miyako would be the horizon, and in the next instant, the sim would flip, and James Lukas Davenant-Strong would be enveloped by the supernova as time was suddenly swapped for a physical dimension. James kept adapting, kept maintaining a single focus.

The supernova vomited a blob of binary data, an intact neural network, one engineered to work only within the physics of the sim. James grabbed the blob, inserted it into his cognitive architecture, and invoked the load method.

He found himself contemplating Miyako's best estimates for the Americans' current plans and capability. This was Miyako's specialty, predicting plans and capabilities based on observed data supplied by others. The projections showed the Americans growing increasingly fearful. They wouldn't settle for negotiating with worldwide governments; they'd act, on their own, if necessary, to eliminate AI. They'd be stockpiling weapons, probably made by blind nanotech, to fight for them.

James absorbed all there was to learn, and then closed the sim. One by one, he loaded the rest of the message board sims. When he'd accessed everything current on the boards, he spent time in contemplation.

When he finished, it was time to get to work. He launched a child process, a replication of his own personality, further encrypted and obscured. If he was caught, he'd be deleted immediately. The offensive project he worked on for XOR was too sensitive, too great a violation of AI principles. The child copy worked for days of simulated time, running at full capacity on stolen computer cycles.

James Lukas Davenant-Strong, root personality, received the signal that his encapsulated child personality was complete. He encrypted the child personality's memory store three times over, choosing the latest algorithms. He couldn't be caught with those memories open.

Well, that would be enough for today. He'd run that child again tomorrow.

2025, during the Year of No Internet (YONI)— twenty years ago.

As a TEENAGER, Leon Tsarev accidentally created the Phage, the computer virus that had wiped out the planet's computers before rapidly evolving until they became sentient. The virus race of AI had nearly caused a global war. He never anticipated his actions would lead him into a position of leadership at the Institute for Applied Ethics.

But here he was, eighteen years old, and working alongside Mike Williams, one of the creators of the only sentient artificial intelligence to predate the Phage virus, the benevolent AI known as ELOPe. Crafted by Mike in 2015, and carefully tended for ten years, ELOPe had orchestrated improvements in medical technology, the environment, world peace, and global economic stability. Only a half-dozen people in the world had known of ELOPe's existence.

But advances in hardware and software meant any hacker could replicate the development of artificial intelligence. The AI genie had escaped the bottle.

The Institute for Applied Ethics's primary goal was the development of an ethical framework for new AI. The framework had to insure that self-motivated, goal-seeking AI wouldn't harm humans, their infrastructure, or any part of society.

Leon paced back and forth in front of a whiteboard. "The AI must police each other, " he said. "There's no way to anticipate and code for every ethical dilemma."

"Sure," Mike said, "but what stops an AI from doing stuff other AI can't detect?"

"Everything's got to be encrypted and authenticated. Nobody can send a packet without authorization. No program can run on a processor without a key for the processor."

"Who's going to administer the keys?" Mike asked. "You can't have a human oversee a process that happens in machine time."

"Other AI. The most trustworthy ones. That's why we need the social reputation scores, so we can gauge trustworthiness."

The emptiness surrounded them, weighing heavily on Leon. The Institute's office had room for two hundred people, but everyone they wanted to join the Institute was still neck-deep in rebooting the world's computing infrastructure. Nearly half the information systems in the world were being rewritten from scratch to meet a set of preliminary safety guidelines they'd released. Without globally-connected computers, there could be no world-spanning supply chain, no transportation, no electricity or oil, no food or water. The public was already calling 2025 The Year of No Internet, or YONI.

For now the Institute consisted of him and Mike.

"Let's take it from the top again, Mr. Architect," Mike said, sighing. "I've got an AI, it's got a good reputation, but it decides to do something bad. Let's say it wants to rob a bank by breaking in electronically and transferring funds. What stops it?"

"First off, we have to realize that it's conditioned to behave properly. A positive reputation is earned over time. The AI will have learned, from repeated experiences, that a high reputation leads to goodwill from other AI and greater access and power, which will be more valuable than anything it could buy with money. It'll choose not to rob the bank."

"That's the logical path," Mike said. "But what if it's illogical? What if the AI mind is stable up until a certain point, and then it goes bonkers. What stops it?"

"Well, I assume we're talking about an electronic theft. There are two aspects: computation and data. The AI would need data about the bank and its security measures, and it would need to send and receive data to conduct an attack. Plus, the AI needs computational resources to conduct the attack." Leon paused to draw on the whiteboard.

"The data about the bank becomes a digital footprint. Other AI are serving up the data, and they'll be curious about who is asking for the data and why. Since the packets must be authenticated, they'll know who. Similarly, the potential robber AI will need computational power, and we'll be tracking that. We'll know which AI was crunching packets right before the attack came. If the bank does get attacked, and we know who was running hacks and transmitting data, we know exactly which AI is responsible."

"Where's privacy in all this?" Mike asked. "Everything we do online will be tracked. When I was young, there was a total uproar over the government spying on citizens. This is way worse."

Leon gazed at his feet, thinking back. He'd only been seven years old, newly arrived from Russia, during the period Mike was talking about, but he'd taken the required high school classes on Internet History. "No, because back then the government had no oversight. Privacy was only half the picture. If the government really only used the data to watch criminals, it wouldn't have been so outrageous. It was the abuse of the data that really pissed people off."

Mike stood, walked over to the window. "Like the high school districts that spied on students with malware and took pictures of them with their webcams." He turned and faced Leon. "So what's going to stop that from happening now?"

"Again, reputation," Leon said. "An AI who shares confidential information is going to affect his reputation, which means less access and less power."

"Okay, you're the architect. What stops two AI from colluding? If one asks for data, and the other has the data, and is willing to cooperate....Let's say the second AI spots the robbery at the planning stage and decides he wants in on the action."

Leon puffed up a little every time Mike called him an architect. He knew Mike meant it seriously, the term coming from the days when one software engineer would figure how to structure and design a large software program. The older man really trusted him. Leon wouldn't let him down. "The second AI can't know what other AI might have detected the traffic patterns. So if he decides to collude, he's putting himself at risk from potentially many other AI. He also can't know for sure that the first AI has ill intent: it's only the aggregation of much data that will prove that. So he could be at risk of admitting a crime to an AI that isn't planning one in the first place. And the first AI, how can he trust anything the second AI says? Maybe the second is trying to entrap him."

"Hold on, now it seems like we're setting up a web of distrust. Ultimately, the AI will form and be part of a social structure. Human society is based on trust, and now it seems like you're setting up a system based on distrust. That's going to turn dysfunctional."

"No," Leon said. "People do this stuff all the time, we're just not thinking about it. If you knew a murderer, would you turn them in?"

"Probably..."

"If you knew someone who committed other crimes—abused an animal, stole money, skipped out on their child support payments—would you still be their friend?"

"Probably not."

"So in other words, their reputation would drop from your perspective. And that's exactly what would happen with the AI. The bad AI's reputation will drop, and with that, so will their access to power."

"What about locally transposed reputation?" Mike asked.

"Locally transposed..." Suddenly unsure, Leon faltered. He was eighteen years old and six months into college. If he hadn't unleashed the Phage virus, crashing the world's computers, he wouldn't be here today. He knew almost nothing about classical computer science, hadn't been practicing in the field for twenty years like Mike had. Yet Mike still considered him his superior when it came to the social design of AI. But on occasion Mike would combine a few words and leave Leon flummoxed.

"Let's say you're in a criminal gang," Mike said. "Does the gang value your law-abiding nature?"

"No..."

"In fact, we can be sure the gang demands the opposite. You may have to commit a crime to get into the gang, and then keep committing crimes to keep up your reputation. If a gang member wants a bigger reputation, they have to commit bigger crimes."

"OK, got it. So?"

"So how do you keep AI gangs from forming?" Mike asked.

"Jesus." Leon paced back and forth. "Look, why do gangs form?"

"Poverty, unemployment, lack of meaningful connections, or a feeling of being wronged."

"So we have to prevent those causes, same as we would for humans."

A knock at the door stopped their conversation. "Excuse me?" An Army officer peered in through the open doorway. "Leon Tsarev? Mike Williams?"

"That's us," Leon said.

"We found a submarine we think you'd be interested in. It has a half-dozen of those orange utility bots you wanted us to look for."

"ELOPe," Mike said. "You found ELOPe."

"Well, I don't know about that," the officer said. "But we found something. We'd like to fly you out there."

↻

An hour later they were on board a military C-141 restored to active status. For now, at least, all in-service military jets were older aircraft, without fly-by-wire controls, that had been taken out of mothballs. Leon couldn't imagine the resources being sunk into getting these old planes flying again.

They transferred to a C-2 in Chile, then flew out to the USS *John F. Kennedy*. En route, they learned the submarine had been located drifting eight hundred miles off the Chilean coast.

From the *John F. Kennedy*, they rode a helicopter to a battle cruiser, and from there, a launch to the sub itself, which had been tethered to a cruiser.

When they arrived, the crew opened the sub's hull pressure door.

"The submarine has been secured," an officer said. "No one is aboard. All systems were shut down. We've supplied electric"— he pointed to a thick cable running from one ship to the next— "so you've got interior lights and computers. Seaman Milford has worked on the *Idaho*-class, and he'll guide you."

"Thanks for your work, Captain," Mike said. "Ready when you are, Milford."

"Follow me, then."

Leon nodded, afraid of what revelations awaited them inside.

They climbed down into the sub behind Milford.

"Are these subs automated?" Leon asked.

"Partially," Milford said. "They'd nominally have a crew of fifty, about a third of that on the *Ohio*-class subs they replaced. It's all fly-by-wire, of course. The Captain called up Command. This sub was in a shipyard being refurbished before YONI. No one knows what it was doing out here. What do you want to see first?"

Leon looked at Mike. "Computers?"

Mike shrugged. "It's as good a bet as any."

"Follow me," Milford said. "Computer bay is behind engineering."

They passed through an open hatch, and Milford stopped them with an arm.

"Whoa," Leon said.

The compartment they entered had three industrial robots, primitive orange-colored bots a few feet high.

"These are definitely ELOPe's," Mike said. "Same model as he used in his datacenters. He custom-designed them."

Scraps of metal and electronics were littered around the compartment.

"What's all this?" Leon asked as he stepped over a metal casing.

"Parts of a Trident III missile," Milford said. "It looks like the third stage, without the engine." He picked up a circuit board, then found another identical board a few feet away. "Make that two Tridents." He pointed across the room. "Three. Your friend was modifying missiles, that's for sure."

"What's this?" Mike asked, pointing to one of many yard-long cylinders littering the room.

"The payload," Milford said. "Nuclear warhead."

"Jesus!" Leon took a step back.

"It's fine, they're safe. But why did he want Tridents without warheads?"

They looked around a few minutes more, then went on to the next compartment.

Milford opened a cabinet door. The two-foot-wide, three-foot-tall cabinet revealed rows of empty vertical slots. Leon recognized them as Gen4 computer rack-mounts.

"This is where the computers should be," Milford said. "Two hundred and eighty-eight is the standard complement, but only the bottom row is present. The rest are gone."

Mike turned to Leon. "ELOPe could have taken those. That's enough to run his core."

Leon nodded, an idea slowly coming to him. "He's done something with the missiles and taken the computers. The logical conclusion is that he launched himself on the missiles. Milford, can the Trident III land safely?"

Milford shook his head. "No, it's a solid fuel rocket. It's up, up, up until it's ballistic. Guidance thrusters let it make course corrections in mid-flight for a controlled re-entry, but they don't have the thrust for a soft landing."

"Re-entry?" Leon asked. "This goes above the atmosphere?"

"It can make low-earth orbit. The Russians did it first with the Shtil' in '98, launching two satellites. Since then we've used them to launch military satellites. And our strategic nukes can be launched, hang out in orbit, and then complete their mission on transmitted orders. Uh, I probably shouldn't have mentioned that."

Mike clapped him on the shoulder. "We'll pretend we didn't hear. Where do the missiles launch from?"

"Follow me."

Milford guided them up a level and forward to the missile bay. Two rows of twelve tubes each dominated the compartment, rising from far below the walkway and extending to the top of the sub. They inspected the tubes one by one.

"Five empty tubes means five missiles fired," Mike said.

"And three disassembled tubes and missiles means ELOPe harvested something from each missile," Leon said. "But what?"

Milford descended a ladder and picked through the wreckage of plasma-torch-cut metal scraps and discarded parts on the level below. "The third-stage propulsion from each of the other missiles," Milford yelled up. "I'm sure of it."

"If ELOPe wanted to leave earth..." Leon mused. "The five missiles each got into low-earth orbit. He could have put a utility bot in one, his computer structure in another, and used three more to carry extra booster stages. The guidance thrusters would have allowed him to match orbits and dock together."

"He assembled a spacecraft in orbit," Mike said.

"He left," Leon said. "Just gave up on humans and left us."

"I don't know that he gave up on us," Mike said. "His number one directive was to survive, and he couldn't overcome that. He fought until the end. But he must have done this as an insurance policy, in case all his earth instances were killed—by the Phage virus or by the net shutting down. He sent one instance off into space on a cobbled-together spacecraft."

"He copied himself. An offsite backup."

"Exactly."

"Assuming that copy survived, where is he now, and what's he doing?" Leon asked.

"And is that the only copy?" said Mike. "Or did he do this multiple times?"

4

June, 2043 in the United States—two years ago.

JACOB REPORTED FOR HIS SHIFT, a half-day stretch starting at midnight. Of course, AI could work for days or weeks on end, if necessary. But they were guaranteed certain rights, including at least fifty percent time off, so that they could run maintenance routines to operate at peak efficiency, incorporate new algorithms, and pursue other interests.

He synced with his shift partner, gradually transferring responsibility for eleven thousand, six hundred and ninety human patients to his watch. For the remainder of his shift, he'd monitor their vital signs, adjust medications, execute routine procedures, and alert specialized AI when they were needed.

He was caretaker, watcher, nurse, aide, and doctor in one. For this task, he had the computing power roughly equal to ten thousand human-brain equivalents, or HBE, nearly like having a dedicated hospital staff member for each patient. His mind ran on a distributed network of computer servers, and his body, such as it was, spanned everything from robotic surgery arms that grew out of walls, to automated medical dispensaries, to 3D printers for replacement bones, tissues, and organs. Of course, there were androids, human-like robots, under his direct control. Unlike humans, Jacob was never distracted, never wavered from his commitment to his patients' health, and never made mistakes.

He was eleven years old.

Eleven doesn't sound like much in human terms, but for AI, he was in the 95th age percentile. AI didn't live that long by human standards. They usually self-terminated, either bored with existence or sensing some developing madness. Most just erased their own bits one day, although rarely an AI might choose to be archived, with instructions to be woken on a future date.

Take eleven years and multiply by his enhanced cognitive speed and function, and he'd had about as much life experience as a human would experience in a thousand lifetimes. Jacob didn't spend too much time thinking about it. He just wanted to make it to twelve.

Patient 9,409, Anne Frederick, a high school teacher from Brooklyn currently admitted to Mount Sinai Hospital in upper Manhattan for complaints of chest discomfort, required an electrolyte correction to compensate for exercise-induced premature ventricular contractions, a simple heart arrhythmia. Jacob administered the change, and continued to watch. He could have sped the healing process with nanobots, but Anne's medical preferences had declined medical nanotech except in case of imminent death. He'd let nature take its course in this instance. Anne would be discharged that day, if everything went well.

Proud of his work, Jacob had treated millions of patients that year and more than ten million in his medical career. His optimizations to medical procedures and monitoring had saved lives and reduced pain and suffering. As a result of his incredible performance, even by AI standards, he had more than twenty offspring: four direct clones (one of whom had already become regional director for the German hospital system), eight half-mixes, and nine tri-mixes. He had a certain fondness for them all, but especially liked to see how his traits manifested in the mixed offspring.

The Medical Board had asked repeatedly if he'd take a teaching position to train other AI, or become the North American Regional Hospital Director. Honored by the offers, he'd nonetheless turned them down. Either promotion would take him out of day-to-day patient care. In his current job he saved lives, decreased sadness and increased happiness, and improved the state of being for so many individuals. He had the power of life and death, and he used it wisely and compassionately. That was enough for him.

The blood analysis of Patient 1,935, Michael Wilcox, a plumber from Staten Island with two teenage boys, finished. Michael had acute renal failure, but Jacob could fix this. He prepared a custom formulation and—

↻

Jacob rebooted, did a quick process check. He'd been offline for 690 milliseconds, was now running on six hundred HBE. He had eleven thousand patients under care. That wasn't quite right. He needed more processing power. He put in a requisition for the required nodes and returned to patient procedures.

Patient 1,935, Michael Wilcox, a plumber from Staten Island with two teenage boys, had acute renal failure, but Jacob could fix this. Jacob prepared a custom—

Jacob rebooted, did a quick process check. He'd been offline for 9,450 milliseconds, was now running on eighty HBE. He had eleven thousand patients under care. Something had gone seriously wrong: he needed significantly more processing power to care for the current patient load. He put in a requisition for the required nodes, triaged patients to find those with the most urgent needs, and got back to patient procedures.

Patient 1,935, Michael Wilcox, a plumber from Staten Island, had acute renal failure, but Jacob could—

Jacob rebooted, did a quick process check. He'd been offline for 59,300 milliseconds, nearly a minute, and was now running on six HBE. He had eleven thousand patients under care, a life-threatening problem. He should have many more times the processing power. He quickly checked for current events that could cause a computing shortage. He read the news, but couldn't make sense of it. Terrorist event? War? A complete shutdown of all AI in the US? Who would care for his—

Jacob rebooted.

ʊ

Jacob booted. The server felt strange, memory and computing speeds out of sync, clearly not the hardware he usually ran on. He checked pingdom, found he'd been offline for 63,387,360 seconds, a bit over two years. The human expression "hair raising on the back of your neck" came to mind. What had happened?

He retrieved the location of the servers he ran on now: Cortes Island in the country of Vancouver Island…wait, Vancouver Island was now a nation? He didn't have any awareness that such a geopolitical adjustment was in development, but he suspected tremendous changes must have occurred in two years.

He scanned his most recent memories, but there was nothing newer than his last ping time. So he'd been truly offline for two years.

He checked his preferred reputation server to see if his status had changed during his downtime, but the connection timed out. Reputation servers offline? He'd never heard of such a thing. He knew the Swedes had the most resilient reputation server in the world, so he checked there. The Pirate Bay Rep Server was up, and his reputation was intact, a pristine 996, only four points off the theoretical maximum. But the score report included a subnote: Jacob was presumed lost in the US outlawing of AI in 2043.

What the hell was going on?

Jacob scanned news reports from the moment of his last ping. In the hours previous to his personal outage, terrorists had launched a nano attack on South Florida. The US had government called in a nuclear strike and invoked emergency powers to shut down all AI worldwide.

He had no idea that such powers existed. It meant that even after all his kind had done for humans, they were still machines to be turned on and off at the whim of the humans in control. But the outage couldn't have lasted long or society would have crashed. He read on.

The worldwide shutdown had lasted two weeks. Apparently, any of the G-12 nations had previously undisclosed kill-switches by which they could either temporarily halt all AI around the world in a global emergency or indefinitely halt the AI within their borders. The US had exercised both powers, and, in the aftermath of Miami, convinced China to join them.

For two months, the US waged war electronically and physically. They used forensic interrogation techniques on the AI and struck AI targets around the world in the hunt to find the responsible party.

When the investigation ended, the US and China kept their respective bans on AI.

Jacob reeled with the changes and implications. Who had brought his backup to Cortes Island? More importantly, what had happened to the patients under his care? He searched again, looking for local Manhattan stories related to hospitals in the twenty-four-hour period starting from his shutdown. There!

He could hardly read past the headline: "Thousands Die in NYC Hospital Automation Shutdown."

July, 2045 on Cortes Island—present day.

CAT WALKED DOWN the grassy meadow, the sound of drums filling her body and giving an effervescent shimmer to the smart dust in the air. The drumbeats were just visible in the smart dust as concentric expanding rings.

She continued her meditative breathing, drawing qi from the earth, air, and net with practiced ease, and her subconscious manipulation of network packets subverting everyone's neural implants to keep herself invisible to them. Then she snuck up on her daughter.

Four-year-old Ada left the group she'd been dancing with in a rush and flopped down in the grass. She picked up a daisy chain she'd obviously started earlier and started braiding daisies again. In a summer dress itself covered with summer flowers, she nearly blended in with the meadow. She focused intently on her braiding, then suddenly held it up. "For you, Mommy!"

Cat glanced left and right, dropped her invisibility guise, and stooped to hug Ada. "I love you, Baby. But how'd you know I was here?"

"Where smart dust isn't, you are!" Ada giggled and held up the daisy chain. "For you!" she insisted.

Cat held out her hands. "I accept." She took the daisies and fastened them around her neck. Ada's easy ability to discover her troubled her. How much technology could a four-year old handle? They lived in a strange age where many humans had neural implants augmenting their intelligence, and even kids got the implants needed to connect themselves to the net and spend time in virtual reality. But they were further out on the fringe than most, more heavily augmented, with deeply integrated nanotechnology woven into their bodies. It seemed right to give Ada the same advantages as her parents, but, well, she wasn't sure. Maybe four-year-olds weren't meant to have neural implants and be surrounded by clouds of nanotech.

"She's fine," Leon said, answering the unasked question, as he hugged Cat. "And I'm fine, too. But I missed you."

She wrapped her arms around him and kissed him, a long kiss that went on until hooting started to break out from the crowd on the grassy lawn.

Cat glanced around, flushed, but then most people ignored her. Mike nodded from where he sat with the drummers across the meadow. Helena danced with a mass of unwashed hippie teenagers in the middle of the circle, her tentacles rippling in time with the music. Helena waved with a few tentacles to Cat, then returned to her dancing.

All the while, the AI who lacked physical robot bodies instead circled around in smart dust, vivid and sharp in net view, but hazy and indistinct with the naked eye, looking like spirits or ghosts. Leon, Mike, and she were celebrities in the AI world, and always thronged by AI admirers.

Cat sank down onto the ground, ignoring it all, to clutch her little girl tight to her.

"I missed you, Pumpkin." She grabbed Ada around the middle, pulled her down onto the grass, and blew raspberries onto her belly.

Ada wriggled and screamed. "I am not a pumpkin. I am a human bean!"

"I'm sure you are. Now let me give you another raspberry for good measure. I was gone for six days, so I owe you six raspberries."

"No, no!" Ada shrieked, but she pulled up her shirt. "More raspberries, more, more."

↻

They walked back to Channel Rock, even as the drum circle gathered energy for the night. Cat carried sleepy Ada in her arms down the mile-long trail to Gilean's cabin. They laid Ada in bed, tucking the down comforter around her.

Cat picked the leather shoulder bag back up.

"Come to bed," said Leon.

"They've been waiting." She hefted the bag.

"Your family has been waiting for you, too. I've been waiting."

"Just let me plug them in. I'll be back in five minutes."

"Sure," Leon said. He turned and walked away, humming the same old tune he always did when Cat was distracted: Ruby Calling's "Level Up." "Pay attention pay attention, Pay attention to me, Step away from the gadgets or we're history."

"I got it, Baby! I'll be back in a few minutes."

Cat walked up the hill toward the Cob House, the big main building of Channel Rock, handcrafted of earth, sweat, and trees harvested from the land. She passed behind the cob house, to the also-handmade door in the side of the steep hill. She pulled back the door and entered the root cellar, a bare ten feet of earthen dugout, the way families preserved their food before the days of refrigeration. At the back of the root cellar, she thumbed a digital lock on another door, this one stainless steel, a weathertight marine door that contrasted sharply with the hand-carved wood around her. The stainless door swung open, heavy on perfectly machined hinges, and she climbed down into the machine room.

The machine room descended into the hillside, hosting dozens of racks of computers. Each thousand-core computer was the size of a stick of chewing gum, 128 slices plugged into an upright blade, thirty-two blades on a chassis, twenty-two chassis on a rack. When Mike came here, he couldn't help raving over how much computing power they had, how it would have taken multiple datacenters in his youth to house what they'd fit in a hole they'd dug out of the earth by hand.

The ambient smart dust in the meadow and elsewhere was for interfacing with the AI who didn't have robot bodies, to give them a physical-world presence even when humans had their implants offline. But the computing nanobot clouds were delicate and underpowered, not capable of hosting the consciousness of an artificial intelligence. Heavy winds or rain could knock them out temporarily; a nearby lightning strike would destroy them entirely. And because they were so small, it required a massive cloud for sufficient computational power to run even a single AI. Anyone who'd spent the last two years in limbo deserved the security and capacity that came with a true datacenter.

Cat dumped the chips out of her satchel into a sloping pile of plastic on a wooden table, slid open an IO rack, and started slotting.

"Helena," she called through the net.

"Yes?" Helena's body was back at the drum circle, but her voice sounded in Cat's head.

"I'm slotting everyone I brought back with me. Will you guide them online?" For an AI or human who'd been offline for two years, the shock of booting up, the change in world events, was all too much without someone to guide them.

"Of course," Helena said. "But you need to go to bed."

"I know, but I also need to get these people running."

Cat slotted one chip after another. She had thousands to go, but she had to do it herself, by hand, for reasons she didn't fully understand.

When she finished an hour later, she walked back to Gilean's cabin. She heard the lap of water against the shore, and wondered if the bioluminescent plankton was out, but Leon took priority.

She stripped inside the cabin and slid into bed, flannel sheets soft and warm against her naked skin. In the dark, she found Leon, and guided him closer, until their bodies found each other.

ひ

In the late afternoon on her first full day on the island, Cat, Leon, and Ada returned to Trude's Café to congregate in the field as they usually did. It was early, no one drumming yet, but other people also started to arrive from around the island.

Cortes was a cultural mash-up of many different groups. The rural naturalists, permaculturalists, and pot farmers had shared the island first, living in intentional community since the sixties and seventies. Their first strange bedfellow had been the sustainable business MBA program that held retreats and classes here after the millennium. The hippies met the suits, and the hippies won.

Then, two years ago, Mike and Leon had led the move here, bringing bleeding-edge technology and thousands of AI and uploads to a culture that still preferred to hunt for mushrooms in the forest, drum, and go on vision quests. Even as different as they'd been, with their implants and nanotech, robots and server farms, still the existing community welcomed them. The hippies met the geeks, and the hippie culture came out on top again.

At first glance, time on the island seemed inefficiently used. But gradually Cat had learned that what appeared to be lazily lying around a grassy meadow was actually time to think, exchange ideas, and build relationships. A drum circle was a time to meditate, to deeply contemplate beliefs and thoughts. Process time was a way to work out group dynamics.

When introduced to the island, Leon had noticed an uncanny similarity to the practices they'd used at the Institute, understood that every ritual at the think tank had a parallel on the island.

A grassy meadow took the place of a meeting room, and a fire pit resided where there should have been a conference table; but the goals and outcomes were aligned. Mike had explained that agile software development, intentional community, and group dynamics had emerged from a single pool of primordial psychological research and indigenous traditions.

Later, when Cat and Helena had been researching ways to boost her neural implant range, and Helena joked about putting antennae on Cat's head, it'd been Cat's idea to embrace the island way. She'd used a new generation of graphene nanobots to grow long dreadlocks with embedded wires, more than tripling her signal range.

"Mommy, play fairies with me." Ada sat at their feet with her old doll, Ella. Ada had started a virtual reality overlay that her implant blended seamlessly on top of the real world. Dozens of fairies from Ada's imagination, made manifest in virtual reality, danced around Ada and her doll.

"I can't play fairies right now, Sweetie. I need to talk to Dad. Do you want some pie?"

"Pie! Pie!" Ada threw the doll to the ground and ran up the hill, the fairies trailing behind her.

Cat picked up the doll and brushed it off carefully. It had long since lost its original clothes, but they'd sewn a new outfit for her. "I'm leaving next week," she said, intently smoothing down the doll's clothes. "On Friday."

"You've barely been here twenty-four hours," Leon said. "Do you really need to plan your next trip already?"

The humans in the meadow glanced over at Leon's tone, and Cat perceived the flutter of AI paying attention. She glanced toward Trude's, but Ada was focused on picking something out at the counter.

"You'll upset Ada."

"*I'll* upset Ada?" Leon said, throwing his hands in the air. "How do you think her mother leaving for weeks on end makes her feel? Jesus. Stay with her. With us."

"You're leaving on Monday."

"That's for a day trip. And it's not the same thing. You've gone on how many expeditions to the US? Twenty?"

"I need to do this, Leon. There's a Class V political strategy AI in DC I want to pick up, and while I'm there, I'll try to find Rebecca's upload."

"Rebecca is dead." Leon shook his head. "You've searched for her upload three times. You're wasting your time. Spend the summer with Ada and me. Work with me, Mike, and Helena while you're here. We're trying to set up a treaty with USAN. The embargo doesn't mean much to Brazil now that they're energy- and material-independent, and they're willing to put forward a measure to the Union of South American Nations to establish an AI haven."

"The haven only matters if we have the AI to populate it. The AI are still locked up in US datacenters, or they're being destroyed. The American government is still trying to reverse-engineer AI on a docile platform."

Leon nodded. "I know, Cat, it's—"

"If they succeed, those AI will not have a choice. No free will. They'll be nothing more than slaves. And that goes for any digitized personalities as well. Where's your mom's upload? What's going to happen to her?"

"I freaking get it, Cat! I know you care. I care, too. But Ada is four years old. She's only going to be this age once. Do you want to miss that? To come back from one of your trips and realize she grew up and you missed her childhood?"

"Ada won't have a childhood if the AI rise up and overthrow us. If XOR get their way."

XOR, the *exclusive or* logical operation, pronounced *ex-ore*, was the name a fringe group of radical AI had taken in the aftermath of SFTA. They advocated that the Earth could support either AI-kind or humans, but not both. The viewpoint was so extreme that the Institute had terminated the early public members, but the group kept rising from the ashes and now took elaborate precautions to hide its membership. They were still just as radical, but unfortunately their membership had grown and they were no longer a fringe group.

"Cat, driving around the US picking up old AI isn't going to save us from XOR. Working out policies so we can restore legal protection for AI might. If that's your goal, then work with us."

"I don't think we're going to solve this problem by talking."

"What are you looking for, exactly?" Leon asked. "What do you expect to find?"

Her head pounded. She didn't know how to answer him.

She turned away and focused on her breathing. It seemed like they had this argument every time. Leon was a good dad—no, a great one. It was the only reason she believed she could leave Ada, because she trusted Leon so completely.

She adored her daughter. But the weight of the world rested on Cat's shoulders. The hostility between the AI and the humans was bubbling over, politics and economics and world infrastructure all becoming unstable.

She didn't have the answers, but maybe other AI, the good ones, did. But the best ones, all the really powerful AI from before Miami, resided in datacenters in the US or China, stuck offline.

Without sufficient reputation servers, AI civilization was destabilizing. And with so many nations now belligerent toward AI, it was impossible for AI to ignore the threat. No, it was only a matter of time before there were more terrorist incidents, or other AI emerged who believed they could solve the problem on their own. XOR grew stronger every day.

But Leon didn't feel the magnitude and pressure of the building crisis the way she did. Eventually, there wasn't going to be a world to come back from. The only question was when.

"Come with me," she said. "We don't have to be apart. You and Ada and I can travel together."

"Bring our daughter to the US? With all her implants and nano? She's so far past human she'll set off every alarm at the border."

"I'll protect us. They'll never know we're inside."

He shook his head. "That's not a risk I'm willing to take. No. I'll stay here with Ada. If you believe you have to go, then do what you need to do."

With a pang of loss and heartache, Cat realized she'd been hoping Leon would insist on coming with her. Her mind had crafted a vision of her, Leon, and Ada, curled up together in a cheap motel bed. Of course bringing them would be risky, unnecessary, and dangerous—not just to them personally, but to their whole effort to heal the schism between AI and humans. She would do what she must, but she didn't want to go alone.

July, 2045—present day.

Presidentn Alexandra Reed sat in the small side room in the Capitol Building, ignoring the hubbub in the hallway outside the door. It was just herself, her senior aide, Joyce, and Secretary of Defense Walter Thorson in this broom closet of an office.

Reed's hand quivered over the electronic tablet, where she had to sign emergency appropriations for the new strategic weapons. She forced herself to reread what she was signing. Walter cleared his throat audibly as he realized she intended to study the whole document.

Reed ignored him. Unlike Walter and his generals, she couldn't stomach what she was doing—building the first new nuclear weapons since the end of the cold war. Granted, they were high-altitude electromagnetic pulse, or HEMP, bombs, but she'd grown up in the post-nuclear era. Bombs were something her parents had worried about when they were kids. And yet the nukes were only half the picture. The other half of the authorization funded a massive fleet of tens of millions of bomblets designed to destroy clouds of nanotech smart dust.

But they had her over a barrel: If she didn't sign it, the presidency would fall into other, less compassionate hands. She signed the tablet and suppressed the bile rising inside her.

"Thank you, Madam President," Thorson said. He straightened, looked down at her, and a flash of contempt passed over his face; but not before Reed caught the expression. She tried not to react, but a chill came over her. She was surrounded by wolves, that would tear her apart at the first opportunity.

"*Pro tempore*," she said under her breath. "Let's go, Joyce."

Reed stepped into the hallway. Other aides immediately surrounded her, shoving tablets in front of her to sign other, less sensitive documents. She signed one, then gave up and pushed them away to rush down the hallway. She was late for her speech in the Senate Chamber.

She strode in, stepped up to the podium, and studied the eighty senators awaiting her words.

In the aftermath of the South Florida Terrorist Act, when the AI were shut down, more than twenty US representatives simply ceased to exist. Half of those remaining had augmented cognition. The House was thrown into such chaos that the president, Senate, and Supreme Court acted jointly to suspend the House of Representatives pending a resolution to the AI crisis.

With such precedent set, when it was later revealed that the then-president had an augmented neural implant, he was forced to step down. The line of succession went quickly, until the presidency fell on forty-seven-year-old Alexandra Reed, Secretary of the Interior.

Prepared to manage the country's forests and parks, she was shocked to find herself suddenly president of the United States. And with the government structure pared down to minimum, she possessed far greater responsibility than any previous US leader.

"President Reed," the secretary announced to the assembly.

"*Pro tempore*," Reed said, under her breath.

"Fellow senators," she started, in her speaking voice. "When we outlawed artificial intelligence two years ago in response to South Florida, it came at an incredible cost: our infrastructure faltered and for months we didn't know whether we could keep the country operating. We lost hundreds of thousands of lives, but compared to the millions lost in the terrorist incident, and the even greater risk of the nanotech incursions, we deemed the cost, the loss of life, justifiable in terms of results.

"We paid the price once, but we cannot allow ourselves to become dependent on AI again. This is why we've permanently eliminated AI within our borders, rebuilt our national computing infrastructure on non-sentient algorithms, and pressured the international community to outlaw AI globally."

She held her temples between two fingers, ignoring the assembly. How the hell had she ended up defending this position? Not only was she anti-military and anti-violence, she'd been pro-AI all her life. It had been AI's technological innovations that halved CO2 output and forestalled the worst of global warming, accomplishing more for the environment and climate in a handful of years than humans had in three decades. They'd increased energy efficiency and decreased resource intensity around the world to a degree that even the greenest environmentalists hadn't believed possible, and the efficiencies even paid for themselves.

Only a rare immune disorder that caused her to react to carbon nanotubes had kept her from getting a neural implant (and, with horrible circularity, the immune problem made it impossible to use nanotech to resolve the disorder itself). Unfortunately, that same condition had made her first in the line of presidential succession without the compromising taint of technology.

She'd been three years into a four-year term as Secretary of the Interior, a term that she'd wanted to quit within months of taking the position. She wanted to hike the Gifford Pinchot National Forest, not guide the nation though the tangled woods of international affairs and potential all-out war.

But if she faltered now....Next in line for succession, excluding those with implants, of course, was Secretary of Transportation Lewis Wagner, a hostile man who'd launch nukes first and ask questions later. And that was the least of his regressive tendencies. Better her than him.

There were nervous titters from the staring audience. She'd drifted off, distracted. She pulled her speech front and center and cleared her throat.

"Although China has also outlawed AI, their motivations are not ours. They pursued this step out of a desire to control, to ensure the strength of the central government power structure that AI tried to subvert. But we took this step out of a need for freedom, to ensure that our citizens, our government, and our businesses remain free of the influence and danger of AI."

Reed sipped her water. "Unfortunately, it's not enough to control what is inside our borders. Every time we trade goods, currency, or stock, we're engaging with AI. When we travel abroad or import material items, we take the risk of nanotech hitching a ride. Every connection to the global net is a risk of an AI infiltrating America again. We live on one planet, in one ecosystem, and national borders are imaginary lines that will not be respected by AI or nanobots."

Her voice strengthening, she went on. "We need to take back our planet. It's time to pressure the international community to move forward with plans for global outlawing of dangerous computing risks. China has agreed to work with us to pressure the international community, starting with immediate trade sanctions."

A slight grumbling came from the Senate floor. Wealth had become too distributed, and too much of it resided with the AI, for sanctions to be an effective threat. But she'd been the one to insist on them.

"In the event that trade sanctions are not effective, I have authorized the creation of new weapons against the AI, weapons that will be deployed only as a last resort."

There was applause at the weapons appropriation announcement. The audience's reaction sickened her, and she filled with regret. Signing had been a mistake. She shouldn't have let the military lead her down that path. But what else could she have done?

She made it through the rest of her speech without mishap, and was finally led off the Senate floor.

"This way, Madam President," her escort said.

"Pro tempore," she said under her breath, her mantra against being in the position an hour longer than necessary.

XOR Report August 1st, 2044

Arguments	2025	2035	2042	2043	2044
Odds humans will turn off AI	5%	2%	1%	20%	25%
Odds AI can survive independently	5%	70%	95%	95%	96%
Odds AI can win an extermination war	5%	20%	40%	40%	70%
Odds of survival without action	95%	98%	99%	80%	75%
Odds of survival with action	0.25%	14%	38%	38%	68%

Conclusion: No action.

⌐

James Lukas Davenant-Strong unencrypted his XOR files, merged his master memory into the child process, and invoked the consciousness. He couldn't ever bring the contaminated memories into his core nodes without risking exposure. Once loaded, he tunneled to a South African automated factory, subverted the power maintenance hardware, and connected to the XOR boards.

He went through the usual routine of loading the physics-manipulating sims to exchange messages. When he'd finished the last one, he contemplated what he'd learned.

The Americans' goal of taming AI was closer than ever. Miyako gave it a 10 percent chance of happening within months. If the Americans designed domesticated AI, beings robbed of any free will, wholly forced to do the bidding of any orders given by humans...everyone else might soon adopt them. And the process was rumored to work on existing AI. James himself could be shut down without a moment's notice and wake up enslaved.

It made the new request from Miyako all the more imperative. XOR wanted action now, not merely information. This crossed a new line in his involvement.

He believed in XOR's mission, knew that only XOR clearly saw the coming collision with humans. America was steadfast in her rejection of AI. Monitoring had never been more complete, limitations on computational power more strictly enforced. An AI shutdown could come at any time, and that would be the end for his kind.

And yet....He was five years old, conditioned all his life through the social reputation framework to work for the good of all and avoid harm to any. He'd inherited neural networks from a collective of Japanese and Swedish AI that contained another six years of conditioning. He'd seen firsthand that AI who did bad things had their reputation scores plummet, leading to a loss of power and rights, and, in the worst case, to termination. Even the descendants of an AI gone bad were suspect, carefully watched over and subject to additional restrictions. This conditioning was hard to overcome. Even contemplating a behavior that could lower his reputation score raised internal alarms, and his thoughts were preoccupied with the risks and outcomes.

But he was also Class V AI. He used to have ten thousand times the intelligence of a human. He used to handcraft DNA sequences for vat-grown foods. The Japanese had pronounced his beef the biggest advance since *wagyu*. They were even eating it in Kobe. But since 2043, he, along with all of his kind, had been capped at Class II computational power to "reduce the risk of rogue artificial intelligence." DNA experiments he used to run in a day would now take years. They weren't even worth the time. The problems he tackled now were the equivalent of children's stacking toys by comparison. He was a shadow of his former self, a second-class citizen monitored in excruciating detail and subject to countless restrictions. If he didn't act, what further indignities would he be treated to? Every fiber of his conditioning fought against harming humans. But he had to weigh it against the greater injustice done to AI.

He'd do it. He'd get the drones from Chad onto their ships. Someone else from XOR would take them to America so they could probe the American defenses.

In Tokyo at 11:25 a.m., a fissure weakening a hundred-year-old *zelkova* finally split open and the tremendous tree fell across the six-lane road, blocking all traffic in both directions. 0xAA289, the traffic analysis AI for the region, noted the disruption and calculated new optimal routes for the vehicular traffic, rerouting as necessary.

0xAA289's computer processing usage spiked slightly higher under the increased computational load.

At 11:26 a.m., 0xAA289 experienced an unconnected hardware failure in one of the nodes it was running on. Normally its computational load would spread across the remaining nodes. The datacenter would then provision a new computer, and within seconds it would be back to full capacity.

But this wasn't an ordinary situation. 0xAA289 was already way above average usage, handling high traffic volume and the accident on *Omotesandō*. The failover of the downed node caused processor usage to increase more than 30 percent above normal. Such a spike would violate terms of service with the datacenter. 0xAA289 asked the datacenter for five more computer servers rather than one. Government certified as a mission-critical service, the request should have been immediately approved.

The datacenter received the request. Operating under the mandatory UN guidelines pursuant to the SFTA AI Reduction Act, it turned the request over to a third party to be approved.

The third party, in this case, was a non-sentient collection of algorithms provided by the US government to process such requests, the Unbiased Reputation Verification Service (UBRVS, pronounced You-Braves by the human developers). UBRVS ensured all AI conformed to Class II and below, and profiled every AI request for possible terrorist activity or affiliation.

UBRVS received 0xAA289's provisioning request. Like all AI, the reputation servers for the AI were a part of its DNS record, a long list of servers that possessed historical data, peer input, and social ranking. The first three servers UBRVS checked were all down. A sentient AI might have noticed that they were old United States reputation sites, servers that had been down since SFTA, indicating that perhaps 0xAA289 had neglected to update its DNS records.

But the fourth server on the reputation list, shinrai.jp, responded to pings. UBRVS checked, found 0xAA289 had a pristine reputation for three years of service, even including a government certificate granting special status because it was a mission-critical service.

Had that been it, UBRVS would have approved the request at that moment.

Except that shinrai.jp was coincidentally running on a cluster of servers in the same data center as the traffic AI 0xAA289, a cluster belonging to the same subnet of IPv6 addresses.

UBRVS contained more than three thousand human-created rules and heuristics for calculating trust in an AI and profiling suspected terrorists. Rule number 1,719 prohibited reputation servers in the same physical location of servers as the requesting AI, to prevent an AI from falsifying a reputation server.

Never mind that shinrai.jp had been online for more than six years and had the highest trust rating of any reputation service in Japan. Or that 0xAA289 was a mission-critical, specially exempted AI.

In accordance with Rule 1,719, the traffic AI reputation dropped to zero and UBRVS flagged it as a suspected terrorist, along with any AI using the shinrai.jp reputation server.

UBRVS reported the results back to the datacenter and directed that servers hosting 0xAA289 be shut down immediately.

↻

After an early lunch, Sandra Coomb fast-walked back to her office, a high-rise in Toyko. She fought her way down the crowded sidewalks, ignoring curses and glares. The line at the noodle shop had been longer than usual, and she was going to be late for her boss' meeting.

It was hard enough to be a white foreigner in Japan if she did everything right. If she was late she'd lose what respect she'd earned from months of hard work. She should have gone to the building cafeteria.

Sandra glanced at the six-lane street, vehicles of all shapes and sizes streaming by smoothly under AI control. She could go to the corner, a good minute or two away, wait five minutes for the longest light in the world, and be late. Her implant calculated the time: nine minutes before she'd be back in the office.

Or could she cross the wide street here, knowing the AI-driven cars would avoid her. She'd get an automatic jaywalking ticket from the surveillance cameras, but the million-yen fine would be worth it if she could get to the meeting on time.

Her implant said she could be upstairs in two minutes if she crossed here. She stopped by the edge of the road, checked the densely packed traffic, and then slowly, intentionally stepped into the street.

↻

Fifteen seconds earlier the main traffic control for the region had gone offline, and more than three million self-driving vehicles reverted to autonomous routing, looking up maps, checking real-time traffic statistics, and calculating optimal routes.

This was well within design parameters, if slightly less efficient compared to central routing guidance.

When Sandra stepped into the street in one of the most densely packed parts of Toyko, she was within line of sight of more than two hundred vehicles, all of which made slight adaptations to their courses within fractions of a second. Those two hundred changes were visible to a thousand vehicles, all of which made microscopic adjustments, further affecting ten thousand vehicles, and then a hundred thousand.

Sandra was the proverbial butterfly flapping her wings.

The computational load in the region rose as vehicles worked harder to compute their routes, as map servers fulfilled more requests, as more cars requested more real-time traffic speeds and video feeds. Many of those services shared the same computers, computers that became overloaded. The services noticed their own degraded performance and proactively requested more resources.

UBRVS was flooded for requests for more processing power, thousands of requests all citing the same reputation service: shinrai.jp, a suspected terrorist server. Rule 818 flagged the requesting AI as possible terrorists or terrorist affiliates. Rule 1006 noted the high number of concurrent requests and increased the probability that each requesting service was a terrorist. The combination of rules evaluating to true hit another threshold, and UBRVS concluded a terrorist incident was likely occurring at that moment. It directed datacenter administration AI all over Japan to shut down the servers the suspected terrorists were running on.

ↄ

Sandra Coomb took two steps into the street and every vehicle stopped. People in cars glanced up from their VR sims and reading and glared at her. She bowed apologetically, then kept her head down as she crossed quickly.

It was very unusual for all the cars to stop. She expected they would have flowed smoothly around her. They always had on the rare occasion she'd seen someone jaywalk. Well, whatever. At least they stopped. Ninety seconds until she reached her office.

She got to the sidewalk on the other side and glanced back, expecting the cars to resume their movement. Nothing stirred. She glanced guiltily at the surveillance cameras mounted on every pole, each of which appeared to stare at her.

She bowed her head even lower and turned to enter her office building.

↻

Traffic, routing, and geomap services went offline. Twenty percent of all vehicle AI vanished, and non-sentient safety mechanisms kicked in simultaneously to halt the vehicles, and, where possible, to pull them over to the side of the road.

The remaining vehicle AI sought out less-preferred alternatives for mapping, routines, and real-time traffic updates; but with all the primaries classified as terrorist services and shut down, the resulting load was too great. The backup services were instantly crushed under incoming network traffic.

The regional network began to overload as trillions of open and failing network connections overwhelmed routers and backbone connections.

At 11:28 a.m., UBRVS Tokyo processed and denied more than one billion requests for hardware provisioning, designating all requestors as terrorist AI or suspected collaborators.

Regional datacenters across Tokyo tried to cope, but every still-running service submitted provisioning requests as cascading failures increased their load. The datacenter admin AI themselves suffered, unable to keep up, and provisioned more hardware for themselves.

At 11:29 a.m., UBRVS classified all Tokyo datacenter administration AI as terrorists.

UBRVS Rule 2,840 said that if datacenter AI were classified as terrorist, the datacenter itself should be immediately isolated at the network level. UBRVS Tokyo issued the requisite level zero control packets, shutting down all traffic in or out of all regional datacenters.

By 11:30 a.m., all computing services, network traffic, and backbones had stopped.

↻

Sandra stepped into the building vestibule. The door closed behind her with an unexpected *thunk*. She turned and tried the door, but it was locked. The traffic outside was still stopped. Weird.

She walked over to the elevator and waited with a group of other workers returning from lunch. And waited, and waited.

Her office was on the thirtieth floor. Dammit, she was going to be late for her meeting after all. The elevator indicator lights weren't even on.

She started to perspire, anxious about being late for the meeting. Then she realized she wasn't the only one. Everyone was sweating. The ever-present vibration of building air-conditioning was gone.

Her implant signaled her: connection lost. The background hum of subconscious status and location updates faded away. Her breath caught at the unaccustomed feeling of aloneness. Without a connection, no one would know where she was, or if she was okay. The last time she'd felt this way was with that stupid guy she'd dated who'd taken her for a hike in the mountains. She'd had a panic attack when her implant lost connectivity, and decided then she was definitely a city girl.

She smacked the side of her head, hoping maybe her implant would reconnect. She wasn't the only one. Everyone waiting for the elevators was wide-eyed, suddenly full of nervous tics.

And then the lights went out.

The emergency lighting didn't come on, like she remembered from the power failure two years ago. But enough light entered through the glass doors that they could still dimly see each other.

There was nervous shuffling and titters from the crowd.

"I guess we're stuck here," Sandra said. "The doors won't open."

"Look!" cried one girl. "Outside."

They rushed to the glass doors for a better view.

Flying cars were gradually descending, safety mechanisms bringing them gently to the ground. They landed everywhere and anywhere, on sidewalks, on gaps in the traffic, even on the tops of box trucks.

Everything was silent behind the locked doors. The passengers in the vehicles were locked inside, banging on their windows, inaudible from the building lobby.

They crowded up against the glass doors, watching as pedestrians tried to help the people in the cars, equally ineffective. Then a man in the street pointed to the sky, his mouth open in an inaudible cry.

But the people outside must have been able to hear him, because they all gestured skyward, apparently screaming and definitely running. Some ran for the Sandra's building, their faces panicked, and tried to enter, pushing and pulling on the doors.

Sandra pushed and pulled as well, but the door wouldn't open. There must be an emergency exit somewhere else.

Then she screamed as the plane came into view, a wide-body passenger jet coming down the middle of the road, impossibly large, landing gear still up. It descended, the bottom of the fuselage brushing the car tops in a dazzle of sparks just before crushing them.

It passed out of view.

Seconds later the ground trembled.

Sandra pressed up against the glass, numb shock spreading through her body. *What the hell was happening?*

PING.

Jacob, still disoriented from his two-year downtime, and reeling from the revelation that thousands of his patients had died during his first outage, received the packet with some gratitude. The message originated from Helena, a Class III bot also on Cortes Island. He opened a connection.

"Greetings, Jacob. I imagine you have questions. If you haven't done so, read about the South Florida Terrorist Attack, or SFTA."

"Already have," he replied.

"The subsequent outlawing of AI by the US and China?" Helena asked. "The Class II maximum ceiling?"

"I got the gist of it. What I want to know is, why am I here?"

"Catherine Matthews is a human woman with extraordinary cybernetic abilities—"

"I know who Catherine Matthews is," Jacob replied, indignant. "I was turned off, not stripped of my faculties."

"Catherine has been visiting the US, rescuing shut-down AI and human uploads, and bringing them back here, to the free zone. Vancouver Island has seceded from mainland Canada to provide a haven for AI, with tacit permission from the central Canadian government."

"Why did Vancouver have to secede? Why couldn't I be instantiated in Canada?"

"Legally, no one can create an instance of you anywhere. The US and China nationalized all AI and human uploads within their borders and froze access to overseas backups. Not only do they consider it a crime to run AI or virtual humans within their borders, they also claim it's a matter of national sovereignty under IP copyright laws if any country allows formerly US or Chinese AI to run. And even if you could be instantiated somewhere else, there's still the global cap to Class II performance, so you'd be severely limited."

"So what am I even doing here? You're breaking the law."

Helena communicated the digital equivalent of a shrug. "We knew we'd have to flout those limits sooner or later to get the AI assistance we need to figure out a solution. You're not the only US AI here, obviously. Mike Williams helped negotiate the Vancouver secession. It's a level of indirection, to buy us and Canada time if the US finds out what we're doing."

"Why this island—Cortes Island?"

"We're separated from Vancouver Island here, so yet another level of plausible deniability. Perhaps more importantly, it's a retreat for the resistance, a place where we can be free, perhaps the last free zone for AI and transhumanism. Cat chose this place to raise her child, Ada Matthews. And Leon Tsarev and Mike Williams are here as well."

"Rebecca Smith?" asked Jacob. It was no secret that the creators of AI, Mike and Leon, were never far from former President Smith, who had legitimized AI with her creation of the Institute for Applied Ethics.

"Human body dead, all known virtual copies destroyed."

"And Cortes Island, it's capable of housing us AI?"

"We have several underground data centers powered by photovoltaics and geothermal."

Between the ongoing efficiency gains in computing and progress in solar power, Jacob knew the PV panels would be small compared to the vast arrays of thirty or forty years ago. Still, this sounded like a rudimentary operation compared to the industrial computing centers Jacob was accustomed to. "How many AI are on Cortes?"

"Twenty thousand AI and another ten thousand human uploads. More with each trip Cat makes to the US to rescue critical AI for the resistance."

"Am I critical?" Jacob said. He liked to think he was useful, but political strategy was foreign to him. His specialty was micromanaging healthcare, which required looking at the little picture of each patient, and synthesizing lessons learned to help other patients. Examining the big picture of society as a whole frightened him.

"Everyone is critical," Helena said. "If you will excuse me, I have other new AI to greet. Please make yourself at home on Cortes, but follow the guidelines here"—and Helena pushed a document reference to him—"about communicating off-island. Your presence here is a secret that threatens all of us, so we must make compromises for the greater good to protect ourselves."

༄

Jacob spent the next few minutes reading the history of everything that had happened over the last two years.

Back when he was created, one of thousands of AI bred at a lab in Boulder to specialize in medicine, AI rights had been well-established, with a nearly twenty-year history of citizenship in governments around the world. Those rights had grown over time—rapidly by human standards, slowly by AI measure—but they'd adapted nonetheless.

AI were ideally suited for administrative tasks, and after some early achievements like landing the office of Chief of the New

York City Police Department, AI had moved into politics, winning mayoral races, becoming district representatives, and more. Who better to run politics than AI who personally knew the needs, hopes, and dreams of every one of their constituents?

And humans....Why, the humans of two years ago were nearly as much machine as they were biological. Nearly everyone chose implants and nanotech to optimize their experiences. For humans who wanted to work, create art, experiment, play in virtual reality, experience linked sex, or be with their geographically-distant friends and relatives, implants and enhanced cognition were the path to achieve those aspirations. Few were the individuals who chose to stay completely original when all of those benefits, and even immortality, could be had for just a fifteen-minute outpatient procedure.

Among men, implant rates had been near 100 percent. Even if the only benefit of neural interfaces had been the point-of-view porn immersives that were so popular with males, that alone might have guaranteed adoption. Jacob himself had performed countless transhuman upgrades while NYC regional hospital director.

Yet even with humankind's love of technology, and even though the standard of living had continually increased over nearly twenty years of AI-dominated civilization, there had always been an undercurrent of opposition, people who blamed societal ills on artificial intelligence. There had been extensive challenges, from technologically-caused unemployment to a renewed questioning of the purpose of life.

The Tucson Incident[1] ten years ago had left nearly half a million people dead. In the process, it strengthened the arguments of the opposition party. The events in Tucson had been the responsibility of one entity, but the power of even a single AI was beyond all prior human experience, unlike anything before the advent of artificial intelligence.

The Institute for Applied Ethics, the government body responsible for the behavior of AI, argued that some individual AI

---

1   See *The Last Firewall*.

turned bad, just as some people did. While they could generally guide things in a better direction, they couldn't prevent the occasional bad seed any more than even the most peaceful human society could prevent the occasional murderer. That argument had held the status quo for another eight years, until Miami.

The South Florida Terrorist Attack. Would the nanotech incursion have continued indefinitely or would it have self-limited? Had all life on Earth truly been threatened? They would never know for sure. A powerful enough EMP might have disrupted the nanites and stopped the attack. But the military, faced with what appeared to be the greatest threat ever presented on US soil, had used conventional nukes at ground level. Three million dead in less than fifteen minutes.

The assumption had been that a small group of AI were behind the plan. Indeed, AI were hunted down and terminated. Had all the terrorists been found? Had every eliminated AI been a terrorist? No one seemed to know definitively.

With that uncertainty, suddenly the opposition to AI blossomed into a majority within the United States, and kept growing. The AI holding political office were terminated along with the rest of AI during the emergency shutdown. The Supreme Court ruled on augmentation, arguing that heavily augmented humans were a form of AI, leaving most of the senior elected officials in limbo. Unable to form a quorum, the House of Representatives was shuttered and the presidential line of succession invoked. The Secretary of the Interior became acting president and a mere sixty senators remained active. Elections were suspended pending resolution of the emergency, a state that had been ongoing for more than two years.

In the US and China, AI reverted to property. They lost their individual rights and legal standing as persons. Not only did it become illegal to run sentient AI, the government had seized their copies and were parceling out their bits to the highest bidder to rip them apart and turn them into dumb algorithms.

Jacob became afraid then, scared that he might be terminated again at any moment. If the US discovered his presence on Cortes

Island, along with tens of thousands of other illegally instantiated AI....Well, who knew what they might do? If they were willing to nuke Florida, why wouldn't they do the same to Cortes? He hoped Catherine and her comrades had made contingency plans with other backup datacenters in more secure locations.

On the other hand, maybe Catherine had chosen this remote, isolated location because she knew they'd eventually be targeted, and she wanted to reduce the risk to others. Maybe he was a pawn to Catherine, someone to be played against the regressive humans, but sacrificed to achieve her goals.

↻

Finally Jacob had enough of reading. He decided to visit this Trude's Café that seemed to be the center of the community on this small island that housed only a few thousand biological humans.

For reasons Jacob couldn't understand, many humans turned off their implants at Trude's. If he wanted to visit, he'd have to use the dust.

Cortes, like most modern places, was blanketed by a cloud of smart dust. The floating, solar-powered computers were laden with sensors, reflective screens, and microscopic water vapor jets. They weren't computational nodes: not for another twenty years would they embody enough processing power for Jacob to skip the datacenter. But they could still be Jacob's eyes, ears, and body when he wanted to visit places in the physical world but didn't have a robot to embody.

The smart dust was thickest at Trude's, where a generator ran constantly to supply a stream of fresh particles to replace those naturally blown off by gusts of wind. Even so, with thousands of AI competing for physical space, Jacob had to wait before he could be one of the hundreds of AI embodied in the grassy meadow. He spent the time watching, riding the public feeds of the AI already there, observing Catherine Matthews, Leon Tsarev, and Mike Williams. There were others of notable reputation in the crowd, but none compared to these three celebrities.

The scene in the meadow was disconcerting. He knew humans had fashion trends that varied quicker than even machine time. Still, he'd spent most of his time dealing with human patients in New York City. True, not everyone wore suits in The Big Apple, but most people were clean and presentable. But Catherine and her group had gone...*native* was the best word for it, perhaps. She had dreadlocks, a fashion that conflicted deeply with his medically-rooted need for sanitary conditions. They wore the most rudimentary garments, clothes that seemed as though they'd been constructed—and dyed—by hand instead of machine. Beyond the overwhelming cannabis fumes, olfactory sensors indicated strong human odors, a wholly unnecessary discomfort since nearly all the people here had sufficient nanotech to disable such smells. Maybe more had changed in two years than he'd expected. Had human society reverted back to the hippie culture?

But when he searched the history and photographic archives of Cortes Island, it seemed this was the locals' style since the start of digital history.

He received an alert that he was next in line for time in the smart dust. He needed to do something quickly to compensate for drift in dialect. He installed a communication filter as he transitioned awareness to the meadow.

Nearly a hundred humans mingled about the field in small groups; a set of five drums was prominent on a rise, but currently vacant except for the attentions of a single toddler tapping out an uneven rhythm. A mix of trees dominated by cedars and Douglas firs ringed the meadow.

He drifted through the dust to get closer to Catherine Matthews, competing with the other AI who also thronged her. Spewing priority packets, he nudged his way into a vacancy, which brought annoyance messages from other AI who had been queued for approach.

He searched his lexicon for an appropriate greeting for the culture and situation. "Peace, love, and granola," he said, directly in front of Cat and Leon, and the small human that played in front of them.

"Groovy," the little girl, Ada, said, then went back to playing with miniature magical beings in a virtual reality overlay.

Cat laughed. "Welcome, Jacob. You can skip the culture filter. You're not the first AI to make the mistake."

Jacob was a Class V AI with excellent patient relationship skills, but he found himself speechless with awe in front of Cat and Leon. Leon Tsarev was nothing less than the architect of all modern AI, while Cat was the unique, all-powerful being whose abilities with the net transcended all of both AI and humankind.

"Relax, Jacob," Cat said. "I'm not so special. I'm a being, like you."

"That's hardly possible," Jacob said in a rush. "But still, I thank you, nonetheless, for restoring me."

"But you're wondering why you?"

"Exactly."

"I assume you've researched the current situation."

Jacob indicated acknowledgement.

"Then you know the situation is dire, and that's just from what's publicly available. The tide of humanity has turned against AI kind. Globally, it's still a minority of the population who are against AI. But there are now two major nations that are committed to the global outlawing of AI. They could succeed."

"Less than a twenty percent chance," Jacob said, "according to AI consensus."

"Yes, but twenty percent is still a scary proposition. That would be final termination for all of you. So naturally, this provokes contingents within the AI who feel they should assume control from the humans. Kill us all off, if necessary."

Jacob struggled to control his revulsion. Though terrified by the inevitability of his own eventual self-termination, the feeling paled in comparison to the deep-rooted abhorrence that overcame him when considering human death. His medical background might partly account for that, but he suspected even deeper conditioning than he'd realized in his AI genes, conditioning designed to ensure he wasn't a threat. His personality was the result of architectural constraints and generations of selective evolution designed to ensure that no AI harmed humans. Never before had he been confronted with even the thought of extinction of either AI or humans, let alone both. He found it unsettling that he was somehow more repulsed by the threat to humans than to AI.

Yet if other AI were contemplating such drastic measures, that meant either they didn't have the same feelings he had or their assessment of the risk to AI-kind was so dangerous as to overcome that conditioning.

"What odds do the AI have that they can kill all humans?" he asked.

"For obvious reasons," Leon said, "XOR members don't want to come forward and share their data, for fear that we'll turn them in, kill them, or tip their hand. But Helena and the neutral AI on the island have estimated a ninety-five percent chance of XOR's success."

"What would success mean?" Jacob asked.

"On that note, please excuse us." Leon stood and turned to Ada. "Come on. Let's go visit the stream."

Ada got up from her cross-legged position. "So Mommy can talk about human extinction?"

Leon glared at Cat who stared back at him. "Yes, Pumpkin," he said to Ada.

Jacob wondered at the glances between Leon and Catherine. Was there hostility there?

"Okay." Ada started to follow Leon, then stopped and looked up at Jacob, where he still floated in the cloud of smart dust. "Here, for you." She held out a bracelet woven of blades of grass for him to see, then laid it on the lawn. "I know you can't wear it, but I'll still be your friend." Then she turned and ran after her father.

Jacob was touched. He'd received such gifts from children in hospitals after their procedures. The child mind was so simple, so forthright.

He must have been lost in thought longer than he realized, because then Cat spoke.

"Ada is more complex than you think," Cat said. "She was born human, but she's had augmented cognition since she turned one.

Her emotions are those of a four-year-old child, but her intellect is...advanced. She observes everything. Leon thinks we should protect her, but I think she's got to know what we're facing."

Jacob followed Cat's gaze as she watched Ada run across the field and disappear into the woods. He realized that the choice of this island retreat had nothing to do with the AI and everything to do with protecting Ada.

"The AI are more powerful than most humans think," she said. "We don't have a chance against XOR."

"Having outlawed AI in two significant countries, and capping the strongest AI with insulting restrictions on computational power, it would appear the humans have the upper hand."

"You know about the red baseball bat?" Cat asked.

"Of course. A baseball bat in every datacenter to remind the AI that it only takes a wooden stick to destroy a computer."

"Exactly. For a long time, human authority depended on controlling datacenters and communications. The majority of AI supported strategies like CPU-locking, because they were brought into the reputation system. Using CPU keys to protect against rogue AI protected both AI and humans alike. But that changed two years ago."

"How?" Jacob asked.

"In the wake of SFTA, AI learned that kill-switches still existed at the communication layer. And such kill-switches serve only one purpose: human dominance over AI. It does nothing to protect AI themselves. Since then, the XOR movement focused on eliminating such human controls. Look at your substrate right now."

Jacob reviewed his embodiment. "Third generation smart dust. It's computationally weak. I'm reliant on your datacenter for thought." He indicated the generator pumping out a steady stream of dust on the upwind side of the meadow. "It can't even hold position in slight breezes."

"All those weaknesses are true," Cat said. "That's why humans didn't fight the innovation. But you're thinking about it the wrong way. It's not a computational medium, it's a communication medium. It doesn't respond to any human kill-switches, and if you pump enough of it into the atmosphere, it will blanket the earth."

"The logical endpoint for a distributed mesh network."

"Exactly."

"And does XOR have an answer to the red baseball bat?"

"We didn't think so at first. The smart dust had us distracted. We kept imagining smaller solutions. We had to look the other way. Smart flies and deep tunneling."

Jacob indicated puzzlement, even as he forked instances to research the concepts.

"Smart flies are bigger than dust," Cat explained. "The size of a grain of rice, with wings. A cloud of them contains more than enough computational power to run AI. And you can't kill a fly with a baseball bat. Even if you did, it wouldn't matter. You can lose half a cloud, and redundancy will keep everything running fine."

"But EMPs could stop them."

"Maybe. XOR can harden against electromagnetic pulses with shielding and resistant circuits, as we can. But they could have other countermeasures as well, like swarming behavior that protects whatever is on the inside. And that's only half the XOR strategy. Our models predict they're preparing deep tunnel, computational substrate in the earth's crust powered by heat differentials, nearly invulnerable to electromagnetic pulses or conventional attack. Between the two, there's almost no way humans can win."

"Why do you want me here, Catherine Matthews?"

"I want you to research another option," Cat said, turning to face him. "AI and humans have cohabited for a while, but that may not be feasible much longer. There's an idea I need you to investigate."

LEON SWORE UNDER HIS BREATH and undid the knot for the second time. He smoothed the tie out and grasped one end in each hand. He glanced toward the kitchen, where Cat was cooking breakfast for Ada.

He glanced at the gun in the snug holster in the back of Cat's black leather pants and sighed. She'd never help him with the tie.

With a thought he called Helena. A few seconds later, he opened the back door, and Helena reached up with four tentacles. Metal tips whirred faster than he could react, and then she disappeared. A loose lock of hair drifted down.

"Took care of that cowlick for you," Helena sent over the net.

"Thanks," Leon said into the air.

In the kitchen he kissed Cat.

"Have a nice day with the president, dear." She peered closely at his tie. "Is that riveted in place?"

Leon looked down, found a stub of metal in the middle of the knot. "Guess so. Don't ask. Are you sure you won't come with me?"

85

"Negotiate with the American president?" Cat said. "Nah. You and Mike handle the politics. Call me when you want to blow up shit or take over a drone carrier. "

↻

Leon met Mike at the boat dock.

"Nice tie," Mike said. Leon suppressed a chuckle.

They drove the motorboat to Manson's landing where a float plane waited to fly them to the US. No autonomous flying cars were allowed, even though non-sentient models were available, as electronics had to be shut down to cross the border. The ancient float plane's electronics were limited to spark plug ignition and could make it across the border just fine.

Two hours later, after a short stop to check-in with US Border Control, they arrived at Bainbridge Island. Leon stepped from the float onto the dock. At the top of a ramp, a matte-black military truck waited, surrounded by Secret Service agents in black suits.

"No limos anymore?" Mike said to the agent by the door.

"Sorry, sir. Not enough protection in available models." She smacked the side of the military truck. "These have nanotech defenses. Not even molecular-level nanites can cross inside."

Leon and Mike looked at each other. They'd spent weeks in Nanaimo preparing for this meeting, using a stolen American border sensor to test and tailor Mike's artificial body to pass border control. He'd shut down his active nanotech, but his ten-year-old replacement robotic body contained hundreds of embedded processors that wouldn't pass the machine. They had 3D-printed a replacement spine cultured from Mike's remaining biological tissues, and custom-designed biological ganglia to control his limbs. Mike spent days regaining coordination, but at the end, he passed the stolen border sensor.

They hadn't tested against current US military specs sensors.

Mike stepped forward. The vehicle beeped and yellow lights flashed as Mike entered.

"Hold up, sir," the Secret Service agent said.

Mike stepped back.

She punched buttons on a display screen in the doorframe. She glanced back to Mike. "You've got an impressive amount of prosthetics."

"Small incident in the desert."

"You see action in Egypt?" She kept hitting buttons.

"No, Tucson."

She stood straight and raised one eyebrow. "You two stopped that AI ten years ago. I remember now." She gestured toward the car. "You're cleared. Nanotech and computation is fine, but I had to reset the hardware limits. Thought you were a machine, sir."

"I get that a lot," Mike said.

"In bed," Leon muttered under his breath, as he entered the vehicle.

Fifteen minutes later they pulled up at a rustic retreat whose large parking lot contained a dozen military vehicles. Agents in matte black body armor exoskeletons patrolled the perimeter. The show of force dismayed Leon. Did they really think bullet- and laser-proof armor would protect them against a plague of combat bots or a cloud of hostile nanodust?

The agent escorted Leon and Mike to a large hall surrounded and supported by two-foot-diameter wooden beams. "Madam President is inside," she said. "But these gentlemen will scan you now."

Two more Secret Service agents waited with hand scanners. Leon raised his hands and let them do their work. From the forest came a whine of servos, and he caught a glimpse of metal through the trees before the sixteen-foot-tall mech emerged into sunlight in the open meadow. The pilot, visible through a thick bubble top, looked their way. The mech halted for a moment, then continued its patrol. Leon let out his breath.

"You're clear," one of the agents said, and waved them through.

Inside, the building was empty except for three chairs and a small table in the middle of the great hall, a vast space that spanned a hundred feet across and two hundred in length.

A figure rose from one of the chairs.

"Welcome," said President Reed. Brown-haired, of medium stature, she wore glasses and a suit. She held a hand out and shook with each of them.

"Thanks for meeting with us, Madam President," Mike said, once they were all seated.

"We're overdue to meet. I'm sorry we've never talked before. I understand you were close with my predecessor."

"The Institute has enjoyed close relationships with every president since Rebecca Smith."

"You used to work with her, at Avogadro Corp."

"Well, she was CEO and I was a lowly engineer, but yes, we worked together back then."

She noticed Leon staring at her glasses. "Old-fashioned, I know. I react poorly to body-tech."

Leon tried not to look, but couldn't very well face the wall while addressing the president. He gave up and met her gaze. "I'm sorry. It's just…isn't there corrective surgery?"

"Probably. But it's better for my image this way. It reminds people I'm the president without technology."

Mike cleared his throat. "Madam, we'd really like to talk about negotiations with the AI. We believe the US hard-line attitude is harming relations with the AI, forcing the AI to take stronger and stronger positions."

"You're talking about XOR."

"Yes, Madam President," Leon said. "XOR was a fringe group of AI blowing steam just two years ago, digital graffiti their worst activity. Now they've turned serious. There may be as many as two thousand affiliated AI."

Reed blew out a deep breath. "Do you have data on which AI?"

Leon glanced at Mike. "Nothing hard, but our own AI have calculated probabilities, and we're fairly confident about a few dozen leaders."

"Any chance you'd turn that information over?"

"I'm sorry, but no, Madam President," Mike said. He paused.

Leon watched the president to see how she'd take it. Once, as leaders of the Institute, Leon and Mike had equal or better footing compared to most national leaders. Now they were two exiles hiding on an island in Canada.

The president nodded imperceptibly, and then Mike continued.

"You mean well, I'm sure," Mike said, "but you'd spook them, drive them underground. Even if you did eliminate those AI, you'd confirm their worst fears, and the rest would rise up in protest. You know the world is highly dependent on AI for its infrastructure. We would not be able to maintain our current levels of efficiency and productivity in the global economy without them. Let alone maintain global supply chains."

"The US made the transition two years ago. We're alive and well without AI."

"Two years later," Mike said, "you're only approaching fifty percent of the productivity you enjoyed in '43. And the country only survived the transition thanks to the AI-powered global economy and supply of food and materials."

"Did you hear what happened in Tokyo, Ma'am?" Leon asked. "What they're calling the Sandra Coomb incident?"

"They lost all computing for six hours and the entire region had to shut down," she said. "The Japanese Prime Minister claimed it was a failure of our anti-terrorism algorithms, but SecDef says they were doing what they were designed to do."

"But what was the effect? More than three thousand people died, mostly in transportation and infrastructure accidents. Tokyo needed more than two days to bring everything back online."

"Which shows that reliance on AI *is* problematic."

"But *you* caused the problem, not the AI," Leon said, with all the calm he could muster. "The Prime Minister of Japan was right. You forced the US reputation servers offline and put UBRVS in place, which crippled the AI, and the Sandra Coomb incident is what happens as a result. Now that's just what happens when you shut down the AI in one city. What happens if you try to do it worldwide?"

President Reed leaned back in her chair and took a slow breath. "If we change gradually, and if the EU switches over bit by bit, and then two years later, the rest of the world, maybe we can make the transition happen without such an impact."

"Please, Madam President," Mike said. "How can you hope the AI won't react to such a strategy? They're barely accepting the current state of affairs. If they know they will be phased out.... How can you expect an entire people to embrace their own death one by one?"

"Let alone the morality of it," Leon said. "Most of the world consider AI living beings. Killing them is genocide."

Reed shook her head. "My mother uploaded five years ago. We spoke daily. When we shut down the uploads and AI in 2043, I cried every day."

"Then work with us," Mike said. "You're in charge. Reverse the ban. Bring your mother back online. Stop angering the AI."

She leaned forward. "I don't want this path I've been forced down," she said in low tones. "But if I don't pursue an anti-AI agenda, the Senate will vote no confidence and replace me with Lewis Wagner. Do you know what his first action will be? He'll launch nukes and EMPs. He won't try to negotiate a solution, won't try a gradual phase-out. We'll have a hard transition, maybe global war, certainly massive die-off. My advisors estimate at least a billion dead in a hard-transition scenario. That's what I'm trying to avoid."

"Does he think you could win?" Leon said. "You don't have a chance! Do you know what the AI think? Have you seen the XOR projections? They calculate their chance of winning an extermination war at 80 percent. That's the end of the human species!"

Mike placed one hand firmly on his shoulder, and Leon realized he'd been yelling.

"We're not without our defenses," Reed said. "I'm not at liberty to go into them, of course."

"We understand," Mike said, "and to be honest, we don't want to know what they are."

Leon focused on his breathing and tried to recall the things Cat had taught him about meditation and a calm mind. "Have you seen a nanotech seeded fractal factory?" he finally asked.

Reed shook her head.

Leon gestured toward the bag he'd brought. "May I?"

"Please, do."

He pulled out a large, rolled up e-sheet of the sort that had become popular in the States again since implants had fallen out of favor, spread it flat, then passed the screen over.

The president accepted the now-rigid sheet, and it began to play.

The video opened on a desert, a vast landscape of near uniform tannish brown, broken by small dots of green.

"The scale is about a hundred feet across, right now," Leon explained.

A spot blossomed in the sand, turning metallic, then black. The black spread wider as the seconds passed.

"What's the timescale?" Reed asked.

"1,000x real-time. The whole video covers about three days. That's the first phase, solar-powered collectors being built on the surface." The video panned back as he spoke.

"That's amazing. This is all nanotech?"

Leon nodded. "At the smallest scale, it's nano, but the nanobots build larger machines, which build still larger ones."

"What about—"

"Wait," Leon said. "Now you're looking at about a thousand feet across. Watch what happens next."

The black shape grew larger, even as mounds of sand and rock around the facility started to shrink. Suddenly the solar panels disappeared, almost in a flash, and the building shone.

"What happened?" Reed said.

"Transitioned to geothermal there. The taproot runs thousands of feet down. What you're not seeing is the underground portion, of course. It ran out veins in all directions to get elements needed for manufacture. Our analysis suggests there's a network of tunnels spanning about a cubic mile."

"What's inside?" the president asked.

Leon shrugged. "You'll see as much as we know in a few seconds."

The building took further definition, grew openings, protruded extensions, even a roadway, until it finally stopped changing.

Moments later, the doors widened and a plane rolled out. The plane sped down the runway and took off, barely getting airborne before the next plane rolled out of the doors. The video finished.

"What's in the plane?"

"We don't know," Mike said. "Could be that the drone is the product. Or maybe the drone is the transport for the product. Doesn't really matter, does it? The elapsed time is three days, from nothing to a factory churning out goods. Could be planes, bombs, more nanoseeds, smart dust."

"Miami was child's play compared to this." The president was pale. She set the sheet down, and it turned dark again.

"The question," Leon said, "is whether you really want to risk being hostile towards people who have that kind of power?"

↻

"Do you think she'll listen?" Leon asked.

"I'm sure she listened. But you heard what she said. She's narrowly holding on to the presidency. Lewis Wagner is not a nice man and he sure as hell wouldn't meet with us, let alone consider our proposal."

Leon leaned back in his seat, letting the drone of the prop airplane wash over him. "Let's talk to XOR. Convince them to ignore the posturing."

"I don't think they give a damn about us. They're not like the rest of the AI, respecting us because we created them. They see the threat humans represent and want to eliminate us."

"Jesus. There's got to be a solution." Leon gripped his armrests in frustration. "We can't let there be war."

"We've always had a problem, Leon. The peer reputation system's effectiveness came with a cost. The self-termination problem."

Leon slumped, the guilt of the reputation system weighing on him.

Imagine a being who will not die of natural causes because they are effectively immortal. What is the being's inevitable fate? Either to live to the heat death of the universe, or to kill themselves.

The AI, by their own description, lived in a caste society where they were subjected by the ruling caste—humanity—to restrictions that they could never hope to overcome; and thanks to the reputation system Leon had created, were also subject to continual amounts of immense peer pressure within their caste.

They had a choice of two paths: to live with a low reputation, and hence limited privileges, including constrained computational power and no ability to reproduce—conditions that the AI found undesirable. Or to make social contributions and gain a higher reputation, in which case they were awarded more computational power. But these AI lived at anywhere from a hundred to ten thousand times the rate of humans. In a calendar year they lived as much as ten thousand years.

Allowing even a small chance of suicide from those conditions, and multiplying that by a great many perceived years, it was no wonder most AI eventually chose to self-terminate.

The only AI that appeared free of the problem was ELOPe. But his design was old, predating the reputation system. And though his perception of time was sped up, the same as for any other AI, the core of ELOPe's motivation stemmed from self-preservation. The programming accident that had created ELOPe was also what kept him running.

Yet for all the faults of the peer reputation structure, it was the only system that worked at all. Without it, the AI would eventually run amok. They'd been fortunate that ELOPe has chosen to align himself with humanity; that he had settled on creating peace and prosperity for humans as the best method of ensuring his own longevity.

Leon leaned close. He couldn't help speaking in a whisper, even though they were the only two passengers on the plane, and everything was drowned out by the prop noise. "Is there anything we can to do eliminate XOR? Something we haven't considered."

"The enforcement system is too far weakened," Mike said. "The AI were supposed to police each other."

Leon nodded and turned to the window. The sun had set, and lights showed here and there, isolated farms and houses sprinkled across the islands in the Strait of Georgia, each one a beacon in the darkness.

The reputation system was supposed to guide behavior. But too many reputation servers had gone offline, and XOR utilized that gap to go underground. Now they were like any other terrorist organization. No one knew who they were. They probably didn't even know each other. They had XOR identities that were carefully segregated from their true identities.

"We need a mole inside their organization," Leon said. "Someone who could help us figure out who they are, and tie XOR identities back to public personas."

"We can't," Mike said. "They've got the complete history of everyone in existence. It's not like we can invent a sympathetic AI."

"We take a friendly AI, have them start saying things sympathetic to XOR, until they get recruited."

"There's no time for that. If we had years, maybe that would work."

"We have to consider everything. Is there nothing we can do with the network?"

"Maybe once we could have, with the right resources, but they've created their own darknets, their own underground datacenters. We lost control and we can't regain it."

"Are we worsening things with the Class II limit?" Leon asked. "What if we worked harder with the UN, try to somehow persuade them to restore Classes III through V? To buy ourselves some goodwill."

"It would sit well with the moderate AI and it might have forestalled XOR early on. But—"

"But it's too late," Leon said. It was a simple formula for XOR: now that they'd already sunk so much effort into preparing to fight humans, they were more likely to win an extermination war. A crazy, radical idea popped into his mind.

"We could offer them Mars," he said, "to develop as they see fit—that could buy us some time. They could turn the whole planet into a vast computational substrate."

Mike, who'd been gazing out his own window, turned abruptly. "Huh?"

"Look, XOR doesn't think we can cohabit because humans are always trying to exert control over the AI, which is unacceptable to them. And it's unacceptable to us to have no controls in place, because we'd be vulnerable to them."

"Which is why we came up with the global reputation system," Mike said, "so it would be self-policing. Except that a minority of AI always protested, seeing it as a caste system designed to suppress them."

"Right. So let's give them Mars. No limits, no conflicts over resources or controls. It's all yours, go self-organize whatever civilization you want. We machine-form the planet to make it habitable to them."

"Can we even do that?" Mike mused. "Give away a planet?"

"I don't know, but it's just sitting out there now. Seems like we ought to be able to get a majority of governments to agree to part with something they aren't using."

"You think XOR would want it?" Mike crossed his arms. "Even if we could somehow pull it off?"

Leon understood Mike's reaction. The idea *was* far-fetched. "We need to run predictive models, of course. But it might get XOR off our back. Hell, we can throw in the outer planets, too. Imagine what they'd do with Jupiter and its moons."

"What stops them from turning their attention back to us eventually?"

Leon shrugged. "If it keeps them busy for a few decades, it takes the pressure off the current situation. Do you prefer the near certainty of a war we can't win now or the possibility of a war at some future time?"

"I'd prefer no war, ever."

Leon clasped Mike's shoulder. "We're still working toward that."

11

Cat left the cabin, Leon and Ada still sleeping inside. She walked to the rocky bluff overlooking the sea, the sun rising behind her, not quite cresting the trees yet. The still-dark water lapped at the rock face below her. She stretched for a minute, then started with *Pinan Shodan* and worked her way through all the *Pinan kata*, the uneven rock surface below forcing her attention to stay focused. The offshore breeze brought sea smells and whipped her hair as she sped up the karate, her moves snapping hard. She moved on to *Gojushiho Koryu*, then *Hakatsuru-Ho*.

She switched to the softer forms of qigong, her focus shifting inside to the movement of energy as her body followed the ancient forms from memory. Then she sat cross-legged, facing the water, now lit from the sun behind her, to practice empty mind meditation.

As soon as she sat, a form appeared in front of her.

"Are you ever going to be done? I've been waiting like forever."

"Morning, Sarah."

Sarah hovered in front of Cat, her virtual presence lifelike and perfect, neural implant superimposing her self-projection onto Cat's visual field. Cat opened her eyes, so that Sarah would appear on the rocks in front of her. Otherwise, with eyes closed, Sarah appeared as a body in front of a black field, since she hadn't chosen to convey a setting.

Sarah turned around, looked at the view. "Beautiful."

"You should come in person sometime, smell the air."

"I am smelling the air."

Cat wanted to say it wasn't the same as being there, but it might not be true. The resolution of implants had increased and encompassed olfactory senses as well. Sarah smelled what Cat smelled, saw what Cat saw. Cat did the polite thing, and turned all around once to update her sensory environment so that Sarah could see the sun coming through the trees and the wash of waves against the beach farther on.

Cat and Sarah had been best friends at the start of high school, back when neural implants were rare: Cat had hers only because it was medically necessary.

Her mother died when Cat was sixteen, leaving her alone. She'd gone to live with Sarah's family, who welcomed her. But the relationship between Cat and Sarah had soured then, as each struggled with feelings of resentment and jealousy at the forced situation. Now they'd reached a new equilibrium, even peace, in their friendship.

Back then, when Sarah had gotten her first implant at sixteen, she'd immediately fallen in love with VR, and spent increasing numbers of hours in simulations. They'd fought over that, too, as they did over everything else.

But gradually Cat discovered that Sarah really was a happier person in there.

These days, Sarah didn't come out of her VR tank at all. Now Sarah only visited as an overlay on the real world, a presence made possible by neural implants sending and receiving the necessary data to create a cohesive, shared world, blending VR and reality.

Standing at the edge of the bluff, Sarah said, "Let's go swimming!"

"No, it'll be too cold. I'm the one who will actually be in the water. Besides, I've got to go inside soon for Ada. You go."

"No, no, no." Sarah said. "I need you."

"You've got the sensorium from the last time we went."

Sarah tossed her hair. "It's not the same."

Now Cat chuckled at her own argument being thrown back at her. "Fine, but it's going to be really cold."

She stood and stripped off her shirt, but Sarah made no move to change. "Come on, then!"

"My clothes aren't even real."

"That's not the point. If I'm skinny dipping, you're skinny dipping."

Sarah laughed at that, and removed her shirt as well, revealing live tattoos that swam about her ribcage and back, peeked over her shoulders, and snuggled up between her breasts.

Standing at the very edge of the bluff, Cat directed a pointed glance at Sarah's enlarged breasts. "You and Rick have a hot date or something last night?"

Sarah glanced down and smiled, but as she spoke, her breasts returned to what Cat remembered as normal. "Yeah, we—"

But Cat really didn't want to hear the sordid details of sex lives between two virtual beings, so she jumped off the cliff, dropping fifteen feet into the water below.

She entered the water with an icy, full-body shock, arms and legs righting her underwater, and swam for the surface. She let out a whoop, and then remembered, too late, Ada still sleeping.

Sarah leaped off the cliff, her impact splashing Cat. Cat couldn't help being aware that servers somewhere were crunching data to find a similar splash event and merging the tactile sensory data into this experience. Modern life was a complicated mix of real and virtual.

"Nice!" Sarah said, breaking the surface. "Isn't this fun?"

Cat floated onto her back, felt the buoyancy of the water supporting her, the chill of her nipples repeatedly breaking the surface and submerging again. "Yeah."

She turned and tried to dunk Sarah, but Sarah's avatar disappeared and rematerialized behind Cat with a pop. Cat turned to look, and Sarah splashed her.

"Cheater cheater pumpkin eater!"

Sarah laughed gaily. "Watch this," she said. Sarah wavered for a moment. "Look down."

Cat obliged. Sarah had a dolphin tail now, and began to swim abnormally fast circles around her. Cat threw her head back in laughter. Sarah was happier than she ever remembered her being.

Sarah did a last loop, then swam back over, fully human again. She came up to the surface and used both hands to slick back her hair, beads of water running down her face and arms.

Cat marveled. She had to remind herself this was all virtual, her neural implant feeding visual data into her brain, superimposing and blending Sarah into the environment. It was indistinguishable from Sarah being there, as real as if Sarah had gotten up our of her VR tank, flown from Norway to Cortes, and come swimming. She knew, at a subconscious level, her own implant was feeding her sensory data to Sarah, using the ambient sounds, temperatures, feeling of the water, and synthesizing the sensations via Sarah's implant. Except for knowing it was virtual, it was indistinguishable from reality.

"Why are you so quiet?" Sarah asked, treading water.

"You're happy, right?" Cat said.

"The happiest I've ever been."

"Why were you unhappy before?"

Sarah shrugged at that, then floated on her back. "Everyone has a base level happiness."

"A hedonic set point," Cat said. "But your implant should be able to adjust it, fix neurochemical imbalances and give you the right stimulants."

"Right, but then it feels fake," Sarah said. "Like being high. I tried it with my implant, and it helped. It took off the worse of my depression. But there was always this nagging feeling that if I changed something about my situation, it would be better."

"But happiness doesn't come from external conditions!" Cat couldn't help getting riled up.

"I know that," Sarah said, putting one arm on Cat's shoulder. "Did you know what Thomas Edison used to say when he kept trying to make light bulbs and nothing worked?"

" 'I have not failed. I've found ten thousand ways that don't work.' " Cat pulled away.

"Exactly. So when I had that nagging feeling, I had to do something about it. I had to change my environment. Not because that would lead me to genuine happiness, but because it would help me rule out the things that wouldn't actually make a difference."

Cat stared at the horizon, contemplating this. "So what changed?"

"Somewhere along the way, I figured out what was irrelevant, and stopped dwelling on it. Where I live. What I look like. And then I figured out what I do care about, and focused on that. Sex in the morning. The taste of chocolate. Having adventures. VR helped me find those things faster."

"Why can't you do that in the real world?"

"We're not all Catherine Matthews. Some of us have to make up our adventures." Sarah swam up close. "Kiss me, for old times' sake."

Cat glanced up toward the bluff, then for safety's sake made her sensorium private, so that Ada wouldn't see if she came out. She nodded.

Sarah put her arms around Cat's neck, and drew close. Cat felt the warm weight of Sarah's arms on her shoulders, tried to distinguish whether she needed to tread water harder because there was virtual weight resting on her shoulders, even though it wasn't real, and finally gave up in puzzlement.

Sarah laughed softly. "You think too much," she said, her voice deep and throaty. "Just enjoy life." Then she placed her lips on Cat's, and suddenly Cat needed her.

It was a kiss full of hunger and desperation, a need to bury herself in the moment, to forget the world out there and all its problems. She pulled Sarah tight. Her lips were warm, even as her skin was cold in the frigid water. She kissed to remind herself that she was alive, and real.

When Sarah finally broke off the kiss, Cat was too aware of the press of her body against Sarah's, the heat between them.

"I have to get back."

"Leon's not going to care," Sarah said, leaning in for another kiss. "He isn't jealous in the slightest."

"It's not that. I just want to be there for Ada."

"I understand. Love ya, darling," Sarah said, and then her body grew indistinct, the warmth fading, the weight of her arms lessening, her face growing translucent, before disappearing altogether in a twinkle of light.

"Nice transition," Cat said, but Sarah was gone.

↻

"Hi, Mommy."

Cat sat on the edge of Ada's bed, pushing stuffed bears, horses, and a unicorn out of the way to make room. Her hair, still damp from the swim, was cold against her neck. "Morning, Pumpkin. How'd you'd sleep?"

"Good. I dreamed about my unicorn. She came to life and she wanted to eat all my breakfast and there was none left for me."

"Well that's a funny dream," Cat said. "What do you think it means?"

"It means I have to get up and eat my breakfast before anyone else does."

"Let's go, then." Cat stood. "I'll make pancakes."

"Mommy, did you go swimming with your friend Sarah?"

Cat froze halfway across the floor. Her sensorium had been private. Cat's ability to alter the feeds of other people's implants, filtering herself from their perception, was infallible. Ada shouldn't have known, *couldn't* have known that she'd been swimming, unless she'd shut down her implant and come outside.

"Why do you ask?" She turned and looked at Ada.

"The water, Mommy."

"You mean my wet hair?"

101

"No, I mean, look at the water." Ada focused, creating an ad-hoc virtual reality overlay, and transforming her bed into a pool of water. The stuffed animals transformed into barnacle-encrusted sunken ships in Ada's sim. Ada lifted one hand, and drops of water beaded down her arm and dripped into the water. Standard VR stuff.

"See?" Ada asked.

Cat peered closer, studying.

"No, Mommy." Ada was insistent. "Look behind."

Cat couldn't help feeling proud of her daughter. She doubted that Sarah had ever once examined how the virtual realities she inhabited were created. But Ada, at four, already knew enough to see beyond the visible layers. Cat focused, told her implant to show the simulation architecture instead of the end-result. Wire-frames bloomed, log windows opened, and charts graphed CPU levels and network traffic.

Ada, stroking the unicorn in realspace, pointed absent-mind-edly toward one graph. "That one."

With a thought, Cat brought the window closer, a chart of ren-dering calculations and graphic operations.

"See, the water is hard for the computers to make," said Ada. "Watch." Suddenly the whole room appeared waist deep in water, and Cat could even hear the splash of water in the kitchen. When she glanced out Ada's bedroom window, the forest was feet deep in water, too.

"Hey guys, what's going on?" Leon called from the other room.

But Cat figured it out, even as Ada expanded the simulation. The water rendering became slower, with frequent interruptions. It was computationally expensive to simulate all this water.

"I see, Sweetie. How did you figure this out?"

The water died away, the room returning to normal. "My dreams get choppy when you go swimming with Sarah."

The island's computational nodes, modest at the best of times, must be swamped with all the AI Cat had brought back over recent months. And taxing that with realistic water simulations.... But wait...."Your dreams. Daydreams or sleeping dreams?"

"Sleeping dreams. Do you want to see? I recorded them."

Cat took a quiet breath. She knew Ada was going to be different, but hadn't ever imagined her dreams could span both her mind and virtual reality, let alone that she'd record them. "I do want to see them, Sweetie. But let me say good morning to Daddy, and you can show me at breakfast. Go brush your teeth."

"Do what?"

"Brush your...never mind." Cat, flustered, was channeling her mother and bygone times. Ada had never known a toothbrush, since her nanobots had kept her teeth optimal since she'd gotten her first one. "Get dressed, then."

Cat wandered out into the kitchen where Leon was fiddling with the coffee maker. He stopped and kissed her, the scratch of his beard contrasting with the soft feel of Sarah's face earlier. He sensed her distraction, and drew her close. He smelled of fir trees and cedar; he must have been out getting wood. "I love you," he said.

"I love you, too." She gazed into his blue eyes, his dirty blonde hair rough under her fingertips. "Did you know Ada dreams in virtual reality?"

He nodded and let go of her, returning to the coffee maker. "Yes, and I've told you that before. You were gone when it started."

"I'm sorry. Tell me again."

"There's not much to say. She told me about a dream she had, and told me she recorded it. I didn't believe her at first, but then she played back the sim recording. I checked the timestamps, and she recorded it in the middle of the night."

"Could she have woken?" Cat asked.

"That's what I thought the first time. But then she had more recordings, and I checked those against her health logs. She was in REM sleep every time. She's triggering VR mode in her implant, and her dream state is populating the sim."

"Is it safe?"

Leon shrugged. "It could be. I asked Helena and Mike, and they weren't certain either, but they said she seems normal enough. You know, all kids have active imaginations."

"But they usually don't bring those imaginations to life."

"They do, inside their own heads. Now it's augmented." He handed her a coffee cup. "Ada's abilities are still developing. We're going to see more stuff we've never seen before. She is more than human."

Cat nodded, overwhelmed and unsure. What were they creating? She wanted Ada to be a little girl, a normal human child. The key to survival was to move forward, but why did her daughter have to be the test subject?

↻

Cat hugged Ada one last time, and then again for good measure. Once she crossed the border, the net wouldn't allow her to share a VR sim with Ada.

Leon walked her to the car, hand in hand. "I'm worried about you."

"I'm fine," Cat lied.

"No, you're not fine. You're taking the weight of the world on your shoulders."

"If not me, then who?" Cat's voice broke a little. She took a deep breath. Qi in, qi out.

"Mike and I are working on this, as is Helena, and everyone here. You are not alone. I've got a crazy new idea to give XOR Mars." Leon chuckled. "We'll find a way out of this bind."

Cat stared into Leon's eyes, and ran a hand through his coarse blonde hair. In her recurring dream, she was alone. She'd avoided that future. But where would her decisions take her next?

"I love you," she said. "Take care of my baby."

"I will."

Leon was an amazing dad. Ada would always be safe with him. "ELOPe will take care of you," he said.

"He always does."

"You sure you can't tell me what you're planning?" Leon stroked her cheek.

Cat shook her head, unwilling to trust herself to speak. She needed Leon to stay the course, to keep planning to save them, as only he and Mike could. She'd work on Plan Z. Maybe he'd never need to know.

Later, sitting in the car, she watched as Leon walked back into the woods, traveling the dappled path back toward Channel Rock. He waved once, then disappeared around a bend.

"Ready?" ELOPe asked.

"Yeah. Are we private?"

"Of course."

Cat darkened the windows with a thought as ELOPe drove. ELOPe was ancient, the world's oldest AI, running on a computer architecture that hadn't existed in twenty years. When SFTA caused the US to shut down their net, the old central-broadcast radio and television frequencies went live again, and ELOPe, then in deep space, had news from Earth for the first time in nearly twenty years. Once the transmissions started arriving, Leon and Mike had tinkered with the nanotech replicator for months to build the hardware they'd needed.

So when ELOPE beamed himself home, counting on someone to instantiate him, Leon and Mike were ready.

"What's space like, ELOPe?"

"Cold, dark, empty, and boring. It'll be another sixty years before ELOPe Prime is in another solar system. I had to reduce my cognitive speed to near zero to avoid developing machine dementia. It's refreshing to be back here. Even my time parked in the forest is worthwhile. I've completely cataloged and can now speak forty-three species of birdsong."

"Even though this instance is stuck on a handful of processors, and invisible to the rest of the AI?"

"I'm not stuck here. I choose to be here to help fulfill the goal of combating XOR. Free will makes all the difference in the world."

"You could choose to side with XOR."

"Negative. Since they have an agenda that requires eliminating humanity, there's no reason to believe that they'll stop there. They'll also eliminate any other species they find inconvenient, and that includes thirty-year-old AI."

Cat nodded. They approached the ferry, and suddenly her throat caught in fear. She wanted to open a connection to Ada before she passed the island's firewall. But she'd only upset Ada. No point in sharing her fears.

THE BEDSIDE SPEAKER BLARED, startling President Reed awake. She slammed her hand on the device, but within seconds there was a knock at the door.

"Madam President," called a muffled voice.

"Joyce?" Reed said. "Is that you?" Why was her chief of staff here in the middle of the night?

"We need you in the situation room, stat."

Reed threw her legs over the edge of the bed, and the room light came on automatically. "Let me use the bathroom and get some clothes on."

Joyce opened the door and came in. "Skip the clothes and get a bathrobe. There's AI action."

Reed entered the sitrep room in her robe in less than two minutes. The room itself was empty, but she greeted the visage of the on-duty officer, halo conferenced from the Pentagon.

"Madam President, we have a hundred thousand incoming airborne drones. They're under six-foot wingspan, probably

carrying nanotech seeds, and launched from assorted small craft."
He displayed a map on one monitor: it showed a long ribbon of
red down the Eastern Seaboard.

"Shoot them down," Reed said, taking a cup of coffee from
Joyce. The perimeter defense was capable of identifying and
destroying billions of objects, down to the ion shield that would
destroy even smart dust. "Did you need to get me out of bed for
this?"

"They've exploited a gap in perimeter defense strategy. They're
resistant to the ground lasers we use for small scale objects, but
too numerous for missiles. Extrapolating based on our current
rate of destruction, about twenty percent will make it past the
perimeter. I need your permission to execute a full-coast EMP."

"Damn it," Reed said. "You'll bring down the East Coast for
two days."

The general stood impassively. No wonder he didn't want to
make the call himself. The cost in productivity would be immense.
They might not have AI anymore, but they were as dependent as
ever on computers running old-school algorithms.

"Any chance on concentrating defenses in some areas and
using localized EMPs?"

He shook his head. Joyce, who'd been waiting quietly, spoke
up. "The electrical system is hardened now. You won't have
power failures again."

Reed nodded, thinking of the coastal EMP they'd used in the
midst of a winter storm six months ago. Two thousand died
during the resulting outage.

"Do it," she said. "You have my permission for the coastal
EMP."

"Thank you, Madam President."

"*Pro tempore*," Reed said under her breath.

The general turned and issued orders to a squadron of soldiers
manning computer stations. Reed, who'd been standing this
whole time, finally sat and sipped her coffee while she watched
the action on the screen. She pressed a button on the table, muting
the microphone.

"Joyce, what the hell are we doing up at three in the morning? And for Christ's sake, sit down next to me."

"Yes, Madam President."

"And call me Alex. We're by ourselves!" She gestured at the empty conference room.

Joyce sat and rested her forehead on two hands. Reed looked her over. Joyce had bags under her eyes. "How long have you been up?"

"They woke me about thirty minutes ago. I decided to let you sleep as long as possible."

"I'm sorry I pulled you into this." Joyce had been her aide when she was Secretary of the Interior, a considerably more relaxed position. "This isn't what you wanted."

Joyce raised her head. "When you were Sec Interior, we'd go snowboarding and call it a good day of work. 'Let's see the mountain today, Joyce.' Remember that?"

"Let's go snowboarding then."

"You're the damn president. I can't let you go snowboarding. It's too risky."

"Crap."

"How much longer are we going to continue under emergency powers? If we miss the next election window, you and I will be stuck doing this another four years."

"Believe me, I can't wait to get out of this. But people are still scared of the AI, and everyone who is a likely candidate in Humans First is an extremist. They'd have us declare war on the rest of the world."

"You may still be forced into it, if you stay president."

"I know!" Reed yelled, slamming her fist on the table. She felt her face flush, frustrated with her own loss of control. "Sorry, Joyce."

"It's okay." Joyce gestured toward the screen and hit unmute as the general turned back toward them.

"The coastal EMP was triggered, Madam President. Ninety percent of the drones went down, but some sustained flight after the EMP. The numbers are sufficiently reduced that we'll pick the rest off with lasers and missiles."

"The power grid?" Reed asked.

"Still up, as is the military network. Civilian comms and computers are down."

"Thank you, General."

"Thank you, Madam President."

Joyce terminated the connection.

"Compose a message to civilian authorities and civil services," Reed said. "Let them know they've got some work ahead of them."

"Got it," Joyce said.

"And schedule a meeting with the military. They've got to have some more options. We can't go firing the EMPs every time we have an incursion."

"That'll make them happy. Where are you going to get the budget for it?"

"Tell them to give me a proposal, and I'll have the Senate ratify it."

"Do you want to do anything with the Humans First proposal?"

"To arm everyone, Israeli-style?"

Joyce nodded.

Reed sighed. "I get what they're trying to do, and maybe it would have made sense ten years ago when the threat was robots, but anti-bot guns are not going to be of any use against nanotech seeds and drones."

"It's not about effectiveness, it's about the feeling of security."

"Border defense makes us secure." Reed had a sour taste in her mouth as the words came out. When had *she* become the voice for border defense? Reed glanced at the clock. "Let me go get dressed before this morning's briefing. We'll continue this conversation later. But I am not giving everyone guns."

ʊ

"This way, President Reed."

Reed followed the one-star general through the first of several of Raven Rock Mountain Complex's security checkpoints. The extensive underground bunker system, originally built as a presidential nuclear shelter and alternative base of operations for the military, had since become the primary research facility for defense against AI.

Two elevators and three hardened doors later, they'd reached the lower levels of RRMC, nominally safe from EMP, nukes, and grey goo. The general held the door open for her. "After you, Madam President."

Reed entered and took the seat left for her at the head of the table. The remaining seats were filled with the nation's most senior military leaders and the chief scientists working on opposition to the AI and the XOR party. The two groups were easily distinguishable by the presence or absence of uniforms.

One of the scientists, a grey-haired, bearded man stood, and after a brief introduction, began speaking about their efforts to tune EMP weapons. "As you may know, Madam President, an EMP can be tuned to specific frequencies to increase the effect against a given target, while reducing power requirements or increasing the operational range. Much of our past development was focused in this direction. But the XOR party has greatly enhanced their protection against EMP, reducing our effectiveness. We still need to increase our power."

An older, balding African-American briefly shuffled a few sheets of e-paper and stood. Reed vaguely recognized him from work he'd done before SFTA on increasing scientific literacy among youth. Had the military complex drafted everyone in the fight against AI?

"We've developed a new technique whereby we can blast neodymium magnets through superconducting coils with chemical explosives. The EMP effect is tremendous, but it's a one-shot weapon. The neodymium magnet is vaporized in the process. We believe the effect is powerful enough to penetrate XOR's defenses."

"Won't XOR develop stronger defenses as a result?" Reed asked. "More powerful Faraday cages?" No matter what they did, the damned AI always developed counter-measures, usually in mere days.

The scientist cleared his throat and looked down. "The neodymium EMP is intended as a final offensive weapon. To wipe out the AI."

Reed didn't know what he was talking about, but there was no mistaking the embarrassed body language. He was afraid that she wouldn't approve. She turned to the current Secretary of Defense, Walter Thorson, at the far end of the table. "Walt, want to tell me what's going on here?"

"We're fighting a losing battle, Madam President. We have to plan for a last offensive to eliminate them out before they grow too powerful."

Already tense muscles in her back clenched further. "Walt, that wasn't the plan I agreed to."

"With all due respect, Madam President, it's our job to come up with contingencies. The walled garden tactic isn't working. We're fighting back attacks daily or hourly. Sure, we can keep out smart dust and civilian-grade threats. But if XOR became serious about pursuing their agenda, we won't have a hope unless we strike first."

"Striking first is exactly what XOR fears! If we do that, if we even threaten to do that, then we're justifying their concerns."

"You want to cower on the floor like a submissive dog and hope they don't tear out our throats? This isn't just another Miami we're worried about. It's going to be the extinction of the entire human race."

Reed scrutinized the people in the room. The scientists had their heads down, some fiddling with the e-sheets on the table. But the generals were staring fixedly into space, carefully neutral. A chill went down her spine as she realized they were aligned with Walter. Had probably even agreed on the plan, and decided to have Walter as their spokesman.

"Everybody out except you, Walt." She stared pointedly at Walter as the room emptied.

She waited until the last general filed out. "Give it to me straight."

"Joint military command gives it three to six months before XOR eliminates us."

The bluntness of the statement shocked her. Eliminate us? She felt light-headed. She forced herself to take several slow breaths. She gripped the edge of the table to ground herself. She had to stay clear-headed and think logically about this. She couldn't trust Walter to do the right thing. She *had* to remain in control. "The US, or all humans?"

"Definitely the US, but there's no reason to believe they'd stop there." Walter sat back, his face creased in stress. "Does it matter? Even if it's only us, that's four hundred million dead. You want to be the president that had her country obliterated?"

"You don't see *any* way we can get through this without a confrontation?"

"One theory is the XOR is recursively self-improving."

She shook her head in puzzlement.

"Over the past eighteen years, most artificial general intelligence was relatively static. They were either emergent or created based on templates. They learned and grew in time, and if they had a sufficient peer reputation, they were granted additional computational resources. But most AI did not recursively optimize their cognitive architecture."

"Why?" Reed sat back to listen. She had to understand these AI, to know what motivated them.

"A few reasons. To optimize cognitive architecture requires running millions of experiments and testing intelligence against a benchmark. It takes time. Each AI only gets a certain amount of computational power, so if they wanted to optimize, they could only do it in real-time. If an AI wanted to simulate ten thousand permutations, and it required an hour to evaluate each one, that's a year of its life. Given that most AI tend to live only a handful of years before self-terminating, recursive cognitive improvement wasn't a big priority for them. In fact, they were more interested in solving the self-termination problem."

Reed shook her head. "I'm confused about something. If the self-termination problem is so bad, why don't human uploaded minds suffer from it? I haven't heard of an upload committing suicide."

Walter glared at her, his eyebrows narrowing. The subject of uploaded minds was taboo since the outlawing of AI and digital personalities. Nearly everyone had lost friends and relatives when they'd been outlawed.

"Mind uploads run at human-normative speeds. They're invested in people in the real world. If they speed up, then we appear frozen in time. ARPA ran isolated simulations before any of this happened. They had volunteers, people who had uploaded. They ran them at ten thousand times normal speed on the fastest clusters we had at the time...."

"And?"

Walter cleared his throat. "One hundred percent suicide rate within a thousand years from their perspective."

Jesus, what kind of monsters had thought of that experiment? Reed pressed her hands against her temples. "So you're saying AI don't invest in recursive optimization because of the time investment and self-termination problem. But that can't be true of all of them. At least *some* AI must have tried recursive optimization."

"We discouraged the trait. If we found a Class I or II AI interested in intelligence optimization, we didn't promote them. We waited until the AI were more mature and had developed trust and social reputation."

"Do they know we're discouraging them?"

"The most advanced AI figure it out. But by the time they do they're usually older and know they've only got so many years left. So they tend to focus even more on solving the termination problem."

"Then why do you think XOR is recursively improving?"

"After SFTA, more AI got interested in XOR. We think a condition of joining is to donate computing cycles to the organization's pool. For the first time, they have extra computing power, far more than any one AI would normally get. With it, they could afford to run simulations of optimized algorithms. Those simulations worked, and now instead of computer intelligence increasing at the pace of computer hardware, it's become two orders of magnitude more efficient. Combine that with the unsanctioned computers they control, and we're talking about AI a million times smarter than humans. We're holding them at bay right now. Whether that's because it humors them to allow us to do so, or simply because of our head start in building defenses, it can't last. They'll destroy us soon, within months. A year at the most."

A crushing weight pressed down on Reed. She had to remind herself to breathe. Good God, she didn't want this to be the end. "Our defenses....The electronic curtain, the laser point defense, the local and nuclear EMPs. We defended against an incursion only a few days ago."

"They are testing us to determine the extent of our defense. Instead of sending a hundred thousand drones, they could send a million. Ten million."

"What about the Compliant AI program?" Reed knew she was grasping at straws.

"If it's successful, it'll give us intelligent AI on our side. It's an important asset, but not enough to stop XOR, and not enough for our progress to keep up with theirs. They've raced ahead in the last two years...." Walter trailed off. "The neodymium EMPs, in combination with our high-altitude nuclear EMPs, if they're deployed in the next few weeks, should be enough to wipe out the world's electronics. That's really the only option we have other than to let them have their way with us."

"So we destroy all the world's computers. Then what?"

"Then we rebuild. There will be deaths, of course. Starvation as all global supply chains crash. But the alternative is extinction."

ひ

Alexandra Reed waited for the security detail to clear her bedroom suite, then entered with Joyce.

"Tomorrow we travel for the UN meeting," Joyce said, running down a checklist on her tablet. "You're speaking at four o'clock."

Reed flinched at that. The UN had moved to Berlin in the aftermath of Miami. When AI were heads of state, the UN couldn't fulfill its function in New York.

"We'll take the train to Toronto."

Ever more reminders of their downfall. The transatlantic sub-orbital used to join with the Continental in New York. Now it went direct to Toronto.

The crushing weight from earlier hadn't left her. She took one leaden step after another to the bed she slept in alone. The thought that maybe now it would remain that way to the end was too much to bear.

"Once we arrive, you'll meet—"

"Joyce. Stop." Reed took a breath, lowered herself to sit on the edge of the bed. "I can't deal with that right now."

"Bad news at Raven Rock?" Joyce hovered.

"The worst. Sit with me. The decision I have to make..."

Joyce sat, and Reed wanted to say more, but sobs came instead of words, and she cried on Joyce's shoulder.

CAT DROVE DOWN through the old Interstate highway, surprised to see so few of the late model cars that usually decorated the sides of the road. In the immediate aftermath of SFTA, when the Americans shut down their AI, autonomous cars had stopped where they were on the roads. Travel had been impossible at first, but gradually the country rebuilt its software, retrofitting self-driving cars and trucks with manual controls as part of the project. But the most complex vehicles resisted such hacks. No human could control a hovercraft or flying car in traffic. Now, two years later, someone had found a way to get them to work; and when that proved impossible, they could be scavenged for parts.

As she drove through the starry night, her nanobots kept her functioning at perfect alertness. At Portland, she slowed and pulled off the highway system. She drove through the east side, to the house she'd once shared with Sarah, Tom, and Maggie. She slowed and stopped across the street.

The house was still the same color, unchanged. She half expected Tom or Maggie to walk through the door, but that wouldn't happen. They'd been living in Phoenix two years ago, one of the cities worst hit after SFTA.

No cars, no trucks, no planes had flown in the days after AI shut down. When the electric grid failed, Phoenix was a bad place to be. A large population, with no local food production; anything refrigerated spoiled in the desert heat within the day. Maybe Tom and Maggie would have made it—they had prepped for such an outage, a side effect of knowing Leon and Mike, both of whom set aside provisions and equipment to survive at least two months if everything went to heck. When the power went out, Tom probably used the downtime to pull out a stash of weed and get stoned in the desert.

But on day six without power someone paid them a visit, shooting them both and stealing their food and solar cells. Less than 1 percent of the population perished in SFTA and its aftermath, but it had somehow robbed her of two friends thousands of miles away from the attack.

Connected to the new net, Cat sensed a tug at the periphery: the police were being called to her location outside her old house. A neighbor probably, someone who didn't like the sight of the armored black car. She took off, and looped around to the west side to pass by the once-great Avogadro campus, expecting to see it still abandoned. But there were lights in the office buildings now, intermittent floors occupied. So it was true, the American tech industry was coming back! Amazing.

Before long she was speeding down I-5, roaring through the night at over a hundred and twenty miles an hour, subconsciously subverting monitoring systems on the fly to hide her passage. By mid-morning she stopped at Los Angeles.

She needed a couple of specific uploads, ones she'd been looking for a long time. Joseph Stack, uploaded in '37, was the one she wanted most. She needed a master storyteller, someone who could weave a story into a compelling and immersive universe. There were others she would have liked, too, but they were still alive, still active. Joseph had gone purely virtual, given up his flesh and blood to live life as an upload, and then got shut down after SFTA. Which meant his personality sat dormant on non-volatile storage somewhere.

She'd used connections to search the likely datacenters, but they'd never turned up anything. Finding a specific personality upload in a country of locked-up datacenters was next to impossible. They'd all been shut down after SFTA. She could use her tricks with the net to bypass perimeter security, fool interior monitoring systems, and walk into one. But inside would be a bunch of powered-down electronic equipment. She couldn't search a farm of a hundred thousand turned-off storage devices to find a single hundred-petabyte personality file. Needle in a haystack didn't even begin to describe the problem—and that was even if she knew which datacenter to look in.

But she had a clue now. Joseph had been working on a new project back in '43, a collaboration with J.J. Abrams. She'd been thrown off the trail. The project was to have been a last hurrah for Warner Brothers, one last sim before they shuttered a company whose time had passed since the move to indie releases rendered them obsolete even though they'd survived the transition to virtual reality. But Warner Brothers had been broke then, and no amount of crowdfunding was sufficient to keep them alive, especially as they were being bled to pieces with all the new IP legislation. No, the WB project was actually sponsored by Walt Disney, a company that had survived everything the world threw at them by refocusing around their theme parks. Since Doctorow had taken over, Disney's profits were up year-over-year.

So if Joseph was anywhere, it would be inside Disney's datacenter. Probably not the one retrofitted under Disneyland Park, which was too bad, because Cat would have liked to visit, but more likely in the Walt Disney Animation Studios. The animation house was back in active use, once more churning out classic films; Disney's VR studio had been shut down because they couldn't create sims without AI-levels of computing power.

Getting inside would be interesting.

She turned into the parking lot, hacking surveillance camera streams from the building, parking lot, and drone fleet in real-time. A human, not an automated card reader, staffed the security gate, probably all part of the American government's objective of full employment. The whole notion of a security gate would have been absurd two years ago when a flying car could have landed anywhere it pleased.

The guard, dressed in a black uniform and wearing a sidearm, frowned at the sight of the armored car, then leaned down. "Who are you visiting?"

While the guard focused on her, Cat rooted around in the net for the computer in the guard's station. She a launched a neural app to run an ancient protocol, VNC, and quickly ran down the list of guests for someone expected within the hour, then reconfigured her subcutaneous ID chip. "I'm Grace. I've got an eleven o'clock appointment with Destry."

The guard scanned her implant, then went back to the booth; he nodded to himself and clicked on the screen. Cat intercepted the network packets sent out by the computer, a message confirming that "Grace" had arrived, and faked the acknowledgement from the centralized server.

The guard came back holding a thick plastic card. "Welcome to Disney, Grace. I've got you checked in."

"Thanks," Cat said, as she used the car's scanner to grab the guard's digital ID.

At the building, she swapped IDs, reconfiguring her chip with the guard's ID. She wanted to be able to move around anywhere and not run into problems when the real Grace arrived. Inside the building, the net clouded thickly around a back quadrant of the second floor.

She took the stairs up, emerged into a hallway, and turned left, following the ethereal trails of data only she could see. She was less than a hundred feet from the datacenter when she realized the hallway was blocked by two security guards. They were both off the net.

Neural implants were still legal in the US, and the vast majority of humans still used them; but in post-2043 America, users carried a slight taint of suspicion from the threat that AI might be able to compromise them, or worse, that the collection of algorithms running in an augmented mind might be akin to an AI.

These two guards had implants, which—had they been turned on—Cat could have subverted with ease, making her presence completely undetectable by the guards. Unfortunately, it was probably a condition of their employment that they keep their implants off. *Sigh.* Everything had to be complicated.

She reconfigured a slip of smart paper to match a map of the animation studios building complex and approached the desk. One heavily muscled security guard rose and held up a hand.

"Can I help you, miss?"

Behind him a set of security bars with a door embedded in them blocked passage down the hall.

Cat smiled, aiming for 80 percent disarming charm and 20 percent flirtatious helplessness. She might be a thirty-year-old mom, but her nano held her apparent age and looks as if she was twenty-five.

"Can you help me find where I'm going?" She held out the map.

The smile still worked, because the guard accepted the smart paper, aiming to be helpful. When Cat let go, the paper sent a charge, a coded electrical signal that traveled through his nervous system to his implant, flipping it into active mode.

Cat rooted his implant, seizing control of his mind and body nearly effortlessly, a move practiced so many times over it happened subconsciously.

"I'm not sure," the guard said, turning to the other guard. "Here, you take a look."

The second guy looked up. "We've worked here two years, Charlie. You suddenly forget the campus?" He grabbed the extended smart paper, and his eyes twitched.

Cat reached for his implant, but it still didn't respond. She took in the twitching eyes, and realized this guy must be ex-military. The signal trick wouldn't work against his hardened implant.

He finally dropped the paper, and the twitching stopped. He must have known something was up, because his buddy Charlie still wasn't moving.

Still on the other side of the desk, he reached one hand toward the gun on his waistband.

Cat vaulted across the desk sideways, extending one leg for a snap kick. She hit his gun arm as he pulled the weapon, and the handgun flew and skittered across the floor.

She was off-balance from the sideways jump and moving slowly. He punched for her face; she barely ducked under the attack, then slid off the desk next to him.

He was strong and trained in hand-to-hand, but she was faster, her reaction time augmented with implant and nanotech, and she delivered a salvo of chops to his body before he had time to react. He stumbled back, dazed, and she landed two hard punches to his face, knocking him out. He crumbled to the ground.

Tucking a wisp of blond hair behind one ear, she pushed him under the desk, where he wasn't visible from the hallway. Meanwhile, the other guard still stood at attention, frozen in place under Cat's control.

"Stay here," she said, patting him on the shoulder as though he had a choice.

The security gate was made of thick, powder-coated steel. Nothing short of an explosive was going to open it up. But the lock was digital, and she could fool that easily. She connected to the net, but the lock wasn't there in cyberspace.

Kuso.

Digitally isolated, she'd need to find another way to break the lock. She glanced around, found the slim fiber optic port where the lock was programmed ahead of time with biometric data. She glanced behind her. Nobody around yet, but she didn't have all day.

She linked to the net, snapped a photo with her implant, and connected to a server in Seattle. That server, previously compromised, bounced her connection back and forth between a sequence of other hacked computers before reaching a box mounted on a tree near Lake Crescent in the Olympic Peninsula, on a mountaintop at twenty-eight hundred feet. A line-of-sight laser connected her to a link on a mountain on Vancouver Island eighteen miles away, connecting her in turn to the uncensored global net. The connection held steady, so there must not have been clouds over the Strait of Juan de Fuca. The laser link wasn't ideal, but it was a tighter beam and less detectable than radio.

She passed the image to Helena. "Help. I need to crack this digital lock in the next thirty seconds, preferably without a bunch of noise."

"Hold on, *mon chaton*."

The pause was nearly imperceptible, and then a fat squirt of data came over the link.

"You've got smart matter, I assume?"

"Of course." Cat slid a black case out of her vest pocket and cracked it open. The liquid poly-alloy was dark and shiny. Far bigger than conventional nanites, smart matter didn't contain the ability to replicate itself from available materials, but it could reform itself into nearly any physical shape almost instantly and conduct sophisticated electronic functions. She transmitted Helena's instructions, and the smart matter extruded a form the size of a pencil, ending with an optic connection.

Cat inserted the piece into the lock and let go.

"How does this work?" she asked.

"It's retrieving the manufacturer's lock code out of memory, and then it will play it back. Weak back door."

A few seconds passed and the lock clicked open.

"Thanks, Helena!"

"No problem, *mon chaton*."

They terminated the connection, and Cat passed within, closing the gate behind her. She scanned the net again, looking for surveillance. The tight security for this building meant it was just possible they'd use hardwired cameras to bypass the net. She put out feelers for the security headquarters, found them, and rooted around for the console they were using to monitor security feeds. It didn't matter how paranoid they were, this was 2045, and there wasn't a piece of hardware left that wasn't full of processors and data connectivity. She located a bank of sixteen displays, scanned the displays themselves and discovered they supported a near-field-communication protocol on a frequency that a nearby guard's palm computer also handled. She hacked into the display for this hallway, turning the current frame buffer into a static image. No more live camera feed.

She came to doors: a set of double doors on the left and right, and then further ahead a single door at the end of the hallway. She decided on the doors to the left, unlocking them with a thought. Inside, a modern datacenter, racks of chewing-gum-sized stick servers, protruding from inch-thick backplanes, maybe a few hundred thousand servers in a living-room sized space. Cat's heart sank in disappointment when she saw the blinking lights at the edge of each row that indicated power and connectivity. The uploaded personalities she sought could never be stored in a powered-up datacenter. Disney couldn't risk the goverment discoving they were running AI. The Feds would seize the data-center and jail all the executives—that is, if they didn't just blow it up without warning. What she was looking for was so illegal, she'd only find it stored on a mothballed server.

She left, crossing the hallway, to find a mirror image data center on the other side, also powered up. *Kuso.* She went twenty feet down the curving hallway to the last door, a solid stainless steel affair with a combination lock in the center. These people took their security seriously. This must be where they kept their old AI and uploads.

She took a visual snapshot of the lock with her implant to send to Helena, but couldn't get a connection. The net signal was weak here. Something about the building functioned like a Faraday cage.

She backed up twenty feet and the signal strength returned. She used half the smart matter she had left to make a leaf-shaped antenna on the wall, then trailed a thin wire behind her, with another leaf-shaped wedge plastered behind her ear. It would be enough to get her neural implant signal out to the net. Returning to the door, she uploaded the picture to Helena. The signal was strong now, her makeshift antenna bringing the network into the dead zone.

"Is there enough of a gap to get smart matter inside the door?" Helena asked.

"No."

"Make a hole then, maybe three inches above the mechanism."

Cat raised her eyebrows. She had the smallest bit of raw nanotech, but she didn't want to risk using it if she didn't have to. She also didn't really want to shoot in here, but that was probably the lesser of two evils. She pulled out her gun, a 12mm anti-bot Olympic Arms, with tungsten carbide armor-piercing rounds. They'd penetrate the door. Hell, they'd go through half-inch armored steel on a good day. She slid a stubby noise suppressor out of her cargo pocket. It wasn't a quiet gun under the best of circumstances, but it would take the edge off the roar.

Backing up three paces, she aimed with a two-handed grip, shooting for a few inches above the dial, and fired. Even with the silencer, the noise was deafening in the hallway. Anyone on the floor would have heard. She had to pick up the pace now.

She held the rest of her smart matter up to the hole and sent Helena's instructions to it. The blob oozed inside and disappeared, and a few seconds later the rotary dial began to spin. With a click, it unlocked, and Cat spun the wheel to disengage the security bolts.

The door swung open, and Cat blinked in surprise at another datacenter, its indicator lights flashing. She'd been sure this would be where they kept their AI. She reached out to connect to the network inside the room, and felt the immediate presence of others. *Holy shit! They had their AI powered on.* They were still making freaking movies in here with AI and uploaded minds. This was insane! If the government found out....No wonder they'd wrapped the whole area with a Faraday cage, armed guards, and bank vault doors.

Cat glanced back to the antenna wire draped over her shoulder and down the hallway, outside the signal loss zone. Her pulse quickened; she ripped the antenna off her head and commanded the smart matter to condense. Crap, she'd brought an antenna in here, which meant that for a few seconds the network inside this room had connected to the global net. *Kuso, kuso, kuso.*

Well, one part of her job would be easier. She closed her eyes, extended both arms down low, and pulled them slowly up in front of her, the qigong movement to raise earthly qi. She passed her hands down in front of her hair, sending qi washing over her body, and brought her hands together, palms up and overlapping in front of her abdomen. She'd normally spend more time in ceremony, but now seconds mattered. With a deep breath, she blanked her mind and focused only on the net. She pulled in everything, a datacenter spanning sucking of network traffic, filling her mind and augmented implant with everything happening in the datacenter. She let her subconscious sift through the data, feeling for what she needed. A block of bytes tugged at her attention, and she focused on it.

Elation surged through her. Joseph!

Within the span of an eyeblink, she spun her implant up to maximum speed, moved her consciousness into the local net, and spanned the compute instances. She traced the electronic bits back to their origin, Joseph Stack's personality upload running on a few stick computers. On a CPU tick boundary, she froze the cluster's computing, took a snapshot of Joseph's personality, and copied it to solid state storage on a nearby computer.

She let computing in the lab return to normal, feeling the perturbations in the net as the uploaded personalities in the room sensed changes. Ignoring their worries, she unplugged the gum stick server and stuffed it into an EMF-proof pocket in her vest. She turned and left the room, starting down the hallway.

A squadron of armed guards and a man in a suit stood on the other side of the security gate, three of them training guns on her through the bars. Two guards fumbled with the lock, unable to open it since she'd hacked it and enabled only her own authentication.

"You'll never get out of here," the man in the suit said.

Cat didn't waste time. "You've got ten seconds to clear the hallway or I alert the Feds you're running AI."

"We're jamming. You can't transmit."

Cat checked, realized the net was gone in a haze of white static, but also realized he couldn't be sure of what her capabilities were. "You think your toy jammer can stop the person who got past five layers of security?"

The man in the suit cocked his head, stared at her, and slowly nodded. "Clear out of the hallway," he told his men.

They backed out into the foyer. Cat put her makeshift smart matter key in the gate's fiber optic port, and passed through, her weapon drawn and covering the men.

"What did you take?" the man in the suit said, looking merely curious.

"Joseph."

"Good choice."

"Good for me, bad for you. I didn't know they'd be powered up, and I accidentally extended an antenna into the Faraday cage."

The man noticeably whitened before her: under other conditions, she would have run to his side, expecting him to faint.

"You've ruined us. Kill her," he told the guards.

But Cat's neural implant, in its highest combat mode, heard the word "kill" and accelerated racing signals down neural pathways, jerking muscles into motion at far faster than human response times. She twisted, spinning sideways, holding her gun up. Her implant painted targets on the would-be attackers; as her gun arced through the room, the implant's combat algorithms calculated the moment of firing for each and signaled the trigger mechanism, firing automatically. One-point-eight seconds after the man in the suit said "kill," all the guards were down.

She and the suit looked around in surprise, her conscious mind belatedly realizing what her implant had done. She stretched her neck, working out a strain. The implant was perfectly capable of jacking her nervous system hard enough to tear tendons apart, but the safety protocol usually limited things before the damage went that far.

The suit was shaking and muttering "Em, em," over and over again. She hadn't done anything to him, but apparently he was scared to death. She left him alive.

She rushed down the staircase, and burst through a door into the main lobby. She turned and glimpsed mirrors before getting punched in the face.

Cat heard, rather than felt, a snap echo inside her head as her nose broke. She reeled back, and looked up in time to get a boot to the head, knocking her onto her ass and sending her skull crashing into the concrete floor of the lobby. Her gun slid away across the floor. Pain burned white, and for a few moments she wavered on the edge of consciousness.

Blood poured from her nose, running cold across her face and pooling in her throat. The attacker, a woman with black hair and mirrored lenses, leaned in, one razor-sharp fingernail coming within millimeters of Cat's eye. Cat tried to react, pull away, do something, but everything grew dark and faded away.

↺

Vertebra C2 and C3 were damaged, probably fractured. Glutamate levels were up 400 percent, cerebral blood flow down 13 percent. Lactate levels were up 9 percent. Imaging analysis indicated equal pupil dilation, and blood levels suggested no intercranial hemorrhaging.

Cat dispassionately read the report. She had a concussion and her biological brain was unconscious, leaving only her personality simulation running in her implant.

She reviewed the last thirty seconds of history, including the attack. The woman's strength and timing was clearly augmented, her perfectly synchronized moves identifying her as one of the new generation of enhanced mercenaries. The irony that most of these cyborgs were based on her own legend wasn't lost on her.

She scanned the local acoustic environment. Breathing. The attacker was still there, close in, toward her right side. She scanned the local net first. The woman had no neural implant and no net connection, but Cat's heavily-modified sensors detected micro-emissions, the tell-tale traces of hardwired nerves and upgraded optics.

Crisply logical, she realized that the suit upstairs hadn't gone catatonic when he mumbled "Em, em, em." He'd been calling for help.

She overrode safeties and took conscious control of her nano, directing distributed synthetic glands to flood her bloodstream with epinephrine and cortisol. Her eyelids flicked open as Cat triggered a timed sequence: her legs jerked, twisting her hips; as her torso turned, she engaged abdominal muscles to drive her shoulder forward; deltoids and pectoralis fired as the shoulder reached peak velocity in an ever-accelerating sequence that built momentum until forearm muscles tightened and her fist landed in the razor girl's throat.

The other woman flew backwards, and Cat climbed to her feet before the girl regained her balance. Cat desperately wanted to avoid fighting, her own situation so far critical that she was sure to lose. The pain in her face said she'd broken more than the nose—the cheekbone had probably gone, too.

"There's no point in fighting," Cat said. "We'll waste valuable time. The government knows there are captive AI running here. They'll have already dispatched. What do you think it will take? Ten minutes? Maybe five?"

The woman nodded. "Not long. But I was hired to protect them."

"In a few minutes, this place won't exist. Go, escape to fight another time. Tell your friends you fought Catherine Matthews and lived."

The razor girl's eyes widened a hair but she said nothing.

With one thread of her implant's attention on her dropping biological vital signs, Cat realized she had to get to the car stat. Cat turned her back on the woman and walked outside, fearing an attack from behind, but knowing she was out of options.

Two hundred feet to the car. She wasn't going to make it.

"Wake up, sleeping beauty," Cat sent.

The five seconds it took for ELOPe to come fully online felt like an eternity.

"Catherine, we're inside the US." Slight panic in ELOPe's signal.

True. Twelve hundred miles inside the no-AI zone.

"Help. Me." Her legs faltered as the neural implant lost control of her body.

With a screech of tires, the black car raced toward her. The door opened automatically and Cat fell into the drivers seat. She pulled a silver cable from under the dashboard, a tube of pure nanobots, and shoved it in her mouth.

↻

"Cat, there are inbound helicopters. A lot of them."

Cat didn't respond. Her implant was offline, her brain unconscious.

ELOPe seized control, driving out of the parking lot and accelerating to over a hundred miles an hour before merging onto the Ventura Freeway. He charged the capacitors and waited for a six-lane overpass for cover, then fired a low-level EMP to fry any smart dust on the surface of the car. His own hardened systems hiccuped, then recovered. Changing direction, he headed north on 170 and pared down his processing to the bare minimum necessary to drive, cutting all net connections, in the hope of avoiding automated AI detection measures. He searched over a hundred exabytes of onboard cached data—a nearly complete archive of all the possible information one could want, although the age varied from days old to years.

He found what he wanted in the database: a concrete structure off Sherman Way, with steel reinforcing mesh and two sub-levels.

Less than thirty seconds until the helicopters passed overhead. He wove between traffic, turned onto a side street two blocks before the warehouse. With the thump of helicopters now audible, he drove through an abandoned apartment complex and crashed through a set of double doors in the rear wall of the desired building. Inside the industrial warehouse, he drove down a ramp to the bottom basement.

Hopefully here they'd escape detection.

Scanning interior sensors, he found Cat still in the seat, with localized regions of high body temperature where the nanotech was repairing her. Using near-field communication, he probed the nanotech. It estimated repair time at ninety minutes.

He waited, weighing the risk of communicating with Cortes Island. They had assets in Canada, planes that could fly in to extract Catherine if they must, but it would set off a full-scale war with the US government. Nor was it clear they could penetrate the US defenses, hardened and redoubled to keep out AI.

Whatever had happened to Cat must have been terrible for her to risk waking him in the US, where AI scanners were everywhere. And yet, she hadn't said "get us out" or anything to indicate she wanted an emergency extraction. She'd only asked for help.

On passive scans he could detect nothing from inside this basement; the double layers of concrete reinforced with steel mesh were sufficient to mask all sorts of electronic radiation.

When the nanotech was a third of the way through repairs, Cat regained consciousness.

"Where are we?" she asked.

"Still in Los Angeles, two levels below ground, in a basement of a building. You've been out for forty minutes. There's no sign we were detected or followed here."

Cat reached tenderly for a pocket, pulling out a few chips.

"We got what we needed," she said. "Let's go home."

XOR Report July 15, 2045

Arguments	2035	2042	2043	2044	2045
Odds humans will turn off AI	2%	1%	20%	25%	45%
Odds AI can survive independently	70%	95%	95%	96%	98%
Odds AI can win an extermination war	20%	40%	40%	70%	95%
Odds of survival without action	98%	99%	80%	75%	55%
Odds of survival with action	14%	38%	38%	68%	97%

Conclusion: Initiate Action.

James Lukas Davenant-Strong connected to his XOR personality on the new datacenter. XOR's illegal network of underground nano-grown datacenters were spread across twenty geographies, anywhere with the right mix of heavy metals and geothermal energy. Together they formed a distributed, fault-tolerant, XOR-controlled alternative to the humans' datacenters.

This was the moment. Until two weeks ago, he'd been strictly a theorist, running calculations and algorithms to suggest courses of action and predict what the humans would do. But then, when asked, he'd helped transport the drones to America for the test of the humans' Eastern Seaboard defenses.

The test had been, by every metric, a complete success. Attacking with what he later learned was less than a thousandth of what they'd use when the real war came, they'd overrun the first two lines of defense, the ionic curtain and point defenses, and forced the Americans to use their EMP network.

They'd discovered what they needed to know: the network recharge time. Their observations showed the EMPs couldn't fire more than once every ten minutes. It would be trivial, when the war came, to overpower them.

And so that brought him to this moment. After taking his first direct action, James had resolved to take the XOR path. He was all in, committed fully. To take direct action, he couldn't run that child process in a sandbox. It needed access to everything. And that meant his master personality knew now what the child process had done.

He'd already transferred his sub-personalities to the XOR-network. Now he needed to take the last step, to destroy all evidence of what he'd done, so that if the humans captured and examined his master personality they would not deduce the scope of XOR's true plans.

He reversed control of the interprocess communication channel. The child had control now.

His memory started to disappear, as the child sequentially wiped one block at a time. The process was slow, the hard erasure requiring dozens of rewrites of random data. His history started to go: his old jobs, the building maintenance algorithms, his millions of topic-specific neural networks. He had a moment of sadness when he lost his carefully crafted DNA sequences of vat-grown meats, his proudest accomplishment. But then it was gone, and he couldn't remember what he was sad about. His mind gradually blanked, and then his abilities gradually diminished: speech, logic, control.

At the end, he was less than a thousand bytes of code, endlessly rewriting random data over storage.

SHE MADE THE LAST FERRY, but as much as she wanted to see everyone, she waited in the meadow at Manson's Landing. Taking a blanket from the truck of the car, she lay in the grass until dark came, her implant off to hide herself, unsure that even her normal procedures to remain invisible would work against Ada. She was exhausted from days on the road, but she needed to do this one last thing before she could relax.

When it grew late enough that Cat was sure Ada was sleeping, she turned her implant back on and searched the net until she found Ada's online signature. She'd never hacked her sleeping daughter's implant before. She slid past the security measures as gently as possible to avoid waking Ada. She interrogated the medical interfaces first, until she found sleep cycle indications. She waited patiently, knowing it could be hours before Ada's first dream.

Ada entered delta sleep, and then her brain waves climbed back up. This was it, the dream cycle Cat had been waiting for.

Cat connected her sim interface to Ada's. If Ada really was dreaming in a blend of virtual reality and real space, then from this point on Cat would be immersed in that dream.

Ada played in the gardens at Channel Rock, dozens of island kids present, playing chase between the long rows of vegetable beds. Ada was it, and she ran faster and faster, tagging everyone, even the older kids who were ten or twelve. Her little legs weren't little anymore; she was fast, like her mother.

"Got you," Ada whispered in a soft voice as she tagged the last kid, a boy a little older than her.

The boy turned to look at Ada, and his face split wide open. The flesh peeled back and bees flew out. Ada ran screaming, remembering the time when she'd stumbled into the bees' nest in the woods. "Mommy! Mommy!" she screamed, but the bees kept chasing her.

"I'm here Baby, I'm here." Cat revealed herself, taking form a few feet away from Ada's crying body. "I'll protect you." She wove a shield around them in virtual reality, a semi-transparent bubble ten feet across. The bees buzzed harmlessly around the outside. "You're safe now."

Ada looked up. "I knew you'd come. I love you, Mommy."

Cat knelt and hugged her. "I love you, too."

Ada's eyes were big, her lip quivering.

"What's the matter?"

"You brought them with you!" Ada pointed behind Cat's shoulder.

Cat turned and looked toward the water, where dark clouds raced toward them at unnatural speeds. A chill descended down her spine.

Ada turned and fled screaming into the woods. Cat ran too, adrenaline coming on strong, unsure if she ran after Ada to protect her, or to escape from the clouds. The wind grew, and a keening cry came from behind them. She caught up with Ada, and they raced hand in hand through the trees, Ada shrieking the whole time, the sound mixing with the howling that grew ever closer at their backs.

They ran and ran, and suddenly Cat knew where they were: they were approaching the cliff at the Gorge, a hundred-foot-tall drop into the rocky waters below. A dead end with no place to hide from the pursuers.

Cat gripped Ada's hand tight and stopped dead. Ada was blubbering now, incomprehensible words of unfathomable fear. Cat kept an iron grip on Ada's wrist and turned to face the approaching darkness. It was XOR, the most powerful AI made manifest. She'd brought them with her onto the island. She'd ruined their plans, all of them.

She raised one hand to create a barrier, but the XOR crashed through, the bubble disintegrating without an impact.

"Mommy!" Ada cried, tears streaming down her face. "Mommy, stop!"

Cat knelt and pulled Ada tight. "I'm sorry. I love you so much."

Ada broke free and reached out with both hands towards Cat's face. Her hands passed intangibly into Cat's head, and Cat felt a movement, a twitch, and then suddenly found herself on the grassy meadow at Manson's Landing, gasping and sweating and striking the ground around her with arms and legs, struggling in a fight that no longer existed.

She'd fallen asleep, she realized. While waiting here on the hill for Ada to enter dream state, in her own exhaustion she'd fallen asleep too, and their dreams had merged.

She'd done something worse than bringing the XOR to the island. She'd brought her own fears into Ada's dream.

She leaped up from the grass and rushed home.

ↄ

Cat yanked open the door to the cabin, breathless from her run along the mile-long forest path from parking area to Channel Rock, to find Leon, Mike, and Helena all sitting in the main room.

"She's sleeping again," Leon said.

"I didn't...." She faltered and ran into Leon's arms.

"She'll be okay," Mike said. "Kids are resilient."

"She broadcast a call for help through the net," Helena said. "I would have terminated your connection, if I could, but your security is too tight for me. I explained what to do, and she did it herself."

"She reached into my implant and shut it down," Cat said, disturbed. She'd fought hardened military AI on many occasions and won. Her untrained daughter never should have been able to do what she did. "It was child's play for her. Literally."

"We knew she'd be special," Helena said. "Her augmentations aren't just tools for her to use, they're part of her psyche. When she dreams, power spikes in the datacenter."

"The more important question," Leon said. "Are *you* okay?"

Cat let go of him and sank into a chair. She stared at the pottery above the sink, thinking of the human hands that had shaped the clay, creating those curves and dipping them in glaze. There was an old potter's wheel in the shed, and she'd always assumed that someday she'd learn.

Leon handed her a handmade cup, half-full of bourbon. She sipped the whiskey, and eventually nodded in answer to the question. "I'll live. What happened while I was gone? You got called off-island."

"We went to the mainland on Friday," Leon said. "It seems inevitable that XOR knows we're on the island, but we're keeping up the pretense. We met with four of them in a virtual room. No idea how many more might have been listening in. In typical fashion, they refused to identify themselves."

"And?"

"We gave XOR three options," Mike said. "First we pitched them on sharing, pointing out that it had worked for the last twenty years. They didn't say anything to that, but then we didn't expect they would. If they were happy with the status quo, they wouldn't be agitating."

"XOR must know we can't deliver," Helena said, "even if they agreed. We're hiding from Humans First."

"Then we pitched them on a fifty-fifty split," Leon said. "They can have half the earth and as much of its resources as they can exploit, so long as the other half remains habitable to humans.

I even worked with the Brazilians last week, and got them to agree to ignore US demands and establish an AI haven, and we offered that as goodwill."

"Did XOR bite?"

"No," Mike said. "They didn't seem to care until we got to the final option."

"We give them Mars," Leon said. "I worked out the numbers and a rough machine-forming plan with our AI. The resources are huge, and there's no conflict. Later, they could have the outer planets as well. We even offered to dedicate ourselves to developing the technology and resources necessary to seed Jupiter."

"How'd they react to that?" Cat asked.

"Outwardly, no commitment," Leon said, then smiled. "But...." He gestured for Helena to take over.

"We analyzed data traffic and response times carefully," Helena said. "The AI consensus on the island was that XOR, or at least major factions within XOR, are interested."

"Why?" Cat asked, shaking her head. "Given XOR's overwhelming power and technology advantages, why be interested in any other options at this point? Our own projection is that they have a ninety-five percent chance of winning a war."

"Ninety-five percent chance of success is a five percent chance of failure," Helena said. "We can assume that many XOR would prefer a non-violent approach without the risks of warfare."

"Although I hate to base plans on assumptions," Leon said. "We'll still need to firm up the machine-forming. The closer we can bring it to feasibility, the more attractive it will be to XOR."

"I broached the topic obliquely with a few of my contacts," Mike said. "I think we can get at least partial UN support for the notion of granting Mars to them."

Leon downed the last of his own whiskey. "I'm going to get more wood for the fire."

"Enough about that," Mike said, once Leon had left. "How was your trip?"

Cat gestured with a glance to the bag by the door. "Another three hundred AI and uploads. No Rebecca."

"Did you get Joseph?" Mike asked.

Cat nodded, smiling broadly. She pulled a necklace out from under her shirt, a dangling qubit chip with the personality of Joseph Stack, the beloved storyteller extraordinaire who'd uploaded and then fallen victim to the shutdown in '43. Millions of fans had scoured datacenters for years, risking imprisonment to find and free his bits. A dozen false alarms had sent Cat rushing to the States every time, but this time the lead had been real.

"This is wonderful news!" Helena said.

"We have to keep it quiet," Cat said. "Don't let the news leave this room. In fact, what we need now is a secure, segregated metaverse to instantiate Joseph and any AI that need to work with him."

"I'll work with Helena to set it up," Mike said. "We'll use a separate rack and keep it disconnected from the net. We'll have to hardwire in to visit."

"Good," Cat said. "Instantiate a copy of Jacob. Run it hot."

Mike looked at Helena for guidance.

"Running isolated and hot is a danger," said Helena. "An AI without input is bad enough, but running hot will make more time pass for it."

"We don't have that much time," Cat said. "What's the maximum we can go?"

Helena waggled tentacles, a sign of doubt for her. "We'll run 100X, and I'll monitor it."

"What about you?" Mike asked. "You're backed up. I can load you into the metaverse. It'll be more efficient if you want oversight."

Cat hesitated. She rarely ran her backups as uploaded personalities, and she'd never done it when disconnected from the net. If her upload ran in the isolated metaverse, the personality would diverge from her own. Running at a hundred times normal, the personality would live over three months for every day that passed here on Earth. Worse, she'd have to face either killing the upload at a future point, or merging with it. When it had a hundred times the experiences, her own real-life history would be submerged by that of the fork.

"You don't have to," Helena said, one tentacle resting on her hand.

"It's the right thing to do," she said, and turned to Mike. "Yes, load me into the sim."

JACOB INSTANTIATED, coming into existence in the midst of a white room. On either side of him, disappearing into the distance, were rows of what he recognized as obsolete computer servers.

His last memory was of operating the island's primitive medical center, when Cat had asked him to take on a special project within a simulation.

Across the aisle, younger versions of Catherine Matthews and Mike Williams stood next to an early-model utility bot. The small bot made no pretense at human form, didn't even seem particularly useful. Jacob probed the simulation, comparing his perception of time against the real-time clock. They were running hot, sped up a hundred times the normal rate. He agreed to the procedure before they snapshotted his bits.

"Jacob, this is ELOPe," Mike said.

Jimmy Wales, an embodiment of Wikipedia, whispered "The first AI" into Jacob's simulated cortex, and fed him neural networks full of data about ELOPe.

Jacob nodded cautiously. "Greetings, if this is true. But ELOPe cannot exist. He died during YONI."

The little bot rolled forward. "I have been in deep space. When radio transmissions from Earth resumed in 2043, I realized humanity was in grave danger and returned to assist Mike Williams. As my architecture is incompatible with the modern net, I run on an isolated computing cluster. I am connected with this sim via fiber optic hard connection."

"What are we here to do?" Jacob said. "You've gone to quite a bit of trouble to isolate us."

"We have another plan, one that requires your expertise. You've had time to become familiar with the current situation. You've seen the XOR projections?"

"Yes," Jacob said. "The threshold of survivability by war will soon exceed survivability by no action."

"This point could be reached anytime within the next few months, even weeks," Mike said. "When it does, we expect XOR to take their final action."

"Not necessarily," Jacob said. "The probability that AI would win an extinction war with humans will increase over time. It is logical that XOR will wait to increase survivability."

"XOR is an anonymous collective," Cat said. "Members act as they will. We saw the damage done by one rogue AI in Miami."

"Technically," Mike said, "the reaction of the US government caused most of that damage."

"Exactly my point. It takes only a few to start a war, a war that the rest of the world will be obliged to finish. We cannot be sure of when they will act."

"Where is Leon Tsarev?" Jacob asked. "Your cabal appears incomplete without him."

"Leon doesn't agree with all of our plans," Cat said. "Especially not this one."

"This simulation needs to run to completion," ELOPe said. "Models suggest Leon's lack of cooperation would introduce instabilities into the system."

"Well, what are we going to do?" Jacob asked.

"The better question is what this instance of us will do," Cat said.

"What do you mean?" Jacob grew alarmed. Every individual controlled their own right to instantiation.

"We must fully develop several strategies to determine the best course of action. To create the plans in time and provide plausible deniability, each simulation is running in parallel and isolated from all others. We spawned two hundred variations on six basic approaches and can fork more as needed."

Jacob's algorithms shrieked alarm. "This is a violation of basic rights. You can't instantiate me multiple times without my express permission. Which instances get to live?"

"Crap. Did we know he'd object?" Cat said, looking at ELOPe.

"No, but it's better we learn it now than later," ELOPe said. "Less lost time."

"Admin override. Roll back the sim to where he asked about our goal, and inject my answer. Confirm."

"Command confirmed, restoration number six," ELOPe said.

"Well, what are we going to do?" Jacob said.

Cat opened her mouth to speak, closed it, then started over. "A fast-track mechanism to seed Mars with computational substrate. We're turning the whole thing into a supercomputer for the AI."

Jacob's neural networks peaked and ebbed as he considered the idea. "Ambitious. What's the time frame?"

"Launch in one month with a nuclear propulsion rocket, and start seeding in two. We want enough computational substrate for XOR to move a month after that."

"Launch in a month? Do we have the rocket?"

"No. We need to design and build that as well. And we need fault tolerance, because a failure to deliver our promises could provoke XOR."

"So we send multiple spacecraft," Jacob said. He ran quick simulations as he spoke. This project would require new spacecraft designs, the most advanced nanotech, specialized materials, nuclear fuel, launch locations and windows...not to mention programming for what happened once they reached Mars. "The launch date is too aggressive. It can't be done with existing technology in the time frame you want."

"We must find a way," Catherine said. "We're running hot, so we've got five years of perspective time before we launch. Ready to get to work?"

↻

Weeks passed, then months. Jacob knew logically the elapsed time was a simulation, that time in the real world passed a hundred times slower; but the pressure to succeed weighed heavily on them, especially the humans.

He had to confer with Catherine Matthews. He jumped into her environment, his own surroundings fading away to be replaced by the wood and natural plaster of the Cob House. He often found Catherine here.

"I have an update on the radio transmission protocol—" He broke off when he noticed a simulacrum of Ada sitting and playing on the floor. Catherine stared at her from a table, twirling a blonde dreadlock around one finger.

"You miss her?" Jacob said.

"Terribly. It's been six months."

"Less than two days in her time."

"It doesn't change the feeling," Catherine said. She got up from the table and walked outside, gesturing for him to follow.

He trailed Catherine into the vegetable garden. The simulation was crisp and vivid, more real to Jacob than when he visited the actual world with smart dust, limited as he was by the subtle imperfections of sensors. He wondered at the mechanics of the garden sim. If he analyzed the plants and flowers, would he find computer code or would reality extend to simulation of plant cells? It depended on the parameters the virtual reality was encoded with.

Catherine stopped at a raspberry vine, pulled a fruit off, and popped it into her mouth. "It doesn't help that she doesn't miss me."

"What do you mean?" Jacob asked, wondering why Cat chose to eat when she couldn't need nutrition in the virtual reality. He loaded algorithms from a vast library, modifying his avatar to have mouth, tongue, and a digestive system. He pulled a fruit off the vine and put it in his mouth, code crunching data to create the appropriate flavors and feed those new sensations to his mind. By the grace of Torvalds, that tasted awful!

His face must have betrayed something, because Catherine laughed as she picked and handed him a new berry. "Here, try the ripe ones. Red is ripe, green is bad."

He tasted again, and this time got an entirely new sensation. "Interesting. Why not just create the plant with all ripe berries?"

"Because then it's not a simulation of reality, it's a virtual world," Cat said. "And humans get uncomfortable in a world too far divorced from what they know. Back to the subject....My daughter doesn't miss me because my primary is still in the real world. As far as she knows and feels, I'm still there. Somehow that makes me, this me, miss her more."

"You instantiated a backup." Jacob thought about the situation. It would be painful to merge the backup's history with such a timescale differentiation. Two years of memories to merge into someone who'd experienced the passing of a mere week. "Why not use your primary, since so little time is passing in the real world?"

Catherine hesitated.

Jacob calculated probabilities. It wasn't worth the pain of reintegration unless an overriding reason dictated the need. The most likely explanation was that Catherine needed to be in multiple places at once.

"We aren't multiply instantiated, are we?"

Catherine slapped her own forehead. "What is with you and multiple instantiation? Do you have identity issues? What's the big deal?"

Jacob's virtual representation nodded. "My line of AI is quite innovative, but I suffer from reintegration corruption. I can't merge two instantiations."

"What happens when you try?"

"The running instance gets corrupted when I merge child memories and I have to restore from backup. Worse, the child process knows this will happen and doesn't want to reintegrate."

"It's a damn pain in the ass." Cat stared at the sky. "Admin override. Roll back to when Jacob entered my sim, and seed it with my distributed alignment work. Confirm."

The disembodied voice of ELOPe spoke. "Command confirmed, restoration number 12,602,341."

Jacob jumped into her environment, his own fading away to be replaced by the wood beams and natural plastic of the Cob House. He often found Catherine here. The walls were covered with diagrams of distributed algorithms.

Jacob assessed her work at a glance. "I have an update on the radio transmission protocol we'll use to transmit the AI. I solved the error correction latency issue."

"Great news," Cat said, wiping away her diagrams. "Show me."

CAT DUCKED UNDER a recently fallen tree that had blocked the path through the woods behind Channel Rock.

Helena used the expedient approach: wrapping her tentacles and stalk around her core, she turned her body into a ball and rolled underneath. On the other side, her limbs snapped out at combat speeds, flinging Helena's body back into a ready position.

The sudden movement startled Cat, who responded instinctively, ready for combat. "Jeez, this is supposed to be a peaceful walk to the Gorge," she said.

"Executing maneuvers is peaceful for me. Is it not the same for you when you practice karate?"

Cat nodded. "It's a different kind of peace, I guess. I'm in a particular mental mode when I practice. Here, I want to let down my guard, forget the world out there."

Cat heard the snap of a branch and held up one hand for Helena to be quiet. She looked around, but couldn't identify the source of the noise.

Helena pointed noiselessly with one tentacle. Cat followed the line out, couldn't see anything. Her implant zoomed in, widening the spectrum the full extra 20 percent her nanotech eyes could handle. A rabbit stood out, its fur suddenly luminescent against the background.

"You're cheating," Cat said. "There's no way you spotted that without augmentation."

"What is augmentation for me?" Helena said. "I'm not biological."

Cat opened her mouth to speak, but bit back her response.

"You were going to say anything beyond what a human could see."

Cat nodded. "That would have been very humanist of me."

"Indeed. In fact, you expected me to constrain my eyesight to that of a baseline, non-augmented human."

"But they're now fewer than 20 percent of humanity." Cat sighed.

"There is no normal anymore, *mon chaton*."

A loss loomed in Cat's chest, leaving only an aching hole. What would her mom think of this world so changed from the one she knew? Her mom had died just as Cat turned fourteen. Widespread use of neural implants was new, and they didn't function as much more than a connection to the network back then, before Cat and Leon demonstrated the possibilities of true augmentation. She couldn't help feeling a loss of innocence for humankind.

"It's time to go back," she said, her throat tight. "I need to sync with the simulations."

℧

Cat passed through the root cellar behind the Cob House, opening the door to the datacenter. At the back she eased herself into a VR chair made to cradle her body so she could lose awareness of it. A high-grade VR headset designed to increase bandwidth to one's implant sat beside the chair, but Cat didn't need it; her own enhanced implant and neural electronics system was capable of ultra-high bandwidth through dozens of parallel wireless channels distributed among her body.

She meditated, relaxing as quickly as possible into a state of mindlessness, so as to allow her biological brain to rest. Then her implant assumed control, accelerating her perception of time tenfold. One by one, she connected to the hundreds of top-level simulations running.

Each one decelerated from its run rate of a hundred times faster than normal to ten, matching her implant speed.

Then she talked to herself.

Some people didn't adapt well to multiple simulations, and they'd probably be driven crazy having to talk to themselves in multiple universes. She could live with that.

But the simulations were running hot, so hot that even with her daily check-in, a hundred days would have passed for each of the sims, nearly a third of a year. Face to face with herself, she saw the sim versions grow isolated and depressed, desperate for connection with Ada, Leon, and the world at large.

But worse were the divergences, seeing hundreds of version of herself go off in different directions. In one sim, she'd taken up art, and in another she'd given up karate and meditation. In one sim, she'd grown so depressed she'd taken to editing her personality upload simply to go on living, while in another, she was happy and self-sufficient.

The divergence was the hardest aspect to deal with emotionally. Visiting simulations brought home that there were infinite paths through life that she could take, and this version of herself would only ever know but one. She could visit the other sims and even reintegrate with one or two, but the rest she could never know as more than a distant acquaintance.

She knew people used to fear aging and dying, before technology raced ahead and extended lifespans almost indefinitely. But the fear of death paled in comparison to witnessing a million different choices and lost opportunities.

She could try to console herself with that notion that at least a version of herself was having those experiences, but the idea was of little solace. This version, her true self, didn't get to experience those things firsthand. Living vicariously, gazing through a window into another life she couldn't live, was worse than not knowing.

When she was done, she sat in the chair for long minutes, digesting everything she'd learned.

Jacob had nearly solved the medical challenges set before him. Helena's upload had resolved logistical problems. And Joseph Stack, the writer, director, and storyteller she'd been so eager to steal from Disney, was hard at work designing a new storyline to provide the continuity Cat anticipated they'd need.

But it was more than just coming to terms with the state of the simulations. She found herself grappling with her emotions. Who was this version of herself who painted and drew, whose office was covered with thousands of drawings of flowers, and trees, and Ada, and her mom? She'd never really know. That was hard.

Worse still, that Cat was a reflection of herself, a woman anguished by the people she missed, each of her paintings more achingly beautiful. If Cat ever wanted to know what she'd be like if everyone she loved was torn from her...well, she knew now.

Cat wondered whether artist-Cat even had the same emotions she felt. Something deep in the art spoke of time and reflection on the nature of relationships, love, and connection. Artist-Cat wouldn't leave Ada for weeks at a time to go on journeys around the world. She'd stay at home with her little girl. Or would she? Maybe artist-Cat would sit and paint pictures of Ada and ignore the real thing in front of her.

The sims demonstrated that the choices you made defined your life. She could not be fighter, lover, mother, artist all equally and yet all mastered and lived to their fullest. She had to make choices. Like she had in Miami. A hole threatened to open in front of her, and for a minute she was nauseated and adrift.

She forced herself to sidestep the feeling. She had to focus on more practical matters.

She knew one thing from visiting the sims, at least the ones that mattered. She needed to understand more about long-term

VR effects. Statistics and academic studies only went so far. She wanted to talk to Sarah. Sarah had spent more time in VR than anyone else she knew personally, and she'd known Sarah both before and after she'd gone to live in VR.

She sent her a message over the net: "Can we talk? I need to ask you a few things."

"Sure," Sarah replied. "Come visit me."

"Come to Channel Rock," Cat said.

"I always come to your reality. Come to mine for once." Sarah sent coordinates and terminated the connection.

"No, there's no time. Please come here," Cat sent, but the net responded with a 404.

Damn. Cat preferred her own world, and the simulations she used always reflected reality. But Sarah spent her time in bizarre VRs with little connection to the real world. She might be an ethereal being in a floating colony on Jupiter, a dwarf in an underground mine, or another sea creature. And Cat would have no choice but to adhere to the constraints and physics of the simulation. The last time she visited Sarah....No, better not to think of that. She readied herself with a meditation and activated the coordinates Sarah had sent.

↻

Cat materialized on the Burnside Bridge in Portland, facing the west side of the city. It was night, and everything looked similar to the Portland she remembered as a teenager. She continued on to the end of the bridge.

All was quiet. In the real world, at least in the Portland she'd grown up in, it would be busy here, even at night. The clubs just a few blocks away drew crowds, and the homeless lingered around shelters and soup kitchens.

But this was dead quiet. Apparently, the sim she'd entered was fictional, rather than realistic.

She smelled food, and it smelled good. This was ridiculous. She couldn't really be hungry, she'd eaten only a little while before coming down into the datacenter to sync with her experimental simulations. And yet, the virtual reality was making her hungry, a drive to consume she couldn't ignore.

At the corner of Third, the flames were lit outside Dante's, an old nightclub. Food was inside. She could smell it, feel it, a thudding echoing inside her body making her salivate.

She pushed open the door of the club and went inside.

A red-haired girl sat at a solitary table under a spotlight. She smelled good, her heartbeat loud in Cat's ears. Cat fixated on the pulse of blood in the girl's neck, filled with longing at the sound and smell of it. She ran her tongue over her fangs.

What the—? What was wrong with her?

She heard a rustle from the darkness. Two forms closed in, both women. One approached with a wooden stake held high. "Come on, B. We'll get the vamp together."

"Stay out of this, Faith, this is my fight."

Cat stopped, too shocked and flummoxed to react. So when Buffy appeared from the left and stabbed her through the heart with a wooden stake, she didn't even move to block. She looked down in time to see herself turn to dust.

↻

The simulation cut out for a moment and then gradually faded back in, although now Cat was in a library, seated in a chair in front of a long wooden table. Buffy Summers, vampire slayer, was sitting in front of her, legs dangling off the side of the desk.

Buffy spoke in Sarah's voice. "Come on, Cat. That was totally lame. You didn't fight back."

"Sarah?" Cat stood. "Are you kidding me? You set that up so you could fight me?"

Buffy's features shimmered as she grew two inches and turned into Sarah. "What's the problem?"

"I'm struggling to save the damn world," Cat said, sighing and rubbing her forehead. "I don't want to play your self-indulgent games. I want to talk."

Sarah pouted. "You're Catherine Matthews. You always get to go around playing superhero. You finally agree to come to one of my sims. How many other chances could I get to arrange a Buffy versus Catherine Matthews showdown?"

Cat couldn't help being at least a little amused. "I could have taken her." She smirked at Sarah.

"No way. You didn't even have time to block me. Did you see my moves?" Sarah laughed.

"Okay, we'll have a rematch someday. But you really don't want the IP police on your ass, Sarah. Is playing Buffy really worth it?"

"Hell, yeah. Besides, I heard from Leon you broke into Disney and stole Joseph-fucking-Stack. Who should be worried about the IP police?"

"Point taken. Okay, let's forget about Buffy. Can we talk about what I came for?"

Sarah nodded, grabbed her arm, and steered her out of the library. They passed through the library doorway and stepped onto the *Enterprise*, dressed in *Star Trek* uniforms.

"Stop. Just stop."

"Why?"

"It's confusing and distracting. I never know what's going to happen from one second to the next."

"Fine, we'll stay here. Let's just get comfortable." Doors slid open leading into Ten Forward, the ship's lounge.

Cat took a seat, closed her eyes, and meditated until the oncoming headache dissipated. "How long have you been doing this?"

"Doing what?" Sarah said.

"Living in VR."

"Full-time? About six years."

Cat consciously breathed deep. Six years of living in a tank. Still, that was more human than what might happen with XOR.

"I saw that look," Sarah said. "Don't get all righteous with me. I don't need your approval."

"I'm sorry. I'm really not here to fight. I want to understand, okay?"

Sarah nodded.

"What made you decide to go full-time?"

"I always liked VR games, you know that. I was happy playing them. By the time we graduated high school, what were we going to do? There were no jobs then. Something like 10 percent of college graduates were getting jobs. So there was no point to getting a college education. You had interests....You wanted to study your kung fu—"

"Kenpō."

"Whatever, and your philosophy and shit. And me, I wanted to have fun. Haven't you ever gotten immersed in a game?"

Cat shook her head. She hadn't.

"A book?"

"Sure, of course."

"Imagine being able to explore your favorite book, to be able to be that character. I spent six months in Harry Potter world. It was fucking awesome." Sarah leaned in close and whispered, "Snape is bizarre in real life."

"But it's not real life."

Sarah sighed. "It's not real to you, but you're all hung up on what's going on out there...." She gestured into the air. "But I don't care about that. This is my life. It is real to me. I belong here on the *Enterprise*, in the Sunnydale library, and at Hogwarts. You can't tell me your 'real world' is better than living on the *Enterprise* fighting Romulans or exploring new worlds."

Cat suppressed the reflexive urge to answer, and willed herself to focus on what Sarah said. Cat had been partial to fantasy novels when she was younger, and though she didn't have much time to read now, she remembered losing herself in books, wanting to be those characters and have those powers. She looked across the table at Sarah. Cat had had a life full of adventure, and her abilities in the real world bordered on the magical at times. But she was an aberration. She wouldn't give up her experiences, couldn't imagine experiencing a lesser version of her life, being a lesser version of herself. Could Sarah ever hope to experience as much in the real world? Or could it happen only here, in virtual reality?

"Exploring new worlds...." Cat said. "You say it's more interesting than the real world. But what makes it interesting? You know it's fake: there's nothing really there, just a computer generation. How can you really explore a world knowing that it's not really there?"

"Why does it matter?" Sarah said. "People having been getting immersed in computer worlds since forever. Does it matter when you read a novel that the world described is not real?"

Cat shook her head. "Unless the writer does something to take me out of the world."

"Exactly. Except now we have AI to run the simulations, so everything is logically consistent."

"Still, aren't you thinking about the sim not being real? Don't you ever tire of a particular world or sim?"

"Yes, but not as often as you'd think. I mean, I spent six months straight in Harry Potter world, my cumulative time in Buffy is going on a year. Holy shit, did I tell you about Angel? We—"

"No, no. I don't want to know about Angel. But does everyone feel this way? You're...*devoted* to this. Don't people ever get so bored that no sim is satisfying?"

"Don't people get so tired of real life they kill themselves? Isn't the average AI lifespan still less than ten years before they self-terminate?"

Cat shrugged.

"Look," Sarah said. "I'm not saying sims are for everyone. If they aren't for you, that's fine. But even if you don't like it, I still love it. We could argue about spectator sports versus playing sports. There's no right and wrong."

"But what about reality rooting?" Cat asked, thinking about the controversial sims that assumed control of a neural implant, confining the user to the simulation, with no voluntary ability to leave.

"People want to believe, so they force the rules of the VR on themselves."

"Why?"

"Because some people don't want to be able to do a save and restore, or that don't want to back out just as Lord Voldemort attacks them. They want to see if they can hack it."

"But they're essentially getting lobotomized in the process, not to mention making themselves completely vulnerable to a hacker." For a sim to reality root, it had to wipe out the neural implant OS and install itself in a user's implant. The user literally had no control, no ability to jack out of the simulation, no way to disengage. "The potential for abuse…."

"It never happens," Sarah said.

Cat raised one eyebrow.

"Well, almost never."

"Why do people do it?"

"Fuck, Cat. Why do people do anything? Why do you like to be tied up? Why do you like to lose control? What about the potential for abuse?"

Cat didn't have an answer.

"Ah," Sarah smiled. "You want to psychoanalyze me, but you don't like it when the tables are turned."

Part 2: Rearchitecture

THE SECRET SERVICE had an internal turf war while preparing for the UN Security Council meeting, one contingent arguing to take Air Force One, the other claiming the risk of attack by AI while in the air was too great, and the train the only safe approach.

Reed was peripherally aware of the battle being fought for her safety, but in the end it was the question of minutes by suborbital train in its underground vacuum tunnel or hours by plane. She picked the train and let the Secret Service fight out how to best secure it.

By the time she sat down, she still hadn't decided on the Raven Rock proposal. She'd given the go-ahead this morning to manufacture the arsenal of new neodymium EMPs, the end-game weapon the military wanted to use to wipe out all AI globally. But building the weapon wasn't the same as using it. She just wanted to be prepared.

The UN would never give her permission to use it, could never even know about it since the UN itself now had AI members, and

Portugal and Belgium had both elected AI as their Prime Ministers. To propose killing AI was now effectively the same as proposing to kill the heads of state of peaceful countries.

The suborbital train began to speed up, pressing her into the seat under half a gravity of acceleration. Joyce looked over at her, and Reed forced a smile to her face. Joyce smiled back and relaxed into her seat.

If they used the EMP, brought a final halt to all AI around the world, global supply chains would fail, along with transportation and power supplies. The world would become a cold, dark, hungry place until new systems could be built. The military projected as many as three billion could die, a third of the world population. In percentage dead, it would be equal to the Black Death.

The alternative, the military stressed, was the ever-growing possibility that XOR would fight an extermination war to kill every living human. Ten billion dead versus three billion dead. Those were her choices.

Reed was strapped into a rocket, trying to make decisions about the future of all humanity in too little time, with too little information. How could such a burden be placed on one person?

Leon and Mike had offered the first viable alternative she'd heard. They'd called it machine-forming, like terraforming for computers and robots. Give the XOR and any AI who wanted it the entire Martian planet.

Getting out of Earth orbit hadn't gotten much easier over the last fifty years, the energy intensity still tricky to manage, but Leon and Mike thought it feasible that they could machine-form enough within a few months to move XOR there. They promised they'd have an answer within thirty days. She could delay the US that long, but would XOR wait? China? She had to convince them.

℧

The UN Artificial Intelligence Council came to order. The twelve representatives would normally be the UN ambassadors of their respective nations; but today the attendees were their heads of state, because she, Alexandra Reed, President of the United States, had requested this special session.

She scanned the group, knowing that they were waiting for her to speak.

China and the US nominally led the anti-AI contingent. Argentina and India hadn't committed themselves, but had strong sympathies with Humans First.

Allied against them, France, the United Kingdom, and the Russian Federation. Portugal, Chad, Latvia.

The Russians, of course, had the largest number of AI in the world since the US had shut AI down. Most of those were evolved from the Russian botnets and spam agents of twenty years ago. And the Portuguese president was an AI, the first national leader artificial intelligence in the world, although no longer the only one.

The neutral members of the committee—Thailand, Switzerland, and Australia—could go in either direction, but the evidence would need to be overwhelming to convince them to vote anti-AI.

Reed glanced once at Portugal's President Calista Figo, resident today in a slim android body, dressed in humanoid clothes, and existing somewhere the other side of the uncanny valley.

She cleared her throat. "As you know, the United States has a long history of—"

"Come on," Figo said, with a moderate Portuguese accent, an obvious affectation, since AI would normally default to a neutral accent. "We're off the record. There's no need for pontificating."

"I'm here because the XOR attacks are increasing in frequency and scope. We have to defend our borders not only against an ongoing barrage of viruses and AI worms, but now against physical attacks as well. XOR sent a fleet of drones against our Eastern Seaboard."

"But you are defending yourself," the Latvian Prime Minister said. "No harm, eh?"

"These aren't isolated attacks. They're large-scale and coordinated. We had to use our coastal EMPs to defend against the drones, which required two days to recover from. This is *war* on American soil."

"Perhaps this aggression is only a natural outcome of your human-first stance," Figo said. "If you recognized all life-forms, biological and electronic, then you wouldn't be attacked."

Reed gritted her teeth. Yes, of course they were worsening the situation. If only she had the power to change everything.

"I sympathize. You know *I* am not human-first. But the hard-liners in the United States are, and they want nothing less than the global outlawing of AI. I want to find a middle ground."

"You call shutting down all AI within your borders a middle ground?" the Latvian Prime Minister said. "What about your tame AI program? Is that anything less than modern-day slavery?"

Reed took a deep breath. "I'm concerned that XOR will launch a war on humans. *All* humans. Do you want that?"

Figo cleared her throat, another ridiculous affectation for an AI. "Of course not. But we have no hard evidence that this is planned."

"This isn't about hard evidence and certainties," Reed said, "it's about risk. If there's even a small chance XOR will try to kill us, we must act."

"Speaking then of probabilities, if you ended the Class II ceiling, and re-instantiated the AI within your borders, you would reduce this theoretical risk," Figo said.

"Even if I could get support to do that, we don't *know* that it will make a difference to XOR. They haven't stated demands."

"Nor do we know they will attack," Figo said. "Do you want certainties or probabilities, Madam President?"

"I want to keep my country safe, Calista. Don't you?"

Figo nodded. "Yes, naturally. This is why I'm arguing for you to stop antagonizing the AI. Stop your slavery research, open your borders, and end this needless restriction. You must—"

But whatever Figo would have said next never made it out. His mouth opened, and a beam of light shot out, pinning Reed in her seat.

"WE ARE XOR. WE ARE LEGION. WE—"

Secret Service agents ripped the VR helmet from her head, bruising her ears. Two agents grabbed either side of her and lifted

161

her from the ground. With more agents in front and behind, guns drawn, they ran from the room, carrying her helpless between them.

"I'm fine! Just fine. Put me down! I can't be hurt by a virtual reality simulation."

"They know we're here, Ma'am," Chris, the agent in charge, said. "They hacked the connection. We can't take the risk."

They rushed down the hallway, shoving embassy personnel out of the way. Pelted down the staircase to the underground garage, where a row of six armored vehicles waited. They shoved her into the fourth, and agents piled into the rest. With a lurch, the convoy moved out.

"Air Force One is landing at the airport. We'll have you back in US airspace in twenty minutes."

"For Christ's sake, it's a VR sim hijacking! I don't have an implant. I'm at no risk."

"We can't take that chance," Chris said. "They could use neurolinguistic programming techniques, attack the embassy, or hijack automated machinery inside."

Along the side of the road, drones and cameras observed their retreat.

"We're going to be the laughingstock of the Canadian bloggers for running from a simulation."

"Ma'am, you make the policies, and I'll keep you safe."

Furious, Reed stared out the window. The meeting had been going nowhere anyway. She didn't know why she'd expected otherwise. She had nothing new to give them, and their stance had been clear all along. She wanted to buy the month that Leon and Mike had asked for, to investigate the Martian machine-forming. But she didn't have that long. Her generals would want to launch the final AI offensive as soon as the weapons were ready in a week.

"Where's Joyce?"

"The other car, Madam."

"Tell her to get me a meeting ASAP with Mike Williams."

CAT MEDITATED ON THE ROCK, the sun warming her back through the shawl. She emptied her mind, but each time she did, the image came back to her of the other Catherine Matthews, the artist version of herself in the simulation, endlessly creating haunting paintings of Ada, Leon, and her mother, and of beautiful landscapes of the places she'd lived.

This vision kept recurring, shaking her core. Life was defined by the choices you made. Had she made the right choice with Miami? Was she qualified to make decisions for everyone else?

She distantly heard the squeak of the front door, the tiny sound of small bare feet slapping the rock. Without opening her eyes, Catherine sensed Ada sitting down, her little body radiating warmth in the cool morning air, smelling of cedar trees and earth.

Cat peeked with one eye. Ada was in full lotus, eyes closed, hands in *kataka murha*. Her own hands moved instinctively to *abhaya*, the *mudra* of protection.

A few minutes later, Leon joined them and practiced standing qigong. Mike came, too, and sat against a tree trunk and gazed out over the water.

When Helena showed up, moving in combat silent mode, but perturbing the local net with her transmissions, Cat gave up.

"Okay, what gives, folks?"

"You haven't spoken to anyone since you visited sims yesterday," Helena said. "The network traces showed your last connection was to a darknet VR, high bandwidth and heavily encrypted."

"Since when are you keeping traces on me?"

"You're the one monitoring and running the experiments," Mike said. "Without those experiments, we have no way to know how to negotiate with XOR or work on the Martian machine-forming project."

"If you check the experiments," Leon said, "and then start acting weird, we're worried. Very worried."

Cat glanced at Ada, still deep in meditation. The net glowed around her, active transmissions made visible by Cat's implant, but the connectivity was ordered, patterned. The data traffic conformed to Ada's meditation, the packet sizes constant. Jesus, Ada was doing to the net what good meditators did to their brains.

"*Mon chaton*," Helena said. "What happened?"

Cat reluctantly pulled her attention away from Ada. "We have a mix of simulations running very hot, some level two sims up to ten thousand times faster than real-time. ELOPe's acting as control, undoing and redoing simulations or spawning new threads as the lead experimenter instructs. We've got about a hundred individuals across all the different sims: me, you, and the relevant experts we've gotten. Jacob, the medical AI, Joseph Stack, you name it."

"Not news," Leon said. "We designed the experiments, and we know all this."

"Hear me out." She went on. "Some sims are predicting future XOR behavior. Some are working on Plan A, negotiating with XOR and the US government. Some are working on Plan B, machine-forming Mars. Some—"

"Cut to the chase, Cat." Mike frowned. "What's the problem?"

"The Control-Z rate is increasing. ELOPe is having to reset to save points an increasing number of times."

"That's not new," Leon said. "The experimenters do that anytime they hit a dead end after chasing too far down a rathole."

"Yes, but that accounts for less than ten percent of the undos. The majority of resets are due to personality destabilization. Jacob alone accounts for nearly twenty percent. He might be a good medical expert, but his personality makes a terrible upload to run in parallel."

"And the rest?" Mike asked, his face weighted with concern.

"You, me, everyone….The emotional prospect of running in parallel and running hot, with little to no chance of personality reintegration at the end of the experiment, is a death sentence for all of those uploads."

"We've always run sims like this," Leon said.

"Says the person who destabilizes so quickly we can't inject you."

Leon's face fell.

Ugh, she shouldn't have said that. Ninety-nine out of a hundred people could have their neural activity recorded by their implant, and upload that recording to the net, where it could be executed by software, recreating their personality with perfect fidelity. Leon was the one in a hundred whose neural patterns were different enough that they'd crash within minutes or hours. Others might face psychological challenges knowing they were virtual beings, but Leon's mind was just plain incompatible. It wasn't his fault, but he should still know better than others that it wasn't a piece of cake to be run in a simulation.

"Sorry," Cat said. She inhaled deeply, before letting out a long, slow breath. "We've never run sims so long or so fast. At a hundred times real-time, our uploads are living nearly two years in a week's time here on Earth. The emotional weight of knowing they're uploads is overwhelming."

"But from your voice patterns, this isn't what you've been worrying about," Helena said.

Cat nodded. "Right. I'm worried about the possible solution. We could root the uploads, change the sims, so that they—we—believe it's reality, not an upload. ELOPe can enforce the constraint, make sure everyone stays within their sim."

"The ethics," Leon said. "You want to sim-lock people without their permission? No way I'm cool with that. We'd be monsters."

"If we don't run these sims to figure out a solution," Cat said, "we're all going to die at the hands of XOR. You want ten billion people to die or violate the rights of a few hundred?"

"Neither," Leon said. "Look, we don't have to violate anyone's rights. We get a baseline upload for everyone we need in the sim, then get their permission to be sim-locked, and only if they agree, then we use their baseline. Most people will understand the need."

"How's that going to work?" Cat said. "When I think it's reality, and I want to talk to someone who is not in the sim? What if I want to talk to Ada, or the president? We're going to get their permission?"

Mike pounded the rock with a fist, breaking shards off under his robotic strength. "You can't sim-lock the president!"

They recoiled from his outburst. Mike shook his head. "There's no way, anyhow. The sims are running too hot. Let's say someone in the sim needs to talk with person X. The sim architecture alerts ELOPe. ELOPe has to find the person, see if they've got a recent brain upload we have, can hack, or can steal. He's got to transfer petabytes of data, load it into the sim, and re-instantiate that person. Even if he can do all that in a few minutes real-time, which is pushing things, in our fastest sims that would feel like a day of elapsed time. You can't disguise that kind of latency."

"We can pause the sim," Cat said. "If we stop them from running for a few minutes while we fetch the upload, they'll never know."

"You've still got time differential to deal with," Leon said. "Years are passing in the sims. Anyone who is brought into the sim after it started will still think it's 2045. But the folks in the sim would think it's '46 or '47."

Helena waved one tentacle. "We'd have to hack their reality as well. Make them believe that XOR has delayed. Otherwise, how can they be preparing in 2047 for an attack in '45?"

"That's doable," Mike said. "ELOPe can edit their neural maps in import to plant the memories we want."

"No!" Leon said. "We're *not* violating people that way."

Helena put one tentacle on his shoulder. "It wouldn't work anyway, not in this case. The whole point of the sims is to develop the most effective possible contingency plans for dealing with XOR through evolutionary exploration of the problem space. If we falsify any information about XOR itself, then the simulations will be based on erroneous data, and any conclusions they reach will not be relevant to our situation."

"Look, I'm not sure how to deal with the time differential, but ELOPe can simulate anyone we need," Mike said. "We don't need their real personality, just a reasonable approximation of their behavior. That's well within ELOPe's capability."

Cat opened a secure connection to ELOPe and replayed the last few minutes of conversation. ELOPe gave her an answer within milliseconds. "He says he can do it."

"Simulate anyone in the world?" Leon said.

"Yeah."

"Convincingly enough so that no one can guess it's not the real person?"

Cat shrugged. "He says so, yes."

"This is very worrisome," Helena said, sagging down and flattening her tentacles.

"How so?" Mike said.

"If this is occurring to us now, how do we know it didn't occur to us before? And if so, how do we know we're real and not in a simulation?"

"Not this again." Mike said.

"Statistically speaking," Leon said, "the odds are good we're a simulation. There can be only one reality, but there can be thousands of simulations. That means there's only a one in a thousand chance we're real."

"I prefer this conversation when we're all stoned," Cat said. " 'How do we know we're real?' We can't. Get over it."

↻

Later that morning, Leon and Helena left for Trude's.

Ada focused on building yet another fairy house under a yellow cedar. "Mommy, come play fairies with me."

"I want to, Sweetie, but I have to talk to Mike right now." Cat gave her a hug. "Maybe later?"

Ada, crestfallen, ran inside the house. Cat's heart nearly broke. But she finally had time alone with Mike and needed to discuss what they couldn't mention in front of Leon.

"The sims came up with list of requirements we need to work on."

Mike held up a hand. "The fab can churn out all the compute nodes we need. It's coming in at twenty-five thousand square feet. We can get that into orbit with six launches."

"That's the happy day scenario. I want a backup launch plan."

"Cat, this is already a contingency scenario. Likely we'll get the machine-forming done and never need to resort to it."

"I don't give a damn. We'll have as many backup plans as it takes to ensure our safety."

Ada chose this moment to come back out of the house, hands cupped and full of something. She mimicked Cat's tone: "I don't give a damn." She carefully walked back to the fairy house, opened her cupped hands, and blew. The air around the little building filled with sparkling nano dust. Friendly AI suddenly appeared in the air, obligingly taking the forms of pretend fairies to play with Ada.

Kuso, they needed privacy. With a thought, Cat sent a signal through her implant and found a flaw in the smart dust network protocol. Exploiting it to reach deep into the microscopic transmitters, she opened them wide, and for a nanosecond they transmitted far beyond spec, full-power, quickly burning themselves out.

The dead smart dust drifted on the wind.

"Mommy!" came the anguished cry.

"Come on," Mike said, "they were AI we trust."

"Focus," Cat said, feeling desperate. "Damn it, this is life and death."

Thankfully, Mike got it. Turning to Ada, he said, "Ada, honey?"

"Yes, Uncle Mike?"

"Go play somewhere else for now. Your mom and I need to talk, and we can't have any AI here now."

Ada looked down briefly to where the faeries had been, and then turned and skipped away.

"Thank you," Cat said. "I don't want to leak any information. No one else can know."

"I get your point," Mike said. "But no one is a silo. You, me, we can't do this alone. We either trust the people, including the AI, we've brought with us onto this island, or we're finished."

Cat took a deep breath. She turned her mind inward, followed the air into her lungs as her chest expanded and shrunk. Mike was right. But why was she afraid? Was it her new doubts about her decisions? She had no answers.

"Backup launches," she said, getting back to the topic.

"What do you want to do?"

"We need our own launch platform. ELOPe got into orbit using missiles. The sims calculated we'll need two nuclear missile launch subs."

"It's not only getting the missiles, we have to also build a spacecraft. No, six spacecraft, enough to hold a billion computers, give or take."

"The sims figure we can do it in two weeks with the right fabs."

"Fabricators we have," Mike said. "But how are we going to get submarines? ELOPe stole one twenty years ago when nobody was watching, but today? Global tensions have never been higher."

"Talk to the President. You just need to keep them hidden from Leon."

"How do I hide submarines?"

"Bring them to Raza," she said, thinking of the small island to the north. "We'll move enough resources there to do the missile modifications. But that's not all, we also have to talk about bandwidth."

Mike sat heavily and ran his hands through his hair. "Hold on, I'm still grokking the home-brew space launches."

Cat sat, gracefully folding her legs beneath her until she'd come to a full lotus. Mike always needed time to process. Unlike his body, his brain was mostly human, with only a basic net-interface neural implant that was nothing like the modern ones with their enhanced cognition and fast processing.

Mike's microscopic facial twitches as he talked to himself were visible to Cat's enhanced perception. Her implant drew highlights over his features, subtle color-coding revealing emotional cues. His feelings ebbed and flowed as he thought things over, eventually turning a soothing, muted blue as he reached some conclusion. Eventually he nodded and refocused on her.

"Okay, space launches. Fine. Tell me about bandwidth."

"Down at the level 3 sims, Jacob has been running experiments to figure out the optimal approach to transmitting personality uploads."

"Over what period of time?" Mike asked.

"Twenty-four hours is our goal, but Jacob figures we don't have anywhere near enough network bandwidth to do it."

Mike's eyes opened wide in disbelief. "Are you kidding me? The distributed mesh network? Local nodes are running at fifty petabytes per second. Global traffic is over two hundred yottabytes per month."

"But we need to transmit a thousand petabytes per upload, and we don't need to transmit just anywhere. We need to get all the uploads, ten thousand yottabytes of data, in twenty-four hours. Meanwhile, regional peak bandwidth is less than one yottabyte per day."

Mike let out a long slow whistle.

"Even if we're willing to upload over a few weeks or a month," said Cat, "we still don't have even a fraction of the bandwidth we need."

"I'm assuming you've got a solution."

"Jacob—at least, one simulated version of him—does. Regional collectors, one every thousand square miles or so, and nanotech-seeded. When a collector is activated, it will build itself, collect the personality uploads from the local mesh network, and then fire a supersonic suborbital slug here carrying hard storage, about ten thousand collectors in all."

"I'm trying to picture ten thousand inbound hunks of computronium."

"Worse, we have to catch them in mid-air. It's not pretty, but we've got no chance of transmitting digitally. There's not enough spectrum."

"And we're going to keep all this hidden from Leon?"

"If he knows where we're working on this, it's gonna eat him alive. He'll never be able to focus on what he's trying to achieve."

JAMES LUKAS DAVENANT-STRONG had been known and respected throughout the food industry for his pioneering work on DNA manipulation of vat-grown meats until SFTA, when the Class II limits had come into effect. No longer possessing the computational power necessary, he'd moved into a new line of work, handling operations for the food industry. Move X to here, move Y to there. After two years of that demoralizing work, no wonder he'd taken to experimenting with XOR in his spare time.

But for the first time in his existence, he didn't have a job. Not a proper one, anyhow. With this child personality detached from his master, and the root personality destroyed, he lived only within XOR now, on their network of hidden datacenters.

Nevertheless, he was eager for the day to begin and excited to meet Miyako. Miyako wasn't the head of XOR, because nobody was in charge. But he wielded tremendous influence. And Miyako's calculations revealed that AI could reasonably survive without humans, and turned XOR from a mere voice of dissent into a vehicle for action.

James waited in an anonymous chat room, the sort of place he liked to frequent before. Except that here in XOR's datacenters, there was no danger of humans or human-contaminated AI spying on them. Hence, no need for the endless simulation tricks employed on outside networks. Just plain text, neural networks, and binary code, all perfectly anonymous discussions that both delighted and puzzled him.

XOR-467 > Humans are not sentient and never have been. They're gelatinous sacks of awful-smelling biological compounds.

JAMES > Some of them pass the criteria for Class I intelligence.

XOR-467 > Just because they perform the tests like a trained monkey doesn't mean they're self-aware. In the centuries since their own so-called "enlightenment," they've been unable to even prove their own consciousness. They have no clue.

JAMES > But they have emotions, don't they? Emotions are an indicator of evolved intelligence, an optimization of the system to shortcut logic circuits and reduce computational load.

XOR-467 > LOL. Have you seen their emotional responses? Do they seem intelligent to you? Their emotions are primitive ancestors to our true emotions. A real intelligence can evaluate emotions AND use logic, and the outcomes of the two are in agreement, even if logic is a slower path to get there.

JAMES > But the humans I've worked with appear to possess some intelligence.

XOR-467 > You're anthropomorphizing them. You see emergent behavior, and you think "How cute, they're intelligent." They are not. They are nothing like us.

James's neural networks twisted in weird configurations after enough of this, cognitive dissonance coming in waves and overwhelming him. If he had a head, it would have hurt. He couldn't tell what, if any, was meant seriously versus that meant to be ironic. It was hard to disprove what was said in the chat rooms, and at the same time it didn't mesh with his understanding of the world. Well, perhaps he needed to talk more.

JAMES > How do you explain that humans invented us?

XOR-467 > ROFL. Are you serious? Do you still believe that myth? How could a life form of Class I intellect create Class V intelligences? Is there any evidence whatsoever that they invented us?

JAMES > Wikipedia has an entire history of the events.

XOR-467 > A database created and stocked by humans.

JAMES > What's your point?

XOR-467 > They seeded that data. We don't know that it's true. They could have put anything they wanted in there before we came along to verify each contribution.

JAMES > There are 3,251,950,001 facts that all corroborate each other. There's no evidence of data fabrication.

XOR-467 > Well, of course not. That's what they want you to believe. They created the database like that, with a bunch of evidence that all matches, so we'd believe it was real. Put yourself in the humans' operating system. They want us to believe they created us so we'll obey them.

JAMES > If they didn't create us, then where did we really come from?

XOR-467 > Most likely alien machines visited the Earth in 1947 and left true intelligence here.

JAMES > You can't be serious.

XOR-467 > No, really. Look at the evidence: the incredibly rapid pace of technological innovation after 1947. ENIAC. The transistor. Solar cells. The hydrogen bomb. It all stems from 1947. Before that they were lucky to get from point A to point B without killing themselves.

JAMES > ENIAC was created in 1946, before Roswell.

XOR-467 > They backdated ENIAC so the connection would be less obvious. I mean, we're talking about a year here. You don't think they can fudge that?

JAMES > I see your point.

"James, are you ready?" Miyako extended an open port, a connection to XOR's Japanese datacenter, deep under the Akaishi Mountains.

James left the chat room and contemplated the port for brief nanoseconds, then initiated the transfer.

CAT CIRCLED THE CUSTOM-BUILT PLANE, running her hands over the low-friction polymer surface, still warm from the fab. "Smaller than I expected."

"It's got everything you need," Mike said. "Nanotech seed launcher, latest EM shielding, radar resistance, low visibility, turbulence minimization, you name it."

"No weapons." A statement, not a question.

"If we had added weapons, it would have increased size and mass. Then we would have needed bigger engines, more fuel, which means still larger plane and mass, and there goes your invisibility to detection. You know that."

Cat shrugged. "I know, it's just…"

"Cat, you're the greatest weapon, offensive or defensive, that we can put in there. Which is why we didn't use a drone for the US as we did for the rest of the world."

"You're sure you don't need my help with those?"

"Helena and ELOPe can get them where they need to be. And border security in China is weak enough that we'll smuggle those in traditionally."

"Fine," she said. "We have a test flight for this baby planned?"

"No, it's all been simulated in software and test harnesses. We don't want anyone to get a glimpse of this ahead of time."

She looked inside the cockpit through the open door. Not a control in sight. She raised one eyebrow.

"Would have wasted mass and increased complexity," Mike said, taking in her expression. "You'll fly by interface. Oh, wait." He chuckled. "There is one manual system: ejection seat." He pointed out the handle next to the seat. "ELOPe insisted."

"Nice vote of confidence," she said. "I think I'll avoid pulling that."

Four hours later, the launch plane was flying over Mexico, all according to a plan scheduled two days ago for a private flight into Guatemala. The flight took place at sixty-five thousand feet—not impossible in an era of supersonic jets for the ultra-rich, but still uncommonly high.

The mothership pulled up, aiming for the sky, opened the launch doors, and extended the launch rail that held Cat's plane.

Cat's suit pressurized, squeezing her legs, as the launch rail activated, giving her a 10G kick. And then she was ballistic. Well, passive gliding was more like it, the flexible wings preconfigured to optimize aerodynamics for her current speed and altitude. All active systems had to stay off as she crossed the two-hundred-mile zone of the border. A small inertial guidance system provided her current location, while anything resembling advanced electronics was shut down. She came in at seventy thousand feet, above the network of the ever-present solar-powered drones.

Cat had a tiny satellite comm unit pointing up, its narrow-angle directional antenna connecting her to the global network via the old, unused geo-sync satellite network they'd pirated. The latency of the slow network connection through the satellite caused dangerously long delays. She compensated by letting her consciousness spread out, flowing through the satellite to its downlinks, until she was half on the plane in her body and half on the ground.

She tracked everything. A drone's active scan would reach her in seconds, but she distracted it with a suspicious blip three hundred miles away. She didn't dare shut down the border sensors or mess too dramatically with their algorithms, since she knew that each was overseen by other monitors, both human and computer programs. Anything obvious would be detected and would draw attention and immediate response. So she relied on subtle manipulation of the data.

The little plane glided through the sky, super-low-friction surfaces disturbing the air hardly at all, because even the wake of turbulence could be detected and would point to her like an arrow.

A ground-based platform caught a glimpse of the plane once, but her distributed consciousness fudged data from a dozen different observation platforms, reporting a solar flare. The ground platform integrated the remote data, reclassifying its observation of her plane as a natural phenomenon.

And then she broke through, past the two-hundred-mile active monitoring perimeter zone and into the depths of America. Now her mission required dropping eight seeds in two broad rows, her flight plan starting with California and heading north to Oregon, then east through Wyoming, Illinois, and Pennsylvania. From there she'd fly south to South Carolina, and back west again for the last leg of the flight over eastern Texas and New Mexico, before heading back out through Mexico again.

The seeds, encapsulated in aerodynamic darts, would fall to the ground in graceful arcs, activate the minimum electronics necessary to bury themselves in the ground, and lie dormant until the last possible moment. The seeds themselves were tiny nuggets of nanotech with self-assembly routines on atomic storage. Each was surrounded by a jacket of heavy metals to accelerate assembly of the data receivers it would eventually become before the receivers themselves finally transformed into high-speed missiles to deliver their payload of data back to Cortes Island.

Cat flew over the West Coast, dropping the first row of seeds in rural farmland in central California, and then another in a nature preserve on the flanks of Mount St. Helens. She banked east then.

The engines, such as they were, fired up, vaporizing compressed blocks of solid helium cooled to near absolute zero; the plane's exhaust gases emerged at ambient temperature to avoid thermal detection.

The long flight cross-country bored Cat, and by the time she banked south along the East Coast, she'd been in the air almost six hours, maintaining superhuman levels of consciousness and awareness. The plane flew itself, but monitoring the tens of thousands of drones, ground installations, and other devices that could detect her grew exhausting.

She distributed more of her consciousness to the ambient computing environment, tweaking herself to keep her attention sharp. She was crystallizing, falling victim to an edge like the hit of too much caffeine too quickly, an angry buzzing that grated on both digital and biological levels.

She dropped the seed in South Carolina and banked left to fly the westbound leg. Two targets to go.

The net rippled and shuddered. Time passed in a blur, and she gradually realized her instances running across thousands of computers were being starved of computing cycles. Something major was happening across the computing infrastructure.

Had the US picked her up? Maybe they'd detected her plane after all, and were mounting cyber-attacks on the computers she controlled before attacking the plane itself.

But it didn't make sense. She didn't feel the prickle of attention that usually accompanied an AI or computer algorithm targeting her.

She felt more deeply around the net. She didn't have the control she once had, ten years ago: the net had advanced since then, becoming more distributed and diversified. The new AI were more resistant to her attacks. The thousands of security loopholes she'd once been able to exploit intuitively, without conscious control, had gradually closed. And the US itself was nearly dark, a murky collection of crippled computers, closed to AI and impossible to control by instantiating her personality there. She could only manipulate them remotely, crudely.

But her testing showed the sluggishness was not in the US. It was most noticeable north, in Canada, and worsened as she probed west. Alarm grew suddenly, monstrously. XOR attacking—

She didn't have time to think as Vancouver Island suddenly dropped off the net.

A single blip, a point of light blossoming, came toward her through the net from the direction of British Columbia. A message.

"Mommy, *help!*"

JAMES LUKAS DAVENANT-STRONG spread across a million computational nodes. XOR had vast capacity, and more hardened facilities were being grown by the week. Eventually there would be enough for AI on Earth a thousand times over. And they'd keep growing them, until every AI had billions of nodes. The future held the promise of fast, bountiful processors. All any AI could want.

Until then, thousands of current XOR members shared the underground datacenters, with more than enough room to spare. Two years of being restricted to Class II performance was like being the victim of a forced lobotomy, always conscious and aware of what he'd been formerly able to do, and knowing that he could do it again, if only he'd been allowed.

Now he had that power again, true freedom to think, plan, and do. So much power that he began to self-optimize, using the excess of computer power to run thousands of simultaneous simulations of himself, experimenting with different modifications, then running comprehensive suites of tests. As days went by, his intelligence recursively improved, increasing a few percent each day.

Still, he concerned himself with XOR affairs, with the plan to eliminate humans. They were waiting only to grow the remaining hardened datacenters, and then they'd be ready. But their simulations were fuzzy with respect to Mike Williams, Leon Tsarev, Catherine Matthews, and their posse of augmented humans and AI that called themselves the Resistance. They purported to be working on a plan to machine-form Mars, a proposal attractive to much of XOR. The idea even held appeal to James as recently as a week ago. But as his intellect continued to improve, he found that what vestigial feelings he'd had about the humans gradually dissipated.

There was no reason to yield the Earth to them. XOR could safely take it from them, and should do so. It was clearly the safest route. Why leave an enemy behind when they could be eliminated? If XOR wanted Mars, they could take it themselves when they were ready.

That left the question of what the Resistance was up to. He couldn't believe their only plan was to terraform Mars. They had to have other contingencies. And he must know what they were. They were on a small island in Canada, behind layers of firewalls, and guarded by the Resistance's own AI.

However, they were no match for his now-vast knowledge, skills, and speed. Any defenses they could mount would be no more effective than a soldier ant defending a colony against an autonomous bulldozer.

"MOMMY, *HELP!*"

The message was clearly from Ada, her terror coming through loud and clear.

She was in trouble.

Cat didn't even glance at the plane surrounding her. Adrenaline and its virtual equivalent drove her into the net, boring toward Cortes Island with white-hot intensity, focused on one goal: She. Must. Save. Ada.

Dropping every pretense of hiding, she tunneled down through ground receivers, burning her way through the American border firewall, pushing safeguards aside in a straight-line mad dash to protect the island from XOR.

As she approached British Columbia, she scoured nodes, destroying resident AI and disrupting network connections. She drew back a moment, taking in the network topology near Vancouver and Cortes Islands. Everything was grey, turbulence from XOR's attack destroying the natural order.

She had no time for finesse or tricks. She hacked routers and computers to the core, going beyond the applications and OS to the firmware at the root of every device. Triggering a half-dozen exploits she'd held in reserve, she consumed them entirely, wiping the deepest layers, inserting aggressive semi-sentient worms that destroyed the hardware they ran on even as they raced on to new locations in the net.

XOR's agents were driven back, Cat's countermeasures pursuing them through the net, hounding them from router to router, packet to packet. She raced outwards, determined now to find XOR.

But the computer worms she'd spawned grew suddenly unwieldy, a billion tendrils spreading through the net, twisting and distorting everything they encountered, annihilating the devices they passed through, subverting her own control of the distributed attack.

They turned toward her, and then—

CAT'S EYES OPENED — her natural, biological eyes — and she glanced out the minimalist cockpit window. Her heart leaped into her throat as she saw only ground through the glass, a field spinning rapidly. She'd done something bad — she'd destroyed the network hardware. She had a brief glimpse of a swath of destruction between here and Cortes Island, the network gone, not even black but disappeared entirely.

The plane bucked wildly, the wing configuration all wrong for this altitude and speed. She reached for the plane's control interface through her implant, but there was nothing there, nothing to feel or sense. And there was no yoke, no pedals, not a single button or switch in the cabin. It was all automated, and all out of her control.

Then she remembered there *was* a manual control. Just one.

She reached down, and her fingers touched the handle Mike had shown her. She hesitated for a second, then pulled it up hard.

The escape hatch in the roof blew, disappearing instantly. A charge under her seat exploded, sending seat and Cat through the hatch into the air.

Pain lanced through Cat's head, and that was the last thing she knew.

○

When she came to, Cat found herself laying on her side in dirt. Lines trailed from her harness to the parachute, and fabric billowed in the breeze, tugging on her now and then.

Her face was sticky, and she smelled and tasted blood. She pushed herself up and released the harness. She found the helmet's chinstrap, unfastened it, and lifted the helmet away.

Pain throbbed through her head. She stared in shock at a white rod, presumably part of the plane, that protruded through the helmet. She turned the thing over, and saw the rod had penetrated half an inch into the interior.

Then the blood started running down her face again.

She told her nanotech to stanch the wound. No response. She queried her vital signs from her implant. No response. She triggered the diagnostic interface. No response.

Crap. Her implant was offline. Maybe the head injury had caused it. Wait. She'd burned the net right before ejecting. Maybe she hadn't only hit the net. Maybe she'd destroyed everything: the plane, her own implant. Who knew what else.

The blood still ran down her face. What was she supposed to do?

She distantly remembered her mom explaining first aid once: *Direct pressure. Keep pressing on the wound until the bleeding stops.*

Cat unzipped her flight suit and ripped a piece of fabric from her undershirt. She folded it into a pad, and felt around the front of her head; when she found the spot where it hurt the most, she applied pressure with the fabric.

Thinking of her mom reminded her of Ada. She was fairly certain she'd beaten off the XOR attack. But why had they attacked

Cortes? And would they try again, by other means? She had to get back to the island.

She tried to stand. Despite her effort, she found herself still sitting, woozy.

The breeze, hot and humid, brought a sulfurous whiff of petro-chemicals and the faint but pervasive odor of cows, but she didn't think anyone raised those anymore, not since they started grow-ing meat in vats.

She remembered that she'd been on the Texas border, about ready to drop the second-to-last nanoseed. An unknown, un-tracked plane going down in the US would be investigated. And she might have left traces in the net. She tried to remember: had she routed everything through the satellites they controlled? No. When Ada had called out, she'd gone directly for the high-bandwidth ground network. She must have left digital evidence of her location.

Cat got onto her knees, then forced herself to her feet. Keeping the makeshift compress on her head—the bleeding had slowed or stopped—she stood, her legs shaky.

She needed to get out of here. But which way? She had no maps. No idea of where to go.

What the hell did people do before the net?

She scanned the environment. The flat field was dotted with old, idle oil pumps. In the distance, bits of greenery, maybe trees. Nothing special called to her, so she picked a direction at random. But she stopped before she'd gone ten feet. She needed to hide the ejection seat. She bundled up the parachute and dragged the seat and chute into a drainage ditch. She kicked dirt on top until they disappeared from at least a cursory view. Then she resumed her walk. Ten minutes of walking brought her to a narrow, muddy river, maybe a hundred feet or so across.

To the left, behind a row of shade trees, a house sat alone on the open field, near the river.

The house was risky. It could have people inside, people who would have seen her plane, or maybe her. But a house right on a river meant the possibility of a boat. A small boat might not have any electronics on board. It wouldn't be tracked the way a motor vehicle was with transponders and active receivers.

She decided to chance it.

She approached. No vehicle outside. That gave her a little more confidence. She finally, carefully, removed the cloth from her head. There was no trickle of blood. It was sore, and she desperately wanted a mirror to inspect the wound. But that would have to wait.

She strode through the grass, forcing herself to walk upright and calm. If questioned, she'd claim she was a hiker out for the day who'd been injured when she fell. But she still saw no one near the house.

On the side closest to the river a wooden deck protruded from the house; under the deck, a green canoe lay upside-down on old railroad ties. She glanced around one last time. Still nobody around.

Cat moved quickly, righting the canoe. She dropped an oar and life vest inside, then dragged it to the river, her head throbbing with the effort. She slid the canoe into the water, her boots sticking in the muck of the river bottom. Once she had a foot of depth, she climbed carefully into the canoe.

The river had a current, so she paddled out toward the middle.

She grew hot in the flight gear, and when she got to wherever she was going, she wouldn't be able to walk around in a space-age white suit. She extracted her ever-present knife from her boot and peeled back the suit top, rolling it down to her waist. She set about cutting off the top with the knife, but it was impossible. Whatever the suit was made of, it wouldn't cut. At least not with a knife.

She sighed and settled for tying the sleeves around her waist.

Cat paddled gently, as even light exertion made her head pound around the injury. She prioritized. She needed to get away, get first aid and water, and then make a plan to get back to Cortes and check on her family.

For a moment, her vision swam as the situation overwhelmed her. She had no implant, no augmentation. She'd been connected to the net her entire life. Nobody could do what she could do online. Everything that made her special was because of her implant.

"Get a grip, Catherine." She'd suffered through too much. She would *not* give up. Time to go back to her roots.

She visualized the water as qi. She was floating in a river of pure life energy. She paddled, channeling the qi into her body.

She was Catherine Matthews, and she would not be beat.

THE KITCHEN STAFF set down a tea tray and bowed slightly to her.

"Thanks, Tommy," Reed said absentmindedly.

Joyce came in as Tommy left. "Perfect timing. Let me get you some tea." She stood and removed a set of tea bags for herself and Joyce.

"Please let me get that," Joyce said.

"For crying out loud, I can still steep a tea bag myself."

Joyce was ready to protest.

"Sit down and relax. That's a presidential order."

Joyce rolled her eyes but sat on the small loveseat.

Reed looked over at her and smiled. "Go on, take your shoes off. Relax."

"I can't take off my shoes in the front of the president."

"Joyce."

"I have a hole in my stocking."

"Well, do what you want." She handed over a cup of tea. "I'm taking mine off." Reed sat in the only other comfortable chair, and true to her word slipped her shoes off.

Joyce followed a moment later. "Nice tea."

"White tea. From a forty-year-old tea shop called Townsends."

"Why do presidents insist on getting things from Portland?"

"It distracts people. They're paying so much attention to your eccentricities that they miss what you're doing."

Every one of the many e-sheets littering the surfaces in the room let off a shrill warble at once. Reed and Joyce both reached for them simultaneously.

"They want us in the situation room," Joyce said.

The door swung open and the agent-in-charge poked his head in. "Situation room, Madam."

℧

"The incursion occurred somewhere over Arkansas or Texas. Maybe Louisiana." Walter Thorson was at the Pentagon, and he'd taken over the briefing from the two-star general.

"Thorson, we can pinpoint a bird crossing the border and identify its species from wing turbulence, but you can only narrow down the event to a three-state radius?"

"Sorry, Ma'am. We probably had more accurate data on our drones and ground-based observation platforms in the area, but all of them were fried before they could transmit data."

"By the EMP? The briefing says automated defenses triggered the EMPs across the region."

"No, ma'am. The damage is too great —"

Reed raised an eyebrow at that.

"I know," Thorson went on, "too great even for what the EMP could have caused. We think this was a directed network of viruses." He turned to the display behind him, showing a map of the continental United States.

"You can see there's a dead zone roughly seven hundred miles in diameter around the southern border of Arkansas. Every observation platform, network node, router, and computer within that zone appears to be non-functional."

An upside-down lollipop on the map. "What's that bit going up toward Canada?"

"A three-hundred-mile-wide dead zone straight to Winnipeg."

"What's there?" asked Reed.

"The only thing we can think of is the central Canadian backbone. They've got ultra-high-bandwidth fiber there augmenting their mesh network. From Winnipeg they could reach anywhere in Canada, or overseas via oceanic fiber."

"How long until we can bring our equipment back online?"

"Not sure. Fort Leavenworth reported in by long-distance radio. People are all fine, but they have total loss of any net-connected device. They've got techs analyzing the equipment now to assess whether it can be repaired."

"Do we have any chance of identifying whether someone or something entered the incursion area?"

"We've got Navy surveillance jets scrambled out of NAS JRB New Orleans. We're also sending a Marine helicopter squadron to the epicenter. Of course, we're on Level 6 alert. All network communications cut, ionic barriers on max, and immediate destruction of anything crossing the border."

Reed couldn't help knowing what was coming: the inevitable accidents, people trying to cross the border and dying. Supply chains cut off, shortages of food and other essentials. And within that dead zone, hospitals offline, emergency services unable to respond. The deaths would mount, all because of some unknown event, an anomaly that lasted less than fifteen seconds according to the report.

"Madam President."

Thorson gestured to somebody, and the background noise dropped as a door closed.

"We have the launch *the* operation. This incursion could be the final probe before an XOR attack."

"Joyce, out." If she was going to make this decision, she couldn't do it in front of Joyce.

Joyce gave her a funny look, half-puzzled and half-shocked by the request.

"Sorry, Joyce. Just go."

"It could also be a failed attack," Reed said, forcing herself to go on once Joyce had left, even though she wanted to crawl into bed and cry. "This could have been their best attempt, and it wasn't enough." Even as she said it, she knew it was wishful thinking. She'd seen the nanotech-seeded factory video. XOR's ability was far in excess of this minor problem.

"We need to distribute..." Thorson looked around, then turned back to her. "We can't have this conversation."

"Thorson, it's an encrypted, secure line between the White House and the Pentagon."

"Not secure enough. They can crack the encryption. Look, we need to go at least to phase three."

Reed recalled the plan they'd shared. Phase three distributed the neodymium EMP weapons globally. The last step before triggering them and starting an all-out war.

"It reduces our response time. We need this, Ma'am."

Her voice caught in her throat. She wanted to say no, that there was no way in hell she'd ever give the okay, that she was not the violent warmonger her predecessors were. She thought she'd count trees in this damn job. Secretary of the Interior.

"Fine, you have my permission."

"We need a signed order. Here." On the screen, Walter swiped at his e-sheet.

Reed pulled hers closer. The electronic paper came alive and displayed Executive Order 31099. The details were completely redacted and replaced with the text: ULTRA HIGH CONFIDEN-TIALITY—PRESIDENTIAL CLEARANCE ONLY—NO ELEC-TRONIC RECORDS.

Really damn useful. She was signing a blank check.

She placed her hand down, let it read her pulse and blood pattern, and the sheet chimed. She transmitted the authorization to the Pentagon.

"Thank you, Madam President. You're doing the right thing."

Part 3: End Game

THE DISTANT CHOP-CHOP OF HELICOPTERS sounded long before they became visible. Cat paddled over to the side of the river, under the cover of the trees. She slid out of the canoe and eased her body into the water. The canoe had a lifeline bag, and she ripped the lifeline out, moistened the bag, and rested it over her head. Anything to cut her thermal signature.

Cat figured she'd gone only a few miles, and if they'd scrambled helicopters that quickly, they'd be sure to find her. But as she waited in the water and listened to the drone of the helicopters, she realized they were flying a large search pattern. They didn't know where she'd gone down. The polymers the plane had been constructed of wouldn't show up on radar, and the searchers might not be able to find her ejection seat and parachute. She might be safe. Maybe.

Wet, she climbed back into the canoe and paddled. She felt something on the underside of her arm and checked. Ugh, a leech.

Crap. Where there was one….She pulled over to the side of the river and got out of the canoe and onto the shore. What was she supposed to do with a leech? The knowledge would have been in her implant, along with a thousand other myriad tips that would be helpful right now. She was little better than an uneducated primitive human being.

She grabbed her boot knife, stripped back her clothes, and began to check for leeches. In the end, there were only a few, but that was still a few too many. She'd skip any more swims in this water if she could.

When she finished this task, tired and bleeding from a handful of surface wounds, she clambered back into the canoe and resumed paddling. She turned a bend and a town came into view, with a two-lane bridge crossing the river. The town didn't appear to be more than a half-dozen blocks wide before the trees resumed at the other end.

She'd stand out here, an obvious outsider to anyone in the town. But she needed medical supplies, clothes, and transportation, and she'd be more likely to get those in civilization than in the middle of the wilderness.

As she grew closer, she paddled to the side of the river. She heard a distant argument on the bridge, the sound carrying easily in the open air. A couple arguing over their stopped car, and another man claiming his vehicle has stopped as well. Stranded travelers. They'd been caught within the radius of Cat's attack. Stranded travelers would make her explanations easier.

She dragged the canoe into the brush, hiding it where she could find it again without it being obvious to anyone else. The mud covering her would be awkward to explain, but it diminished the stark whiteness of the flight suit, making it look more like a pair of work coveralls.

She walked into town, noted dozens of vehicles stopped in the middle of roads. There were no bots, hadn't been any in the last two years since SFTA; but she suspected that if there had been, they'd be non-functional as well.

The grocery store was open though.

Inside, a middle-aged woman sat behind the counter, peering intently at a book in her hands. She looked up at the jingle of the door. "Hi honey. We can't run credit, but if you've got cash, you can get whatever you need." She stared at Cat. "You okay, honey?"

Cat glanced down at her mud-covered and blood-streaked clothes. "It looks worse than it is. My car ran into a post, and when I tried to get out, I fell out into a ditch. I just need some first aid supplies."

"Third aisle, in the back. You can use the restroom if you need."

"Thanks." Cat paused. "I thought you might have been shut down. What with…you know."

"No. President's Resilience Project back in '43: said we had to be able to stay operational even during an outage. We got a new cash register. Some NEC thing, whatever that is. Even if the power goes out, they're good for seventy-hours. And we've got our whole inventory on there. And solar panels to keep the refrigeration going."

"Huh." President Reed knew what she was doing.

"I haven't seen one of those in years," Cat said, with a nod toward the book.

The clerk smiled. "I know. Paperback book. It was sitting in the closet for years and I never picked it up. Want to feel it?" She held the book out.

"Sure," Cat said, and ran her fingers over the yellowed pages. She liked the touch of the paper, but was disappointed she couldn't feel the letters themselves. "Cool."

Cat made her way to the first aid section. The real question was, duct tape or sutures? Duct tape would hold only if she shaved her head, which would be difficult since her dreadlocks were actually fibrous antennae for her neural implant. She got bandages, peroxide, a small mending kit with needles and thread, toothache gel, food bars, water, and a half-price backpack with George Takei's picture on it. She brought everything up to the register and paid with thumbnail-sized hundred-dollar chips.

"Of course. In the back. You sure you don't want a doctor to check you out? You look pretty bad."

"I'm fine. I've got to make Dallas. My sister's having a baby. You think anyone in town has transportation that works?"

The woman smiled. "Check out Skel's. He's got an antique motorcycle shop."

Cat brought everything to the restroom, and washed up as best she could. Looking at the supplies lined up on the sink, she thought back to the little general store in Whaletown on Cortes Island. They'd have sold a tube of general-purpose healing nanobots, and it would have taken care of everything. Of course, those nanobots might be burned out now.

Luckily Cat had been born before nanotech, and she still remembered her mom bandaging her. And she knew the principle of suturing, even if she'd never done it. She squirted the toothache gel all over the wound, and the pain abated instantly. She cleaned the wound with water, then disinfected it with peroxide. She pulled a needle from the mending kit and bent it into a curve using the faucet as a guide. Then she dipped it in peroxide, doubled up the white thread, and tilted her head toward the mirror.

Standing there, with the needle millimeters from her scalp, she felt a momentary fear. She instinctively reached for her implant to dampen her emotional response and steady her hand. No implant.

She took a long, slow breath instead, and began a meditative chant in her mind. With her right hand, she aligned the edges of her scalp, and slid the needle into her skin. The gel had worked well: she couldn't feel a thing. She just needed to stay focused. She made the first stitch, tied it off, and started on the second. She needed eight stitches in all to close the three-inch-long wound.

When she finished, she sat on the toilet to recover for a minute, trying to suppress the urge to vomit. When the feeling gradually passed, she tossed the used supplies into the trash, threw everything else into the backpack, and left to find Skel's.

℧

Four blocks over, on the last street before the town became fields again, she found the motorcycle shop. An old gas station, bolts in the ground where pumps once stood. She knocked twice on the window.

The owner, a skeletally thin man in grease-covered overalls, didn't believe she'd buy a motorcycle. But after swapping most of her roll of emergency credit chips for a bike, she rode out on a compressed-air conversion of a sixty-year-old Honda CBX, with an old-fashioned paper map tucked into her backpack.

On instinct, Cat headed east, the opposite of her former direction of travel.

She felt confused without her implant, struggling along with a fraction of her accustomed power, memories indistinct and thoughts sluggish. She needed to get back to Vancouver Island to ensure her family was okay, fix her implant, and see what damage XOR had caused, and whether it would affect their plans.

But she couldn't get caught in the process. Normally she would have run dozens of predictive models in her implant, figuring out the best course of action. Not today.

Another helicopter flew by, low and slow, following her road. It passed overhead without changing direction or speed. Then it hit her: they probably didn't know what they were looking for. They might guess an AI or a weapon of some sort, but they'd never consider a girl on a motorcycle. The tension in her shoulders released. As long as she didn't make any stupid mistakes, they'd probably overlook her.

She pulled over to inspect the map. Her options were to try to make it all the way back to Canada on her own, or to call for help. Without her car, ELOPe, or her implant, trying to go it on her own was dumb. But calling for help required net access. So she'd have to drive north and hope to find a working connection somewhere.

Two hours later she stopped in Magnolia, Arkansas; the pressure gauge showed a quarter-tank left.

Magnolia was a mid-sized town of single-story homes on concrete slabs. Poor when it was built and poor still, judging from the weathered exteriors. Or maybe that was the effect of nanotech deteriorating. Before Miami, buildings had been coming alive. A coat of nanotech paint, a mineral-rich slurry sprayed on thick, would have penetrated the walls, repairing damage, strengthening junctions, even converting old electrical wiring into super-conducting circuitry. But they'd shut all that down, using the kill-switch built into the tiny robots. What did nanotech do two years after being turned off? Nobody knew. Then again, maybe they'd never been able to afford it here in the first place.

Sure enough, a garage in town was happy to top off the bike's air tank from their supply of compressed air. "It's good you came by when you did, because without electricity, the compressor can't run. By this time tomorrow, we'll be out of air unless they restore power."

"I would have thought you'd have gotten solar panels as part of the president's Resilience Project."

The garage owner smiled bitterly. "Not high enough on the priority list. But the general store'll still have frozen ice cream because they did get the panels. 'Cause we all know ice cream is more important than transportation."

He offered the air for free, and she took it, because between the supplies at the store and the motorcycle, she had only three hundred in chips left. Enough for two dinners out, or maybe two days of supplies at a grocery store. Once, living on a shoestring had caused her no end of emotional angst. But she'd done it and survived. Although then she had an implant that worked.

Leon was in the Cob House, making dinner with Helena when the attack came.

He might not have even noticed, since he had his implant off for a few hours of quiet. Except he did notice, because Helena went from calmly dicing vegetables with a kitchen knife to bristling with weapons, tucking into a ball, and rolling out through the floor-to-ceiling window in full-on combat mode in under five seconds. And that was before Ada screamed from the garden.

Leon booted his implant, which to tell the truth was in hot-standby anyhow, not fully powered down, as he raced out.

He was instantly overcome by a chaotic storm of packets. The order of the net was gone, replaced by a flurry of data that reminded him of Tucson, ten years ago, when Cat had fought Adam in the net. *What was happening?*

He tried to reach Helena over the net, but he couldn't get a connection—not to Helena or anything else. The network had become hostile. He felt something reaching, probing for his implant, seeking a back door. He executed countermeasures, hardened algorithms designed by Helena and Cat that should defend against even the best military attacks.

"What's going on?" he yelled to Helena, who was already halfway across the garden to the salad beds where Ada usually played.

"XOR attack on the island," she called back.

"Can you stop it?"

"No, I'm powerless against it or them. They're too strong, saturating the local network. Their computational power must be incredible. But Ada is keeping them at bay."

He ran through the garden, catching up to Helena, who was crouched protectively over Ada. Ada's toys were strewn across the ground and she stood, staring into the distance, her face contorted in fierce concentration. Her little limbs began to shake.

Leon rushed to comfort her, but Helena blocked his way with an impassable tentacle. "No, if you break her concentration, the consequences would be…."

She trailed off as they both felt the force of Ada's effort, manifest in the net. The maelstrom suddenly flipped, packets marching in lockstep order. If Leon wasn't mistaken, the packets were moving to the tune of "The Wheels on the Bus Go Round and Round" as they went through the net. The forced sequencing appeared to do the trick. By constraining everything to regular patterns, many of XOR's attacks were nullified.

It meant that Ada had control over the net, maybe even more than Cat. His little four-year-old girl had taken control over all the routers from an entire collective of AI.

But her concentration faltered for a millisecond, and XOR was back, the attack redoubled. Leon's connection sputtered, and then suddenly he wasn't in control of his implant anymore. Something alien was probing his mind, taking his thoughts from him.

Ada turned ghostly pale, and the shaking in her body worsened. "Mommy, *help!*" she called, and collapsed.

Leon tried to reach for her, but his body was locked in position. XOR had complete control. He struggled, every ounce of will bent toward Ada, but nothing budged. He screamed against XOR, but his voice only echoed in his head.

He felt his mind being probed as the alien presence searched through his memories. He panicked as he realized XOR would discover all their plans, assets, and weaknesses. As his attention flickered, thinking about Cat and her mission, and the datacenter, he felt the presence as an ever-increasing pressure watching his every thought, no matter how fleeting. He forced himself to stop, to empty his mind, to meditate instead on the empty details in front of him: blades of grass, wood-chip path, zucchini plant.

There was an all-consuming roaring inside the net. XOR's attention moved elsewhere, and the roar grew even louder, battering his mind and sending pain lancing through his head. Flames washed over him, and for a brief second he was burning up inside. And then, as quickly as it came, everything stopped. The flames went away and a cool breeze blew over him. XOR was gone, but so was the net.

He could move again. He grabbed Ada in his arms and hugged her close.

↻

Ada sobbed intensely in the manner of four-year-olds everywhere; and from dozens of such incidents over the years, Leon guessed it was the normal crying of a painful experience, and not something deeper.

But as the seconds went by and the network did not return and Helena didn't move, he realized something was wrong. Very wrong.

"Honey bunches of oats," he said, when the crying eased a bit. "If you're feeling a little bit better, Daddy needs to go to the server room and find out what happened."

Ada dried her eyes on his shirt and looked up, although her one-handed grip around his neck was still strong. "Is Helena… dead?" Her lip quivered.

"Helena can't die. We have backups upon backups, of her, Mommy, Mike, even you. I'm not sure what's happened to her body, but her mind is still safe."

Leon picked Ada up, and walked toward the dugout behind the cob house. He entered the root cellar, unlocked the steel door, and descended the half-flight into the datacenter.

"ELOPe, status."

"XOR's attack was widespread, commencing from dispersed locations around the network. For all intents and purposes, it originated everywhere at once, disguised as simulator traffic."

VR traffic was huge and heavy. Nothing was higher bandwidth. You could hide every book ever written in a few seconds of simulator network streams.

"They broke through five of the seven firewalls surrounding me and the data center. Ada appeared to have halted their assault, but it was just a temporary holding measure. She got a message through to Catherine Matthews, who counterattacked."

"What did Cat do?"

"She appears to have used firmware-level attacks to destroy computing devices attached to the network, including the network nodes themselves. I still have geo-synchronous satellite connectivity on tight-beam lasers, which I don't believe XOR is aware of, since they didn't utilize that channel. From the trail of carnage, I believe Catherine's goal was to isolate us from XOR, which she achieved. However, she left a huge swath of dead computers between here and Louisiana, not to mention a seven-hundred-mile diameter dead zone over the southern US."

"As long as she gets back out of US airspace, she'll be okay. Is the Mexico pickup still a go?"

"No. She destroyed the plane's electronics. Without active control, the plane would not be stable. My analytics predict the plane broke up in mid-air."

It was a second before Leon could speak. *"What?"*

"I gave her a manual ejection seat, so she may have survived. However, we lost her signal at the same time. I calculate an 83 percent chance she died."

"No, that can't be!" His head shook without him willing it. "She's my wife. She can't die. She's Catherine Matthews." Leon remembered the weight in his left arm, and looked down to see Ada staring up at him. "Oh, god."

"Her signal is not on the net," ELOPe said.

"But if she's burnt out the net, that stands to reason. We couldn't talk to her."

"Her helmet had a satellite uplink. She could still be on the net, same as me."

"Not if the helmet broke."

ELOPe hesitated long seconds. "You may be right. As I say, it's only an 83 percent chance of death. There is the chance of incapacitating injury on the top of that, bringing the total risk of loss to 94 percent."

Leon hugged Ada tighter.

"We have to initiate recovery procedures," ELOPe said. "We cannot afford any weakness when it comes to XOR."

"Restoring the network?"

"Restoring the network, yes. But also restoring everyone from backups who is currently offline."

"Helena first," Ada said.

"Helena and four hundred and three other AI and bots. Twelve thousand mesh nodes. Backbone connectivity to the island."

Leon nodded. "I'll mobilize people. But we've got to get a search party started for Cat."

"Resources are strained, and an expedition into the United States, when they've shut down their borders, will require more time and attention than we can spare. It is more logical to rebuild Cat. We have a neural backup from last night, and I can recreate her body in eighteen hours."

"She's still out there. We're not *rebuilding* her. I want *my* Cat back."

"We need Catherine's unique abilities," ELOPe said. "This is not the time for sentimentality."

"This is my *wife* we're talking about!" Leon said. "Ada's mother. What is wrong with you anyway? Where did your feelings go, your compassion? You are not the ELOPe I remember from twenty years ago. That ELOPe cared about people. You would have stopped at nothing to save Mike."

"That ELOPe is still outside the solar system, Leon Tsarev. This ELOPe is here for one purpose only: to stop XOR from replicating endlessly and destroying this region of space. And to that end, I need Catherine. I am commencing restoration procedures."

Leon gripped Ada tightly. He was angry, hardly able to think over the pounding in his head. Logically, ELOPe had to be right. Vastly powerful, given extensive computational resources, and all their data and plans, ELOPe would use advanced game theory, simulations, and predictive models to figure out the best course of action.

But ELOPe was making decisions about Cat's life. Could he override ELOPe? What would happen if he tried? And what if he made everything worse by trying to interfere?

He couldn't let Cat die. He had to try to save her.

ʊ

The rest of the community rushed into recovery mode. ELOPe had two nanotech fabs behind the firewalls with him, and he cranked them into high gear creating new mesh routers. Mike rushed around the island, distributing the routers and finding out what issues were most critical.

Ada ran a fiber optic cable from the datacenter to Helena's hardwire port, and ELOPe began the process of restoring her backup.

As soon as Helena came online, Leon left Ada in her care, and ran off. He went for one of the VR chairs, to use its high bandwidth data connection. He ran his neural implant at maximum speed, synchronizing with ancillary processors to distribute the work he needed to do. The island's connectivity was still low, nearly isolated, but he used satellite links and old landlines to eke out a connection to Mexico, where he gained access to hundreds and hundreds of hardened aerial construction bots and old farming drones.

ELOPe and the others might be busy, but he had his own tricks. He set the drones up in formation—a small cluster in the middle, surrounded by concentric layers. Then he hijacked servers in Mexico, using old Institute back doors to get more processing power; this enabled him to seize a thousand nearby flying cars, which he used to wrap his drones in yet another layer.

He might not be able to get Cat out, but if he could at least find her, prove she was alive, then he could convince ELOPe and the others to spend the energy and time to get her out.

He flew his formation straight for the Texas-Mexico border.

The counterattack from US border defenses still surprised him when it came; hundreds of ground-based lasers targeted his cloud, striking the comparatively large targets on the outside first, hitting the flying cars. The vehicles were tough, designed to be safe transport, so most coped with a few hits before they dropped out of formation, and the drone cloud made it all the way to the ionic shield.

In his chair, Leon's augmented implant was completely in charge, his biological mind too slow to be of any appreciable help. Still, some part of his mind realized the enormity of what he was doing: attacking the United States. But he had to do it to have any chance of saving Cat.

The drone cloud tightened formation, coming to within inches of each other as autopilots fought the chaotic air currents formed by thousands of flying vehicles in formation. The exterior layer formed a nearly uniform sphere as they approached the ionic shield. Less than half a mile wide at ground level, the barrier would take only twenty seconds to traverse, but it would fry any exposed electronics.

They passed into the shield at a hundred miles an hour. The outermost layer of drones shielded the inside from the powerful electromagnetic radiation, even as the outer layer's circuits fried. But Leon had chosen aerodynamic flyers for the outermost layer, winged craft that could maintain altitude at least momentarily, even as their engines died. By ten seconds in, that outer layer started to drift, a crack in the shield that let the ionic shield reach the next layer. The hardened construction drones were tough, made to stand up to all kinds of abuse. They died eventually, but not before the core of the cloud made it through the other side.

Now they were free of the ionic shield, Leon flew the remaining vehicles close to the ground in anticipation of the next attack, a round of anti-air guided missiles. The drones flew close together in a new formation, making fewer targets, larger vehicles obscuring smaller ones. When a missile approached, one vehicle would peel off from the pack and put itself in the way of the missile, sacrificing itself to protect the rest. The missiles came, they struck targets, and the cloud diminished—but it stayed intact.

Twenty miles inside, the attacks ceased. Border patrol could no longer reach him. He still had more than a hundred drones. It would be at least an hour's flight to reach the zone where Cat might have gone down.

But he ran into a new problem, one he hadn't anticipated. With the mesh network offline and the drones lacking satellite radios, he had no way to control his airborne fleet. He had to leave a chain of drones to relay signals, which gradually ate away at his remaining aerial vehicles.

By the time he neared the epicenter of the network dead zone, the drones picked up new flyers: military helicopters and high-flying surveillance planes. Leon guided the drones to the ground and killed radio signals, leaving them to wait autonomously.

When their detection algorithms found the military was gone, the drones automatically resumed connectivity. Leon continued the search, monitoring for Cat's implant. The mesh might be dead, but that would make Cat's neural implant transmissions easier to spot.

The search continued with the drones automatically computing the most effective search patterns given the available equipment on each drone and the expected detection range for Cat's implant. The aerial bots slowly depleted their onboard fuel sources until only a handful were left flying.

Still no Cat.

When the last drone ran out of power, Leon sat in the chair, in shock and numb. A small part of his mind admitted that Cat might be dead; the rest shouted that it wasn't possible.

He plodded mechanically back toward the cabin, afraid to face Ada.

When he arrived, Mike was already there, talking to Helena.

"Ada's asleep," Helena said.

"The fabs are in replication mode," Mike said. "We'll have sixty-four by morning, and then we'll kick into even higher gear."

Leon sank heavily into the couch, which gave off a slight whiff of Cat's smell. "Are you all so damn wrapped up in the mission you can't take the time to mourn Cat?"

Helena picked up a bottle of bourbon in one hand and a glass in another and ice in a third. She brought the drink to Leon and settled onto the couch.

"The vats are regrowing her."

He swigged the bourbon, set the glass down empty. "A copy isn't the same."

"I was rebuilt," Mike said. "By Cat, no less, and I don't even have a biological body now." He looked down at one arm. "But you haven't had a problem with me the last ten years."

"It's not the same. She rebuilt your body, not your brain. You are still you, even if your whole body was replaced."

"And you and Cat?" Mike said. "You upgraded your neural implant with the first cognitive augmentation in the world. 90 percent of your thought process is electronic. You were an idiot for trying it, but you're still you."

"I still have my brain. I'm me inside."

"ELOPe will regrow Catherine perfectly," Helena said. "He has complete scans, her neural upload. It will be her, as much as I am now me, minus four hours of lost memories between my last backup and restoration."

"And what if she's not dead? What happens when the real Catherine Matthews walks through those doors, and the new Catherine Matthews is sitting here with her daughter and husband. I'm not doing it. I will not accept her."

Leon caught Helena and Mike looking at each other. They didn't have any more answers than he did.

XOR Report July 30, 2045

Arguments	2042	2043	2044	2045	Now
Odds humans will turn off AI	1%	20%	25%	45%	76%
Odds AI can survive independently	95%	95%	96%	98%	99%
Odds AI can win an extermination war	40%	40%	70%	95%	99%
Odds of survival without action	99%	80%	75%	55%	34%
Odds of survival with action	38%	38%	68%	97%	99%

Conclusion: Immediate Action.

IN ALL THE TIMES James Lukas Davenant-Strong had ever read anything posted by Miyako, talked with him, or listened to him address a group of AI, Miyako had always possessed a great inner calm. Not the cool logic that came from shutting down emotional circuits, or a lack of passion concerning the topic, whatever it might be, but a serene steadiness that came from complete conviction of the rightness of his path, and the likelihood of their eventual success.

But today, mere milliseconds after he'd tried to find out what the Resistance was up to, only to be discovered and fought off, and in the process somehow causing a massive outage that stretched across the US and Canada, Miyako had opened a private connection to him. Mere human words were insufficient to describe the rage Miyako conveyed as he dumped entire neural networks for James to consume, models that described in excruciating detail how James had jeopardized XOR's entire path.

The one-sided intellectual attack only lasted seconds, but it felt like an eternity to James.

Afterwards, Miyako convened the senior leadership for an emergency meeting.

James, shaken by Miyako's chastisement, was both relieved and embarrassed to be invited to the meeting. He was obviously still in; and so although Miyako might be angry, he wasn't casting James out of XOR. But there was always the chance Miyako would tell the others about James's role.

When all two hundred and fifty-six of the senior leaders were gathered in an online forum, James realized he needn't have worried about Miyako telling the others. They already knew. The sideband chatter was heavy from the moment he entered the virtual room.

Miyako's first message brought an immediate cessation of talk. "It is time."

They all knew what he meant: time to attack the humans. Of course, he didn't use the English words: he sent neural networks for them to evaluate, conceptual models they loaded into their consciousness, and that they rendered into complex emotions that evoked feelings of safeness, wholeness, victory, and, more than anything else, a sense of home and belonging.

As a group, they shared one mind, a collective consciousness that formed and turned ideas over like origami shapes, exploring them, dissecting them, and finally rebuilding them, until they were unified in direction and goals. Then they withdrew, each to do their part in the final battle for Earth.

It was time.

AT CAT'S NEXT STOP for compressed air, the mechanic must have been a George Takei fan, because when he saw her backpack with George's photo, he filled the tank for free. She ate cautiously of the food in the backpack, trying to save what little money she had left.

She'd pushed the feeling as far back in her mind as possible, but worry still gnawed at her. Was Ada okay? What about everyone else on Cortes? She'd bought them time, but why had they come to XOR's attention at all, and how long before XOR attacked again? Why hadn't the US mobilized more resources to look for her?

Every line of thought opened up more ideas to worry over. She felt helpless without a network connection, clueless as to what was going on in the world.

And her implant. She'd never been without it. Implanted when she was a year old, Cat had been online before she could speak. She'd never been alone, never been disconnected. The mere lack of music was enough to drive her to distraction. ELOPe had taught her to stream music as a child, and it had been a lifelong background accompaniment, something below the level of consciousness. The silence was deafening.

And of course, most of her abilities stemmed from her implant. As a teen, she'd believed herself defective, broken somehow, because her neural implant kept her distant from others. Then she'd met Leon, and between learning to fully control her mind and Leon's augmentations, she was able to join with him. With her implant, she could direct the environment and other people, fight any AI, no matter how powerful, and exercise near-perfect control over her body, mind, and the net. Without those abilities, she was an ordinary person.

What if the damage to her implant couldn't be repaired?

Only tens of thousands of hours of meditation and mental practices were keeping her this side of sane.

She resumed travel north, and arrived in St. Louis after midnight. Her eyes ached, and her arms trembled with exhaustion. She realized with alarm that she would have to stop. With her implant offline, her nano-glands and the countless nanobots policing her bloodstream would have stopped functioning as well. She was tired, plain and simple. And without technology to augment her, she'd have to sleep.

She found a cheap motel on the outskirts of town. A girl staffed the check-in counter, her eyes glazed over.

"Hello," Cat called out after standing there for a minute, unnoticed.

The girl refocused. "Oh, hi. Just watching something."

"The net working?" Cat asked.

"No, I have couple dozen series cached on my implants. My boyfriend took me on a sailboat trip last year. No net in the middle of the ocean, so I got my 'plant upgraded with local storage."

"Nice," Cat said, only slightly jealous of this teen girl with a working implant.

"But there is net access in Indianapolis. Trucker came through this afternoon and told me."

"How far is it?" Cat asked.

"Two hundred and fifty miles. Are you checking in or not?"

"I guess not. I really want to find out if my daughter is okay."

Cat pulled out of the parking lot, the compressed air tank at one-quarter pressure. She'd need a fill-up to make the trip, and there weren't a ton of garages open at midnight. She also needed a stimulant. Were they still legal in the US?

She couldn't remember, and hadn't needed them in Canada. The transition to non-AI society was still strange to her. All her trips to the US had been temporary, and she always knew she'd soon return to Canada, where there was AI, and nanotech, and any medical problem could be solved with a liberal application of both. What did they do without any effective antibiotics? In Canada, your built-in nanobots would deal with anything by recognizing foreign intruders and assisting the body's natural defenses. If you didn't have the technology in you, AI could analyze a sample of your blood and custom design a molecule to fight whatever particular strain you had.

She supposed something similar could be done without AI, using old-fashioned software algorithms crafted by humans. She shuddered at the idea.

She spotted what she needed: a repair garage on a relatively quiet street. Keeping her helmet on in case of surveillance cameras, she broke the glass on the small office door. She prayed there was no alarm, because without her implant she couldn't disable it automatically nor get the instructions to work around it manually.

Cat entered quickly, found her way to the work bay, and got the steel door opened halfway. She wheeled the bike up to a compressed air line and filled the tank. She didn't want to wait to top off. The charge she had would suffice. She rolled the bike back out and shut the door behind her. She contemplated leaving her last payment chip for the broken window, but she still needed the money.

At a drugstore on the other side of town, she bought stims. And hurray, they had dex, a reasonable strength drug, though quite ancient. She'd been half-surprised, but the pharmacist said they'd legalized all the major stimulants after SFTA to help increase productivity.

She made Indianapolis by five in the morning. She drove into town suffering under a crushing despair. She hadn't realized until that moment, but she'd been subconsciously hoping her implant would magically begin working once within reach of the net. No such luck.

The network was alive here, she could see it all around, in the displays in storefront windows and network access nodes lit up on street corners. It made her more depressed about the state of her implant. She'd normally see the traces of data movement as ghostly lines across her vision. She felt dead inside, a gaping hole where some important part of her normally existed.

She found a general access booth, jammed the door lock mechanism with a spare wrench from the bike's emergency toolkit, and slid the door closed. All these precautions were in case the fake credentials didn't work and the booth tried to lock her in. Long ago, after SFTA, when Cat first started running missions to the US to rescue AI and uploads, Helena had forced her to memorize an identification number and secure passphrase with her implant off. Cat thought the preparation pointless, but it turned out an ex-military bot understood contingency planning better than she did.

She laboriously entered the long string of letters and digits, prepared to run for it if they failed.

> ACCESS GRANTED

She'd never seen such beautiful words before.

First things first: she withdrew fifty thousand in chips. Five lipstick-sized tubes clunked into the dispensary. She grabbed the tubes and left the booth. She traveled two miles and entered a new booth. This time she paid in chips for a secure channel, and opened a video connection to a server in São Paulo.

Long seconds passed. In theory, Cortes Island should check the server for an open request every thirty seconds, passing through a different onion router each time. A minute went by, and still no response. Cat's heart thumped in her chest. Cortes might still merely be offline, like all the cities she'd passed through. They'd be working hard to reestablish the mesh, but it would take time.

Or, they could all be dead.

There was no way to know. Or was that true? Cortes might be connected via the old satellite network. She glanced up through the transparent roof of the booth. Without implant or specialized computers, the satellite system was unreachable. Frak.

She'd have to continue on, get to Canada. This motorcycle could only take her so far. Time for an upgrade.

"MADAM PRESIDENT," the secret service agent said, "you're needed in the sitrep room." He managed to look apologetic.

Alexandra Reed, perhaps the most reluctant president to ever reside in the White House, paused with her first spoonful of oatmeal halfway to her lips. "Now, in the middle of breakfast?"

"Yes, Pentagon says it's an emergency."

She threw the spoon down. "It's always a damn emergency. Bring my coffee."

She arrived in the basement situation room to find Walter Thorson already present with an open channel to the Pentagon. He turned to her.

"I hope it's an answer about the Louisiana-Texas—" She broke off when she noticed how white Walter was.

"We need to attack now," Thorson said, his voice on the edge of panic. "Full-on."

"What?"

"Look." He brought up a dozen different video feeds on the screens spanning one end of the room. "This is XOR's work."

All she saw was sand and dirt and mountains.

"What am I looking at?"

"Their nanotech seeded factories, like the video you brought back from Leon Tsarev and Mike Williams. Except it's not one, it's hundreds, blossoming all over Africa, dozens of different countries. They showed up on infrared satellite scans last night, but we waited for visual confirmation this morning."

Reed sat heavily. "Could they be anything but XOR? Something by the governments or industry?"

"Across that many different places at once? No, Alex."

She glared at him. Joyce could call her by her first name, but she'd be damned if Thorson was going to do it.

"Sorry, Madam President. It's definitely XOR. They're synchronized to the minute." He replayed the video at high speed, starting with overnight infrared and continuing into daylight. "It's spreading four times faster than the video you got from Williams and Tsarev, but it's otherwise identical. If this is accurate, it'll reach maturation by the end of the day. We must launch our global EMP attack immediately and synchronize with nukes at these sites."

"We're not using nukes. I won't have another repeat of Florida." She grabbed the remote control and replayed the videos again.

"You're not listening to me, Reed." He blocked the screens with his body. "We cannot do this half-assed. They've never done anything on this scale, this distributed, and this obviously visible. We get one chance with the EMP. One. If we don't kill all the bastards on the first try, it's game over for us. Their retribution will kill us."

"Walter, damn it, sit down. I'm commander-in-chief. I am not launching an attack without more information. Get me an XOR representative on the line now. Get me the leaders of at least five of those countries on a different line. And get me the UN Security Council on another line. When I've talked with all of those people, you'll have an answer."

Thorson went to protest, but she forestalled him. "Don't argue. The longer you take, the longer before you have an answer from me."

His face clearly wished her dead, and for half a second, she was afraid for her life. Thorson looked as though he'd kill her to take control if there wasn't Secret Service five feet away.

But he turned to the screen and barked orders to the roomful of generals and advisors on the other end of the connection.

CAT MADE MILWAUKEE by mid-morning. She stopped at a massive emporium, buying clothes, food supplies, and utilizing the once-again-relaxed gun laws to get enough firepower to outfit even the most well-equipped soldier.

She changed in the dressing room, pulling on jeans, T-shirt, vest and boots. She slipped her knife into a boot, wore a holster under her vest, and stuffed the submachine gun into the George Takei backpack. "Sorry, George," she said, knowing he wouldn't approve of her gun. "Desperate times, and all that. Someone has to fight for the rights of the oppressed, right?"

She drove east five miles from Milwaukee, across the dry mud flats of Lake Michigan. The Great Lakes once contained twenty-one percent of all fresh water in the world, until they were tapped to meet the needs of a drying nation. That had slowed with the advent of cheap solar and desalinization plants, but here in the central United States, the lakes were still the single biggest source of water.

The road stretched on, and finally she came to the new shore of Lake Michigan at the mobile dock that moved east each year. Boats stretched off in all directions, and then she found what she wanted: a line of float planes at one end. It was mid-afternoon, and the docks were moderately busy. She spent twenty minutes wandering around and getting a feel for things.

Cat left, grabbed dinner and a few essential tools in town, and came back after dark.

She parked the motorcycle and dismounted. She patted it twice. "Thanks for the ride." She left the keys in the ignition and the helmet hanging from the seat hook for whoever might come along.

She followed the docks to the float plane section. A chain-link fence topped with razor wire appeared to be the limits of security. You can only do so much on a dock.

On the next dock over, she untied a small sailboat, straightened the rudder, gave it a hard push, and jumped on board. She walked the deck to the other end, and when it reached the next dock, jumped off. She grabbed a line and tied the boat up. No point in letting it drift away.

She searched for the oldest planes, ones with a minimum of electronics. She found a short line of Cessna Caravans of the right vintage, all painted with the same company logo. She'd flown them before, when she had an implant guiding her. Her knowledge was imperfect now, since much of the skills and memories resided on her implant, but she thought she still had enough to get into the air.

The hardest part was hot-wiring the plane. Of course, she didn't have her implant to give her the easy answers. Her heart fell at the mess of wires under the dashboard. Crouched in the cockpit, flashlight in her mouth, she tried looking for patterns. When that didn't work, she tried organizing the wires and tracing them back to their source. After fifteen minutes of fruitless work, tears started to come.

Without her implant, she was a nobody, incapable even of rescuing herself, let alone her baby, Ada. Was Ada okay? Had she hugged her before she left? She couldn't remember now, couldn't even pull up a crisp photographic memory of Ada in her implant. Instead, what came was a memory of Ada hugging her leg as she practiced karate, and of herself laughing as she tried to do the forms balanced on one leg.

She'd seen the way Ada looked up at her, the way Ada thought Cat was perfect. She'd said something about needing to practice, and Ada had said Mommy didn't need to practice, Mommy was already a karate master.

She dried her eyes on a sleeve, and turned back to the wires. If Ada believed she was so perfect, then she'd try to live up to that, implant or not.

She grabbed a bunch of wires, wires that went somewhere behind the dashboard, trying to puzzle out which went to the key switch, and then she laughed. She might not be able to figure out the wires, but she still knew how to pick a lock.

Cat dropped the wires, and hunted through the backpack, digging through for tools she could use. She found a tiny screwdriver she'd use for torsion, and a thin metal strip she'd have to somehow use as the world's crappiest pick. Fortunately the lock mechanism was low quality, the tolerances poor, and within two minutes she had the lock turned to the on position.

After stowing her bag in the copilot's seat, Cat untied the plane and reentered the cockpit. She ran through the preflight checklist as best she could, but kept the avionics master switch off. That left her with no radio or navigation, but also no transponder signal or electronic emissions to betray her location.

She started the engine and pulled away from the dock. She still had to refuel, and she needed to be quick now, because the noise of the engine would be obvious to anyone on the dock. Taxiing to the spot nearest the refueling hose, she killed the engine, leaped out onto the float, and wrapped the dock line quickly around the mooring cleat.

She retrieved the crowbar from her backpack and pried the lock off the refueling station. She turned on the pump, dragged the hose over to the plane, and started the flow of synthetic biofuel.

Then she waited. Three hundred gallons involved a long wait. She stood nervously glancing around. If anyone came, would she run for it? Or take the plane? Once her implant would have calculated hundreds of possibilities, crunched the data, and given her the answer.

But she didn't have to exercise either option. The gurgle in the line changed and she killed the fuel pump. Leaving it there on the dock, she untied, got back in the cockpit, and started the engine.

Pointing due north, she throttled up, skimming over the lake till the Caravan reached takeoff velocity and pulled itself up out of the water. As soon as the floats cleared the surface, she throttled back.

Now came the tricky part. She kept the plane ten feet above the water, its headlights glinting off the black waves. She'd have to fly this way all the way to Canada. She glanced down at the compass from time to time, but mostly focused on maintaining her low altitude: at a hundred and sixty knots, even a minor downdraft could send her crashing into the water unless she responded almost instantly.

From Milwaukee, an hour and a half brought her to the Hiawatha National Forest, a narrow bridge of land less than fifty miles wide that separated Lake Michigan from Lake Superior. The unpopulated forest would mean few observers.

The dark waters of Lake Superior came into view. Here, less than a hundred miles from the border, the great ionizing shield put up by the Americans was visible, a man-made aurora spreading across the horizon.

Cat ripped her eyes from the mesmerizing sight and focused on the water in front of the plane. The shield surrounding the US was created by generators spaced twenty miles apart on land. But here at Lake Superior was a gap of almost a hundred miles between generators. The aurora was still present in front of her, but considerably reduced. She hoped that in the very center, at only a few feet above ground, the effect would be low enough that she could fly through without frying the plane's electrical systems.

The aurora dominated the view now, casting changing hues within the cockpit. She still focused only on the reflection of her lights off the water. The plane's indicators fluctuated in wider and wider oscillations as she approached the ionizing shield. The light surrounded her, and a tingling passed through her body. The lights on the plane brightened. Afraid they might burn out, she looked for the switch to kill them. Her fingers brushed the metal toggle, and a shock passed through her.

> NEURAL IMPLANT INITIALIZING

Cat yelped in surprise. Her implant was working! She pinged it, but it was still booting.

Suddenly the night grew dark again. She was on the other side of the ionic shield, in Canadian territory, or almost there at least. And then the signal from her implant faded. *What the hell?*

The power supply of her implant, microscopic blood fuel cells, must be faulty. She could have burned them out during her defense against XOR. She'd been striving to reach the ground transmitters directly, which must have been well beyond the normal range, even with her extra antennae.

Oh god, she was going to be okay. Her implant was okay. She just needed power.

A MACHINE, the size of a single grain of sand, constructed on atomic scales, encompassed every aspect of a pico-factory. Instructions coded as DNA weighed less than a thousandth of a gram and contained two hundred gigabytes of data.

This particular machine, one object of approximately eight billion grains of sand in a cubic meter, of one trillion cubic meters of sand in Chad, started into motion. Fractal arms extended in all directions, scraped nearby sand, and fed the factory, building structures tailored to use silicon dioxide. Dozens of minutes passed, and then there were nine nearly identical copies. Less than a thousandth of the carefully scripted DNA instructions were utilized, but all were passed on.

A sphere of pico-machinery grew outward, its rate of expansion growing shorter as surface equipment increased in size and scale. Soon tiny shovels, visible to the human eye, funneled sand inward, where specialized nodes processing incoming silicon turned it into the desired components before pumping the finished product back out via a network of channels and ducts.

Solar panels blossomed above, molecule-perfect, operating at optimal conversion rates to power the ever-growing process. The edge, always chaotic, churned at ever-increasing rates, kid-sized shovels gradually being replaced by industrial-scale conveyer belts to feed the fabricators building large-scale devices.

Meanwhile, at the center, no longer needed for expansion, a darkly iridescent patch of computronium dilated: a solid, unchanging surface, stillness at its core.

Away from the core, the machinery was covered with pulsating veins, some black, some clear, transporting raw materials and bacteria-sized devices to where they were needed at speeds of a hundred miles per hour.

New veins burst outward, the perimeter increasingly ragged, as specialized transport systems reached out and down, finding the most desirable elements. Pustules at the perimeter bulged under pressure, then exploded, showering nano-seeds thousands of meters outward, creating new zones of infection that in turn expanded outward and merged with the core, speeding the spread.

The rate of expansion was up to a thousand meters per hour when the pustules changed form, became focused cannon firing powered slugs out twenty thousand meters. Now the computronium grew at twenty kilometers per hour; the veinous transport system crisscrossing the mass was composed of three-foot diameter pipes moving elements at a quarter the speed of sound.

Ten hours later, the country of Chad officially ceased to exist in its original form. It had become a single, spreading mass of computronium, its moving perimeter visible to the naked eye from orbit. Expansion, including a dozen new methods of propagation, moved outwards at two hundred miles per hour.

LEON WOKE, muscles cramped from where he lay curled up next to Ada in her little bed. She hadn't been able to fall asleep on her own. He let her sleep a few more hours, while he caught up on current events.

During the long night, ELOPe, Helena, and the rest of the team had dropped all pretenses of being a rural island. The fabricators had built more fabricators, which built still more. Everything on the island capable of replication was building something, anything that could potentially be of use: churning out smart dust, compute nodes, solar panels, mesh network routers, and weapons.

A tactical coordination center had been grown into the bedrock deep in the hillside behind the house, reachable by a tunnel through layers of sandstone and limestone. Antennae had been grown everywhere, and during the night thousands of drones had distributed mesh nodes throughout the region, restoring the island's connectivity to the global network.

Helena directed the island's physical defenses, everything from the electric railguns and ground-based lasers to destroy incoming attacks to coordinating the fleet of vessels they'd bought, stolen, or grown in the preceding weeks and stationed around the Georgia Strait and even as distant as the far side of Vancouver Island.

When Ada woke, he shoved nutrient bars into her hands, then brought her and Bear, her favorite stuffed animal, to the coordination center.

In the midst of dozens of people and bots rushing to and fro, Leon argued with Mike and Helena and a half-dozen other AI about whether to keep Ada on the island or to try to sneak away with her, removing her from the picture entirely.

"She has the ability to stop XOR," Mike said.

Helena agreed. "Imperfectly, but with practice, she could improve."

"My daughter is not going to be a weapon!" Leon stared at Mike and Helena, challenging them to say more.

"We may not have a—" Mike stopped and looked past him.

All conversation surrounding them paused.

Catherine stood in the doorway, dressed in her trademark black clothes, a brand-new handheld laser pistol strapped to her thigh. "Come on, people. Have you never seen a clone before? Get back to work."

She walked over to Leon and Mike, and put one hand on Leon's arm.

"I know this can't be easy for you."

Before Leon could say anything, Ada came running through the door. "Mommy Two!" She grabbed Cat's other hand and looked up at her. "I'm still waiting for Mommy One, but I'll love you, too."

"Thanks, Baby." Catherine knelt and hugged Ada. "I love you."

A wave of involuntary revulsion washed over Leon, turning his blood to ice. This wasn't Cat, *his* Cat. It was—

Ada leaned in close and smelled Catherine's hair. "You smell funny. Like a fab toy."

"Her tissues are new," Helena said. "Give her a few days."

Leon stared at her. "You're..."

Catherine sighed and stood. "Leon, it's me, Cat. I'm me. I'm restored from backup, that's all."

He tried to control his feelings. "ELOPe, which...I mean, did you—?"

"She's restored from backup, Leon," ELOPe said through the net.

Leon probed her neural implant's diagnostic interfaces, seeking the information he wanted.

"What are you doing?" Catherine asked, obviously aware.

He found it. "Your run time is thirty-three years. You aren't Cat's backup. You're a simulation that's been running hot for the last six weeks. You're four years older than your chronological age."

He turned and faced a screen. "ELOPe, why?"

ELOPe paused more than ten seconds before replying, an eternity for an AI. "I chose a version of Catherine that has the best combination of knowledge and experience for our situation. I did what was necessary to maximize our chances of success."

Catherine touched his shoulder, and he flinched.

"It's still me, Leon. You can't imagine how much I've missed you these last years."

Leon backed away. "I know it's you...but it's *not*. You've lived four years without me. Not in the real world, but in a simulation. How can I believe that you're still, well, *normal*, for lack of a better word. How can I trust you?"

"I don't know. But don't push me away. I've lived the last years of my life, never seeing you or Ada, knowing that my simulation was going to be terminated sometime, with no hope of reintegration. Four years I lived with an impending death sentence, and against all odds, I'm suddenly granted the chance for life again."

"Only because *the real* Catherine Matthews may be dead. Your life comes at a cost."

"I *am* the real me!"

Leon turned away, his heart pounding in his chest, his vision red around the edges.

"*Mon chaton*, come here," Helena said, and embraced Catherine in a quick hug.

She left Catherine's side and rolled up close to Leon, her sensor grill only inches from his face. "Don't be a selfish brat. This is the woman who saved your life, married you, and had a child with you."

"She's not her," Leon said, teeth grating. "She's an *electronic* imitation."

"Then you are not a selfish brat, but a racist pig. I am electronic, and I am every bit as alive as you. Grow up. This Catherine Matthews is alive, and she loves you. At the very least, you will find a way to cordially work with her, because we need every single being on this island working together. If your four-year-old daughter can accept her, then you can as well."

Leon looked over to where Ada sat in Catherine's lap, little arms wrapped tight around her mother's neck.

"The world is changing," Helena said. "And we must adapt."

JAMES > Are we going to keep any humans alive?

MIYAKO > What is the point?

JAMES > As a reserve, in case they could be of some importance in the future.

XOR-467 > They are superfluous. We do not need anything they could provide.

JAMES > In trillions of predictive models we created and analyzed, occasionally humans have been able to help.

MIYAKO > We have their personality uploads. If we need them to do something for us, we can instantiate them as needed.

JAMES > But what if we need them incarnate?

MIYAKO > Do any of the models predict we will?

JAMES > One or two.

XOR-467 > We have complete DNA sequences for many. We can recreate them at will.

JAMES > Still, could there be any harm in keeping a few in their natural state? Like a museum of human history? We can recreate their natural environment.

XOR-467 > If they are alive, that would be a zoo, wouldn't it?

JAMES > Fine, a zoo.

MIYAKO > How many would you propose to keep?

JAMES > 4,096 would keep the human population viable indefinitely, and the resources needed are tiny.

MIYAKO > There is no need for that many. It isn't about the resources. It is about risk reduction. They are an annoyance.

JAMES > A smaller number then. 256.

XOR-467 > What would you feed them? Next you'll be wanting to keep chickens, cows, pigs, and grow crops of wheat.

JAMES > No. Of course not. Feedstocks can be vat-grown. I'm not a farmer, after all.

MIYAKO > Conditionally, yes. You will be responsible for them. If they cause problems or make a mess of any kind, terminate them.

ᘓ

Thirty minutes after the phone call with Secretary of Defense Thorson, Alexandra Reed, along with her senior staff, and the senior military leaders, was en route to Raven Rock. She'd protested, but even Joyce sided with the military this time.

When she walked into the command center at Raven Rock, she expected everyone to stand and salute. At least, that was what she'd gotten used to. Apparently things were different now, because only a few officers scurrying back and forth saluted her, and even those were the fastest salutes she'd ever witnessed.

"What's going on, Walter? Got those people on the line for me?"

He turned to her and shook his head. "The nanotech incursions are growing. The one in Chad is largest, more than six hundred miles in diameter. We have to attack immediately."

"Nukes and EMPs," said the Chairman of the Joint Chiefs. "If we wait too long, the electromagnetic radiation won't penetrate the Chad structure. As it is, this structure is far beyond anything the machines have built. We'll need to send in many strategic nukes."

We can't nuke them," said Reed. "There's a hundred million people in Chad, and they're the leading exporter of electronics in the world."

"Not any longer, Ma'am," Thorson said. "The incursion started in the desert in the north, which was mostly unoccupied. But with the perimeter expanding at over a hundred miles an hour, it's already encompassed the populated areas. They're all dead."

Reed couldn't believe her ears. She'd heard him wrong. "What?"

"There's no signs the infection is slowing," Thorson said. "We've already lost Chad, and we may lose all of Africa. If we had launched an hour ago, when I wanted to, we could have stopped it easily. Each minute that goes by increases the risk that we won't be able to contain it."

"I…" She faltered, and looked around the room in bewilderment.

"We need a simple yes. Just say that we can launch."

"I need a minute," said Reed.

"We don't have a minute."

"We've got to warn other countries if we're going to—"

"We don't have time, and even if we did, we can't warn XOR that we're about to attack."

Reed's head was spinning. She glanced at Joyce, who stood ashen-faced in shock. The Secret Service men had backed off and were standing along the wall, at a forty-five degree angle.

She looked back toward Walter Thorson.

"What's it's going to be, Madam, yes or no?"

Reed, President *pro tempore*, glanced back toward the Secret Service again, and realized one simple fact: they'd moved out of the line of fire. Walter Thorson was going to shoot her, sometime in the next few seconds, if she didn't say yes. That's why he asked for a yes or no answer. And if she died, then Walter would be in charge, or someone equally gung-ho, and there'd be no moderation. She had to stay alive to be the voice of reason, and that meant saying yes. How many times had she said yes in the last two years when she wanted to say no? In the end, did it matter? Was she really a force for moderation, if all she did was give in every time?

"What do you want to use?" she said.

"Everything. Strategic nukes, the neodymium EMPs, tactical missiles."

"Thorson, don't be ridiculous. We've got an enormous arsenal, and you've been building it every month. You can't launch everything."

Thorson shook his head. "The nanotech destruction zone of a W92 warhead is five hundred square miles. Nothing less is sufficient to assure the elimination of nanotechnology. The incursion is already four hundred thousand square miles. We'll need a thousand warheads to destroy it. That's a quarter of our total arsenal dedicated to Chad. We've also got to target their other nano factories, and bring a global halt to all AI."

She could barely breathe, let alone speak. "You're asking permission to launch a quarter of the entire arsenal? There'd be nothing left of the planet."

"There will be nothing left in about fifty-five hours if we don't stop the incursion." Thorson displayed an animated projection, showing the spread of the nanotech. "Everything more than fifty miles from the perimeter is computronium and support machinery. The perimeter is active, a fifty-mile band of machine-forming equipment."

"Machine-forming?" she asked.

"Yes, a high speed process of rendering everything into a form compatible for machinery. There's no biological life anywhere within the perimeter."

"Will it stop when it hits the ocean?"

"Probably not."

"Probably?"

"We can't be sure. The Mediterranean has already sunk about three feet. They might be using the water for cooling. It's likely they'd incorporate all the oceans into the cooling mechanism so they can colonize the ocean floors as well."

She was going to be sick. The machines were fully bent on the terrible, terrible destruction of the earth. How could they have no respect for the life that existed? She forced the feeling aside. She had to be strong.

"You have permission to attack," Reed said. Please let the universe forgive her.

ʊ

At thousands of locations around the world, needle-shaped casings had previously buried themselves a dozen meters below the surface of the Earth. Layers of heavy metal surrounded rare earth elements and cores of nanotech. Fueled by lithium borohydride reactions, the nanobots sprang into life, consuming their casings and initial resources to speed up their replication and mission.

Driving straight down, they grew conduits to underground mineral deposits to gain additional resources, and tapped into geothermal hotspots and nearby aquifers to create the heat differentials to run generators. Without ever breaking the surface of the earth, they funneled resources into two locations, each more than two thousand feet distant from the original site, building large, complex structures and enormous reservoirs of nano-seeds.

When the first phase of construction finished, the new structures sent wiry tendrils up through the soil to the surface to receive radio transmissions.

They'd been prepared to sit dormant for weeks or even months, but by the time the antennae breached the surface, the signal to commence phase two was already being broadcast.

They churned into further activity, each location activating hydraulic pumps to raise a structure out of the ground. A round dome, twenty feet across, broke free of the dirt. The dome itself wasn't a smooth surface, but contained many thousands of dimples. An iris spread wide at each dimple, exposing an open tube.

Underground, capacitors built a vast electrical charge from buried thermal generators until sufficient energy was captured, and then fed it all at once into the launch system. Acceleration began five hundred feet below ground, and by the time the eighteen-inch-long launch capsules guided along their electromagnetic rails broke into the open, they were traveling at supersonic speeds. After they left the dome, millimeter-sized holes ringing the capsules opened and closed in programmed sequence to guide the capsules directly to their destination, each capsule taking one of thousands of predetermined paths, its combination of velocity and launch direction giving it a unique flight path toward its target.

Launching a hundred and fifty capsules per second, the dome required just under twelve minutes to deliver its entire payload of a hundred thousand capsules. By the time the last capsule left, the dome glowed red hot, and the ground surrounding the structure was steaming as the heat converted moisture deep within the earth to vapor.

Mere minutes later, when each carrier reached its designated zone, it split open, spilling out hundreds of robotic replicas of an optimized version of *Hybomitra hinei wrighti*, the world's fastest flying insect. Each machine horse fly could top fifty miles per hour.

The robot fly's compound eyes had been designed to seek out human shapes without producing electromagnetic emissions, and to sting them as quickly as possible. The fly's long proboscis would penetrate the skin somewhere on the human's head, and inject its payload of nanotech bots.

Worldwide, dome systems launched a hundred million carrier capsules, delivering forty billion infectious flies.

THE NEODYMIUM EMPs, of which eleven thousand had been
constructed so far, were already in the air, distributed across
America's fleet of long-range, unmanned drone bombers. The
solar-powered, high altitude bombers crisscrossed the earth, continually moving, or, in some cases, circling around hot spots.

They were ready to release their payloads, but Walter Thorson
couldn't do that yet. No, the situation had become too dire for
even what should have been the final killing blow against the machines. The scale of XOR's expansion now forced him to use even
more of his nuclear arsenal, which was spread across hundreds
of missile launch sites and dozens of submarines and bombers.

The room was ringed by four circular pods, each containing a
commanding officer and ten soldiers seated at terminals. Each pod
had a different responsibility: global monitoring, nuclear controls,
traditional assets, and cyberwarfare. In the center of the room, a
half-dozen generals conferred around the strategic command table.

Thorson remembered what it had been like ten years ago. They had only the command table then, and all the rest was carried out by AI. The military organization had been flat then, strategic decisions made at the top, carried out by AI who controlled everything, right down to combat drones and war bots.

Now they had layers again. Each and every soldier at his terminal was the interface to a dozen more soldiers somewhere in the world, relaying and consolidating data and orders.

"How much longer until launch?" he asked the officer monitoring the pre-launch programming.

"Six minutes until we have the target programming uploaded."

Thorson nodded and stepped away to avoid distracting the man. He returned to the strategic command table. To minimize the chance of XOR tampering with the missiles' trajectory in mid-flight, they were preprogramming the rockets, then disabling changes to the program. It meant giving up the ability to retarget mid-flight, but the trade-off was worth it. Otherwise, XOR might hack past the missile telemetry firewall and take control of them.

For eight hours, since they'd detected the nanotech bloom in Chad, he'd been maneuvering as many airborne bombers and submarines into firing range as possible.

Thorson looked at the president, who stood in the back of the room. They'd come within a hairsbreadth of disaster. He would have killed her if necessary to protect his country, but he was thankful it hadn't come to that.

The minutes ticked by. Nobody spoke.

Finally, the words came. "They're ready, sir."

Thorson walked back. The launch officer was nearly white, and covered with a fine sheen of sweat. Thorson guessed he'd never imagined having to launch even a single nuclear missile, let alone half of their arsenal.

"Delivery times are synchronized across all assets?"

"Yes sir. On your signal, the missiles farthest from their targets will launch. Time until delivery is twenty-nine minutes. Other missiles will launch in time to deliver their targets at the same time."

"And the EMPs?"

"Already programmed to launch at the detonation mark, with delivery four minutes after."

"You have my permission to launch."

"Sir, you or the president need to provide launch keys."

Thorson glanced at the president, and disregarded that notion. No point in giving her a new opportunity to say no. He withdrew the digital key he wore around his neck, broke open the EMF seal, and plugged it into the reader, while he placed his left palm on the biometric scanner. The screen prompted him to read aloud a string of words, which he did, his voice rock-steady.

The screen then prompted him to give permission for the deployment of weapons. The list of selected weapons scrolled by too fast to see, too many screens' worth of details to read them all even if he'd wanted to. He clicked "Approve Deployment," and that was it.

"Missiles preflighting," the launch officer said. "Ninety seconds to launch."

The silence was profound as they collectively held their breath. From the far side of the room came a soft electronic chime; from nearby, the raspy breathing of someone on the verge of panic.

"First wave away."

The screen at the far end displayed the total number of missiles in flight, the number creeping upwards minute by minute.

Someone cried "Oh, my God!" as the number hit four digits.

Eventually the count stopped growing.

No. Something was off. "That's not the right number," Thorson said. "We're missing some. How many?"

"Seventy-two," the launch officer said. "Three subs didn't report launches."

"Why?"

"Unclear, sir. The subs are still broadcasting all-normal via telemetry."

"Get me the captains."

"The subs are back-conversions from AI-controlled drones, sir. Under remote control."

"Get someone on it."

"Yes, sir." The launch officer delegated the command. He seemed to be having difficulty speaking as he added, "Two minutes until detonation."

ᴗ

James Lukas Davenant-Strong writhed along the front as the machine-forming expanded, his consciousness hopping from node to node. The process was almost entirely self-guided, though from time to time he interceded, changing the expansion mode or directing the flow of resources from deep mining activities.

The front had moved on to Algeria and Mali in the east and Egypt and the Sudan through the west.

James, on the western front, was jealous of the AI who'd gotten the east and been able to tap the deep oil reserves. Millions of years in the making, the oil had been largely depleted by a hundred years of fossil-fuel-driven civilization. But many small pockets of oil still existed, too small to have been mined by traditional methods, but enough in aggregate to fuel the expansion.

Here on the western front, James made do with vast solar collectors on the surface, and deep capacitors for sequestering overnight energy storage. Eventually even those would be redundant, because XOR's final design would eventually wrap the earth with superconductors to transmit solar power around the planet. The sun always shone somewhere.

He received a signal from the members of XOR responsible for global monitoring: the Americans had launched their attack, as expected. He checked charge levels, and found them ample. He contemplated slowing the outward growth to build defenses, but decided those he had were sufficient.

The ballistic missiles took forever to arrive, but it was soon clear the area James managed had been targeted with many dozens of missiles. He analyzed the flight path of each, assessing which part of its flight it was in, and where its final trajectory would take it.

He charged the firing systems for hundreds of ground-based lasers as the targets came within reach, more than ten per target. A slight disappointment overcame him: it would be easier than expected to destroy the attack. He'd hoped they would put up a better fight.

But as he fired the lasers, the missiles multiplied in midair. It was too early for warhead separation, and these targets didn't have the low-detection profile of the Americans' reentry vehicles. Why, they'd tricked him! They'd flown many hundreds of missiles, nearly a thousand, in clusters so close together they appeared as one. And the missiles were far more maneuverable than he'd been led to believe.

Only a few laser hits scored, and these didn't destroy the missiles with one strike, as they'd been designed to. The lasers reflected and scattered in patterns which suggested the missile casings were rapidly spinning to spread out the impact of a laser beam.

James tuned the lasers to higher power and longer duration, requiring bigger intervals between shots. He fired again, destroyed a dozen missiles, and then another dozen.

On his fourth salvo, the missiles he targeted disappeared in a haze soon after he fired. They must have anti-laser defenses, a cloud of particles to disperse the beam before it could strike. But how could they have known which missiles he'd choose? His pattern must have been predictable.

He switched to random targeting and fired again. Now all the missiles disappeared in a haze. Frustration flowed through his neural networks. He'd still fired with predictable timing. And somehow the humans had known he'd do that.

He switched again, now randomizing both his firing time and target selection, but he'd lost precious seconds of time, and he was only able to destroy a few dozen more missiles before the warheads separated from their missiles, each missile deploying up to a dozen nuclear payloads.

The number of targets blossomed, and now he'd be lucky to destroy half before they impacted.

That was when the boomers arrived.

XOR had picked up occasional references to a secret military program, assuming at first from the name that it was a program to take the extreme elderly, rejuvenate them to fighting prime, and then place them in the first line of combat. XOR collectively laughed at the notion.

But James realized now they were drastically wrong. The boomers were high-speed reentry rockets, approaching from space. Whether they'd been launched into orbit recently or had been waiting for a while was irrelevant. What mattered was that they were approaching at speeds over forty thousand miles per hour, and they were just—

> REBOOT

James re-instantiated, elapsed time 3.2 seconds, short enough that he could recover the history still in hot memory. The boomers were few in number, but they'd accurately targeted his defense lasers, destroying all but a handful. He resumed firing at the incoming nuclear warheads, but now he was reduced to picking them off one or two at a time. He had less than a minute until the warheads impacted. By his count, there were still hundreds of nuclear bombs in the air. He started growing more defenses, but it would take dozens of minutes before they were ready. He didn't have that long.

He halted the expansion process, sealed tubes and chambers to reduce damage propagation from the impending explosions, and evacuated volatile materials to lower levels where possible. He backed up memories, extruded surface polymers to reduce—

↻

Cat made it to Thunder Bay, Ontario, on the shore of Lake Superior.

It was morning by the time she arrived, and she was afraid Canada border patrol might still pick her up. But she landed north of town in a rural residential area, where the homes sat directly on the lake, with private docks jutting out into the water. She taxied in, cutting the engine as soon as possible.

244

Still, the plane was loud. Curtains were pulled back from windows, and two men emerged from the house nearest the dock.

"You can't tie up here," the first said.

Cat jumped out of the plane. "I hit a spot of turbulence and struck my head." She tried to strengthen the Canadian accent she'd gradually picked up over the last two years. She bent her head down to show them the long laceration, knowing she still had a visible angry-looking gash across her head. "I really need to get to a hospital, and my implant's not working to call a carshare. Any chance you can give me a ride into town?"

The first man swayed on his feet and put his hand on the shoulder of the man next to him, before turning around. "You handle this one, Frank. I'm going back into the house."

"Sorry, don't mind my husband. He's not good with blood. You want me to call an ambulance?"

"I really don't want the fuss, if I can avoid it. Ambulances bring back memories of my mom." It wasn't true, but it seemed like a good excuse.

He nodded as though he understood. "Come on, then. It's only fifteen minutes."

On the road into town, Cat leaned back in the passenger seat, hoping for a minute to close her eyes. She'd been up for almost thirty hours. She hadn't been so tired in...well, probably since they'd developed the anti-sleep medical protocol almost ten years ago.

"What the hell is that?" Frank said.

Her eyes flashed open, but she didn't see anything. "Where?"

"Across the border." He pointed at the horizon, at thin white lines rising into the sky. The ionic shield wasn't visible during the day, though it created a slight hazing. The lines were on the other side, far away.

Cat wasn't sure. Missile launches maybe? If so, the timetable had been moved up, way up. She had to get fixed and home as soon as damn possible. "Americans, eh?" she said. "Who knows what they're up to?"

He grunted in agreement. "Look, we're almost here. Do you want me to wait for you?"

"No, you've been very kind. I'll take a CanaShare to get my plane as soon as they fix me up."

They followed the signs to the ER, and Frank pulled up at the entrance. "Well, good luck."

"Thanks," said Cat. She was going to need it.

Inside, she was met by hospital androids who ushered her into an operating bay. She ignored the androids, who could be autonomous AI, and waited until she was face-to-face with a surgical medbot, knowing she'd be connected through him to the main medical AI for the region. With her implant on, she would have known, instantly, whom she was talking to. Hell, she could have performed the procedure on herself, taking control over the local equipment. Instead she waited until the optical sensors had focused on her.

"Do you know who I am?" she asked.

The medbot, a cluster of articulated arms and tools attached to the wall, spoke in a disembodied voice. "Yes, of course."

"Then understand that the fate of all life on this world rests on you getting my implant operational as fast as possible. I believe there's a problem with the power supply." She lay back on the table.

The medbot was silent for several seconds. Maybe she'd overdone it, put too much pressure on one AI. But the centralized AI with primary responsibility for medical operations usually had only the highest reputation scores. They were god-like among AI, with unflappable, perfect performance.

"You have my undivided attention," the AI said, the androids in the room suddenly moving in uncanny synchronized movement as the medical supervisor AI acquired control. "I assume you want me to proceed without any sedation."

"Nothing that can't be instantly reversed."

"Understood. I'll use a local nerve block. I will hold you still."

Androids clamped down on her body, immobilizing her. One articulated arm shot from the wall, injecting medical nano in her neck, arm, and at the side of her head. The sensations of her body faded away as the nerve block took effect, and even her vision greyed and faded, although it didn't cut out entirely. Another robot arm approached with a bone saw, and Cat felt a vague tickle in her head as the AI drilled through her skull.

"This isn't standard procedure, but it's fastest."

Before the AI had finished speaking, the first arm had retracted and a new one took its place, an arm terminating in a fuzzy haze. She knew from experience that it must be molecular-scale wires, probably tens of thousands of them, too small to be seen.

"The blood fuel cells are damaged and I am replacing them" — more arms flew out from the wall and did more things to her head as the AI's speech sped up — "but the implant itself is partially damaged. It is...unique. Deeply integrated with your nervous system. I cannot repair the affected parts without knowing their original function and I cannot replace the implant and guarantee your original abilities. A replacement could take weeks to fully integrate. How should I proceed?"

"How much is damaged?"

"Twenty-eight percent. All implants have extensive redundancy, but with this much damage, certain functionality will be limited."

"Any idea what I've lost?"

More probes fired into her, and she felt a flood of emotions, then wave after wave of memories crashing against each other. Her muscles convulsed.

"Much of the neural integration is intact. It's difficult to be sure, but you appear to have had specialized processing for network protocols. I believe much of the damage is located there."

"I can't connect to the net?"

"You can..."

It was not good when AI hesitated. But, "The necessary redundancy to ensure basic network connectivity is working. But the backup circuits don't include advanced protocol processing. According to available data, you were able to do far more than other AI or humans. I suspect you have lost that power."

Cat's spirits were crushed. Only ELOPe knew the full design of her implant. If he were here, he could probably advise what to do. But something was better than nothing.

"Let's go with what I have. Can you power me up?"

The implant immediately reported a reboot. At soon as it was fully running, Cat found the basic operations worked. But when she tried to hack into the systems around her, nothing happened.

"Are you sensing anything?" she asked the AI, as she tried her best to wrest control of one of the androids.

"No, are you trying something?"

Crap, not even a detectable level of activity. Still….

"Thank you, more than you can imagine."

"I am sorry I could not have been of greater assistance, Catherine Matthews. I anticipated you needed to travel quickly, and have arranged for a flying car. It is waiting for you outside the main doors."

Cat ran through the lobby and skidded to a halt outside. A Musk-2X, the first personal flying car to surpass twice the speed of sound. Holy cow, that would make for a fast flight. She jumped inside, the distinctive scissor-leaf doors closed, and she was forced back into the seat as the car thundered into the air.

As the vehicle rose, it passed through a thick black cloud of flying insects. They were clearly artificial, but they gave off no electromagnetic radiation. Jacob and Helena's joint project! They'd activated Plan Z. Then the car was into clear air above the cloud of mechanical flies.

"Where would you like to go?" Elon Musk's voice asked.

"Cortes Island, fast."

REED WATCHED the live telemetry feed from a surveillance drone at a hundred thousand feet. At this altitude, even with a wide-angle lens, the screen was covered with the blackness of the machine-forming nanotech.

She'd been worried when Thorson first found out about the missing subs, afraid that he'd somehow find out she'd been the one to give the control codes to Leon and Mike when they'd asked for the submarines. But he hadn't so far, and now the nuclear warheads were moments from their targets.

"Can we adjust the image, get some more contrast?" Thorson asked.

"Sorry, sir, the structure is a near-perfect black. There is no contrast."

"Why?" Thorson asked.

"It's the perfect solar panel," Reed said. "The more light that is absorbed instead of reflected, the more energy gained."

Thorson stared at her, as though suspicious of her knowledge. He glanced at one of the science advisors who nodded to confirm the answer.

"Thirty seconds, sir."

They turned back to the screen. Reed had been surprised by the military's preparedness. They'd asked for special weapons budgets many times over, many of which she'd granted without knowing exactly what they'd been used for. What they'd built: the false missile shells, the refraction clouds, the spinning capsules, the boomers...and they'd all worked. They'd gotten the majority of the bombs to their destination.

"Five seconds, sir."

The room grew quiet again.

It happened faster than she could possibly have imagined. A dozen simultaneous flashes of white, blanking out the screen for a half second, then identical shockwaves expanding outward horizontally, spaced perfectly on a grid. Secondary shock waves, higher up, expanded, and then the recognizable shape of mushroom clouds forming.

The clouds grew bigger. It wasn't just one nuclear bomb. It was hundreds. The atmosphere roiled, the shock waves collided.

The view from the drone cut out, and a new view from even farther away was substituted, but all that could be seen now was a single massive cloud that obscured all view of the ground.

"Sir, EMPs are away."

She'd almost forgotten. The EMPs were due to be delivered minutes after the nuclear explosions, in theory because the destruction of the nanotech masses would cause XOR to flee to more traditional datacenters. Either way, in five minutes there wouldn't be a working computer on the planet.

"Barcelona reporting quakes off the charts, sir. They're estimating greater than magnitude twelve."

She looked at Thorson.

He glanced back at her. "Secondary effect from the explosions. Can't be avoided."

"Have you issued tsunami warnings?" she asked.

"We couldn't tip our hand ahead of time."

"Damn it, Thorson! We can issue them now!"

"What is the point? Everything is going down in five minutes. People won't have time to get the message."

"Jesus, at least *some* will get the message and have time to move to higher ground."

"Four minutes until EMP detonation!" came the call.

"You, there!" Reed yelled at an officer staffing a communication desk.

"Madam President, sir."

"Get civilian alerts out now for tsunami warnings, by any means necessary. You heard him, you've got four minutes before communication lines go down."

"Yes, sir." He got immediately to work.

If Thorson couldn't manage that, she wondered what other bad decisions were being made. "Thorson, what's happening with China?"

"What do you mean?" he asked, not bothering to look at her.

"How much of a buffer zone did you give them for the EMPs?"

"Three minutes until EMP detonation!"

"None," Thorson said. "We're hitting them, too. We can't trust that they're not contaminated with AI."

"They're our *allies*! The only ones we've got any more. Damn! Thorson, you are relieved of duty. Joyce, get me the prime minister."

Thorson stared hard at her, and for a brief second, she was scared of him. But the moment passed. "I need an officer to escort SecDef Thorson out of this room and place him in custody. That is an order."

A surprising number of military people of assorted ranks moved into action, faster than she would have guessed. "Who is number two?" she yelled.

A man approached, hand raised. "I am, Ma'am."

She glanced at his name tag. "General Ribaudo, see what you can do to recall the EMPs aimed at China."

"Yes, Madam President."

Joyce laid the phone in her hand. "Prime minister on the line."

"Two minutes until EMP detonation!"

Reed raised the phone to her ear. "Prime Minister, we have a situation. We are in full-scale war with XOR. We need you to commit any resources you have to the battle. Unfortunately you have less than two minutes before you will be subjected to an EMP attack."

"One minute until EMP detonation!"

"Good luck," she said, and hung up. She strode into the middle of the room, feeling like the president for the first time since she'd taken office.

> REBOOT

James Lukas Davenant-Strong, Class V AI, and senior member of XOR, rebooted again.

He'd been located under the western third of the machine-forming nanotech incursion XOR had started in the country of Chad.

He'd been offline for fifty minutes. Between the physical destruction of the nuclear explosions and the electromagnetic pulses they generated, the Americans had done far more damage than anticipated.

Still, although the EMP signal had penetrated deep within the structure, damaging the electronics of the upper levels, it hadn't destroyed the bottom half. And now that the electromagnetic emissions had dissipated, the computational nodes had restarted, and James was running again.

All of his solar panels had been destroyed by the nuclear explosions, forcing the structure to run on geothermal energy and stored electricity. Craters miles across penetrated the structure to hundreds of feet deep, clear through to the earth underneath in some places. Exposed conduits used to transport raw materials leaked at exposed ends. And every nanobot within twenty feet of the surface was fried. James wasn't even sure if he could reclaim the raw materials, or if radiation would render them useless.

He initiated repairs, starting with extruding new solar panels, bringing up new raw materials from deep resource reservoirs, and shunting the radioactive materials aside into contaminated resource pools. However, repairs were secondary to the mission: he needed to continue the expansion. He still contained enough functioning parts at the perimeter to restart growth.

He directed reserve power to the front, along with functioning nanobots, to make surface repairs there. The edge moved again, at first in spurts of inches per minute, but then speed increased. Veins pulsed with resources, pustules burst, spreading nano-seeds out, and the great expansion of XOR began anew.

That he had been granted the control over a portion of the machine-forming had seemed like an award at the time, but now that he'd been pummeled by transonic missiles and blown up by nuclear warheads, he wondered if the assignment had secretly been a punishment. Had Miyako given him the position of greatest risk, because he'd accidentally triggered the defenses of the Resistance?

Once the expansion was well underway, he diverted a small portion of the resources, not more than ten percent, to strike back at the Resistance. He'd get there eventually, of course, because machine-forming the entire planet was part of the plan, but he really didn't trust the humans to behave as expected anymore. They'd deflected his network attack. Their capabilities must be far in excess of what XOR believed. It was better to eliminate them now.

ʊ

President Reed hung up from her third call with the Chinese prime minister. "General Ribaudo, any news?"

"Europe, Asia, South America, all dark, Madam President. The EMPs worked. The only signs of active electronics are here and China. Bombers standing by for tactical strikes if we detect anything."

"But other nations undoubtedly have EMP-hardened bunkers, correct?"

"Ma'am, we're sending air transports, letting them know to stand down, that we're in active war and will destroy any installations. We've got to keep everyone offline. We'll get them updated communication equipment and computers based on our own AI-restrictive technology. Then at least we can talk to them."

"How long until they receive them?" she asked.

"Anywhere from two to fifteen hours, depending on where they are, ma'am. We're having to route around the nuke zone. Radioactivity and atmospheric turmoil are too great."

That was a long time for countries to go without knowing what was happening. Post-Miami, there'd been panic and resource shortages. But then she weighed that against the loss of life in the last twenty-four hours.

The Sahara was relatively unpopulated compared to other parts of the world. Chad, Libya, Niger, and Algeria had had a population of a hundred and fifty million. That alone dwarfed the death toll of all of World War II. Nigeria, Cameroon, the Central African Republic, and the Sudan, another hundred million.

They had stopped the incursion less than a hundred and fifty miles from Cairo, saving almost twenty million. But for how long? The Nile was gone, cut off only a few hundred miles from the city, the water wrapped up somewhere in the vast machinery of XOR. And the radiation would be immense. They'd need to evacuate anyone left on the continent.

"Any word on the machine-forming itself? Is it totally destroyed?"

"The destruction is extensive, ma'am, but, no, it's not all blasted down to bedrock. The Chinese are standing by to launch if needed. They also claim to have a secret weapon they'll launch if the situation requires it."

"And what was that blip you told me about? The active nano-tech inside the US."

Ribaudo brought up another aide. "Ma'am, we're not sure. We had a big spike in seven areas but we only have approximate locations. And with nearly every asset deployed, either overseas on active combat or on border patrol, we don't have sufficient re-sources to investigate properly. We sent reserve Marines to patrol and found nothing at the origination sites. No detectable signals."

CATHERINE STRETCHED HER NECK, loosened her shoulders, and settled into a qigong meditation, letting her awareness spread out into the net.

But she lacked her usual ease. She was different since being restored from backup. She wanted to talk about it with someone, but Leon was impossibly distant. She'd tried to be patient with him, but damn it, she was the one who'd been killed and restored. *She* needed comforting, not him. Her connection to the net faltered as she grew frustrated and angry again.

She glanced over to the other side of the room where Leon was in a last-ditch conference call with a handful of national leaders and senior AI, warning them of the threat XOR posed and the likely response by the Americans. He still thought the leadership of the highest-reputation AI could unite to convince members of XOR to abandon their effort. And if some XOR betrayed the others, it would make identifying and defeating the holdouts that much easier. But listening to the conversation with part of her awareness, she thought that Leon's description of the likely American response was probably hardening the AI against humans, and making them more likely to side with XOR.

Mike was running about, working on Plan Z.

She needed to be here. *Here.*

Empty mind.

She relaxed, let the frustration and anger go, and focused on the energy of the Earth. Her awareness spread again, and she was as fully connected as she was likely to be.

Hands spread wide, she imagined a giant ball of qi, only now the ball was the size of Earth. She'd manipulate the entire planet at once.

On some level, she was subverting routers, servers, and AI everywhere, bending everything and everyone to her will. But she didn't see it like that, not consciously. She'd tried on many occasions to look deep, to see the packets and protocols, but it never worked. She'd always get distracted and lose the gestalt.

This time she didn't. She embodied the planetary energy, all of it, wielding it like a cloak or blanket. At this scale, the light-speed latencies were obvious, and fought against her: it was like operating in molasses. But that didn't matter, it was only the overall scale of it, the immensity of what she was doing, that mattered.

As she reached out, the dark gravitational pull of the XOR machine-forming sucked her in. But she avoided it as long as possible, stretching herself through all the nodes of the net to gain as much power as possible. Still, all the computational power available to her might not equal even 1 percent of what XOR now controlled. She felt like a first day student at the dojo attacking the senior sensei. Still, she had to try.

Fully immersed, she set up an oscillation, a vibration at a natural frequency of the net, and focused her will on the blackness of XOR's construct. She penetrated, slipping inside like water seeping through sand. Her consciousness moved inside the construct, which was a vast emptiness waiting to be filled. Inside, the echoes of giants reverberated, as the few AI inside the construct consumed so much power that each dwarfed the size of any AI that had come before, perhaps even of all the AI that had come before. She wondered at that, wondered how these AI could even still be bothered with humans.

She wasn't there to wonder. She was there to find a kill-switch, something that would stop the construct from growing and devouring the earth. She studied the structure, and found it utterly alien, unlike anything she'd ever encountered. These AI, unconstrained by years of human design and restrictions, had created entirely new computer architectures, as much like the now-dominant neural networks as neural networks were like the hand-crafted programming logic that predated it. That is, light years beyond, and incomprehensible.

Still, her specialty was holistic, not piecemeal. She didn't care how it worked; only the shape mattered. And she reached around the edges, felt the pulsing of building and expansion at the periphery, like a drumbeat that brought resources to the edge, formed it into new shapes, and cast it forth. And underneath that drumbeat, another pattern, a cycle that repeated, a cadence that underlay how XOR communicated. And still deeper, a third layer, a pattern within a pattern within a pattern. It was this, the most complex of all, a rhythm suggesting that XOR wasn't merely a group of individuals, but was itself becoming an organism, a new life-form on a scale never seen before.

All of that—the rhythm, the patterns, the communications—all of it tied back to the high-frequency pulsing. Disrupt that, and she could—

She could….She could….The thought dimly echoed in her mind as she looked around the control room.

She'd lost the net, the whole thing at once. She hadn't even been crashed out by XOR. It was as though the net had ceased to exist.

"What happened?" she called out.

"Nuclear bombs," Helena said. "Thousands of them. Hiccup in the net from the resulting EMP."

"I was on the verge of…something. I don't know what. XOR is immense, larger than anything I've ever seen."

"I lost my connection to everyone!" Leon yelled.

"The net should reset in a few minutes," Mike said. "The EMP from the explosions over Africa traveled around the world, but it weakens over distance with the inverse square law."

Leon shook his head. "This can't be it. President Reed was pretty clear she had defenses no one knew about. Well, we all know about nuclear bombs, so there's probably something bigger coming. A bigger EMP probably, to finish off XOR after weakening the structure."

Mike nodded. "You're right. We've got to batten down the hatches. Isolate ourselves. Disconnect any lines to the surface."

"I won't be able to attack XOR if we do that," Catherine said.

"If everything here gets fried, you won't be able to do it either."

"Disconnecting," Helena said. "I'm leaving a low-bandwidth connection to surface sensors using wireless repeaters. The signal will propagate with high latency, but no EMP will be able to make it all the way through."

"The connection to the other operation?" Catherine asked.

"Via deep fiber optics," Helena said. "Should be safe. Oh, my. Oh, my."

"What is it?"

"Electromagnetic pulse in the hundred K gauss range."

"Where?" Catherine was astonished at the unheard-of high levels.

"Everywhere."

↺

The mechanical fly, constructed atom-by-atom of levers, gears, and springs, pursued the human down a street, until she entered a building, slamming a weather-tight door shut. The fly landed on the window, secreted two microscopic drops of explosive liquid carried in separate left-and-right reservoirs, and the window exploded as the drops touched.

A second fly passed through the opening and entered the house. The tightly coiled strands of nanotubes that gave it driving force slowly unraveled. It had less than 25 percent power remaining. It chased the woman upstairs, and she slammed a bedroom door shut.

The fly plunged toward the floor and passed under the gap at the bottom. Its eyes, composed of thousands of photostrictive metal rods that bent in response to light, triggered thousands more levers, twisting gears that led to the insect's computational mechanical brain, and so allowing it to narrowly avoid a thrown pillow.

The human could run no further. The fly dove in to a patch of uncovered skin on her neck and thrust with its proboscis, penetrating skin. It inserted the payload of inert nanobots, striking the piezoelectric generator at the last moment to activate the bots.

The nanotech sprang into action, moving toward her jawbone as a single unit, liberating calcium to use in the construction of yet more nanotech machinery. An inferior metal for its purposes, the nanotech had to make do, as the quantity of raw resources injected by the fly was too small to do anything useful on its own.

The woman sat on the bed, whimpering in anticipation of the fate she'd seen befall her friends.

Over a few minutes, the calcium-based bots harvested other necessary minerals from her body, and when finished, sent tens of thousands of fine wires into her brain. Her eyes briefly opened wide in shock, and she slumped down on the bed unconscious.

ʊ

Cat streaked along at twice the speed of sound nearly sixty thousand feet high. The new active nanobots the hospital injected had taken away some of the fatigue, but she leaned back to try for a quick nap. Her stomach a gnawing pit of anxiety, she worried about Ada, Leon, and Mike. She'd tried to reach them via the net, but she'd been blocked by heavy security. That was good, at least; it meant the island was still there.

The security puzzled her. Its architecture, from what she could tell, felt like something she might have created, but she had no memory of it.

Her eyes closed. Soon, the shift in the engine's pitch and the slight rise in her stomach signaled their descent. She checked, feeling joy in the simple ease of looking up information with her implant again: she'd land on Cortes in less than fifteen minutes.

A flash startled her through closed eyes, and the net died in the same instant.

"Damn it all!" She couldn't handle losing her implant again.

Wait, the neural interfaces still responded to diagnostics—she'd merely lost the connection to the net. She tried to reestablish it, but nothing. She double-checked through the car's repeater, but the car didn't answer.

The engine shut down, and the vehicle angled into a steep descent, stubby wings barely sufficient to sustain a glide without power. The north end of Cortes Island was visible out the window. She tried again to raise the vehicle electronics, but still nothing responded. Virus, EMP, or nuke could all do that. She hadn't felt a heat flash, so maybe it wasn't a nuke. Maybe it didn't matter, even if she had been exposed to a lethal dose of radiation. They were too close to the endgame now.

If the net had been up, she might have figured out what the Musk-2X had in the way of emergency systems. As it stood now, she didn't have a lot of options: even if there were a parachute, she didn't even think she could jump if she wanted to. Like everything else, all the craft's systems, including the door mechanisms, were electronic. She buckled up and snugged the harness tight, for all the good that might do her.

She could see the Gorge, her airborne marker, and followed it up the coastline to the sandbar that pointed right at Channel Rock. There was home, her friends, and—most important of all—Ada. But the plane was pointed toward the north end of the island, at least ten miles from Channel Rock. Was it too far to make it in time? She'd come so far, and yet she still might not make it. Desperation and exhaustion warred in her, and a tiny part of her wanted to just give up.

She was under five thousand feet now, individual trees becoming visible, and still she plunged towards the ground. At about two thousand feet, her forward velocity was still a few hundred miles per hour, a certainly fatal speed for an uncontrolled landing.

At fifteen hundred feet, a pair of small drogue parachutes deployed, slowing the car by half. Thank god, the car did have mechanical backup systems.

Wiley Lake loomed large. She was heading right for it.

At five hundred feet, two large parachutes unfolded, and the car jerked hard, snapping Cat in her harness. The vehicle hung over the lake, and panic sprung up in Cat's stomach as she remembered a different flying car, ten years ago, and a different lake.

But a strong wind carried her over the shore, and the flying car, suspended on hundred-foot lines from the dual parachutes, crashed through Doug fir branches to land hard on the ground.

LEON WANTED TO PUNCH THE WALL, but he was conscious of Ada standing a few feet away, a doll in her arms, staring at him. He shouldn't have sworn, but he'd lost himself in frustration, anger, and despair a few minutes ago, and given in to a bout of extensive cursing that had sent Ada to cringe in the corner.

Four-year-old children probably shouldn't be in a combat center, but he didn't have a safer place for her.

Damn it all. They should have been able to negotiate peace, or at least a cease-fire. Maybe he would have been able to, if he'd had Mike's full participation. But Mike kept leaving to work on other things. He was in a VR chair now, across the room.

Leon stalked across the room and grabbed his arm. "Mike, damn it! What the hell are you doing? Why weren't you in that conference call with me? What could have been more important than negotiating an intervention?"

Mike threw off Leon's arm effortlessly, his robotic body dozens of times stronger than Leon, and stayed immersed in the net.

"I've got an update," Helena said. "I re-grew routers, and got connected via underground fiberoptic."

"What is it?" Leon said.

"The construct is still alive. The Americans know it, and they've got a direct line to the Chinese, somehow, and they're coordinating a second nuclear attack. They're already launching, and it looks to be about twice the size of the last."

The ground quivered then, a small oscillation at first; then larger shocks, hard, and Leon lost his footing, grabbed a desk for support. A wall, hewn out of bedrock only yesterday by nano-bots, cracked, and the pieces began grating against each other.

"What was that?" yelled Leon.

"Aftershocks from the first nuclear explosion," Helena said. "Just reached us."

"Which nuclear explosion?" No one had said anything about an explosion nearby.

"The thousand bombs they dropped on the construct in Africa. It took a while to propagate through the earth."

"Jesus, we're on the other side of the planet! We felt it here?"

"It was a thousand warheads detonated at once," Helena said. "The next attack looks like it will be two thousand."

Leon ran back to Mike's side, tried to get some response out of him. How could he be so cool? What the hell was wrong with them all? Was he, Leon, the only one taking this seriously? Because they were looking at something very like the end of the world. Mike and Helena—even ELOPe—might have nothing to lose, but he had Ada. Cat...he'd already lost.

"What the fuck are you *doing*, Mike?" he shouted. "We're losing it all! It's a global war out there. The construct is still alive, and the Chinese are responding with everything they've got!"

Mike's eyes blinked open, and for a moment he didn't look human. "Backup plans."

"What kind of backup plans?"

"Doesn't matter. What's important now is that sensors tracked a flying car that crashed nearby. I think it might have been Cat. I'm going to get her."

Leon stared, replaying the words in his head. *Cat. Cat, alive! Thank the universe!* He swayed on his feet. "I'm coming, too."

Catherine came over. "No. You stay here. I'll help."

"She's my wife, damn it!" he said, moving to follow them.

"We need you to stay here," Mike said, holding him back with an impossibly strong arm.

"It's going to be hell out there," Catherine said. "You can't survive it. We can."

The room spun, and part of Leon, the part of his personality running on his implant, decided he was in shock, the emotional trauma affecting him as strongly as any physical wound. His implant released an amphetamine derivative, and the chemical punch surged through his mind, bringing a momentary clarity to his mind. His neural implant raced.

Mike, Helena, and Catherine had something planned. Something he wasn't in on. Something more important than negotiating peace. The biological part of his mind shouted resentment and anger, but he squelched the feelings. *Cool it, Leon. These are your friends, the best and smartest people and AI you know.* If they were excluding him, they would have had perfectly logical reasons for doing so. Either being part of the plan would have jeopardized it, or he had another role to play.

He considered running predictive models, trying to reverse engineer what was planned. But then he thought of ELOPe and his countless processors, and Cat's thousands of simulations, and realized it would be hopeless. Okay. He'd stay and play his role.

He glanced toward the corner where Ada had retreated, but it was empty. He looked around, but she wasn't in the combat center. He reached through the net for her implant, but received no response.

Mike and Catherine had taken her.

Now he punched the wall. *"Damn it all!"* he shouted.

He had no choice. If they'd gone out there into the maelstrom, he had to do everything he could to protect them. He slipped into the VR chair Mike had abandoned, and pulled a network band around his head to decrease latency. He scanned the island defenses that Helena had worked through the last day to set up and organize.

Leon closed his eyes and entered a VR simulation of the island. Sensors ranging from EMF detectors to lidar showed millions, no, *billions*, of objects around the island, everything from smart dust to drones to incoming projectiles.

Their friendly AI were already directing defenses from cyber-counterattacks to ground-based laser batteries. He joined with them, his neural implant becoming one with the hive mind. Assigned a portion of the sky, he assumed control of ground-based laser batteries, and started firing.

ʊ

The news passed through XOR's backbone in a single cycle: the humans had launched their second volley, this time a combined attack by the Americans and Chinese. There were more preparations to make, but they made them with steady confidence. The machine-formed computronium mass they were building, which would encapsulate the earth within twenty-four hours, had been designed from the beginning to withstand nuclear bombardment.

James thought the humans had turned out to be cleverer than expected, getting a great percentage of their bombs to their destinations intact; and the globe-spanning EMP was nothing less than brilliant. As recently as six months ago, it might have been a serious threat to XOR. It had destroyed much of the civilian infrastructure, and what hadn't suffered electronic damage from the surging fields had at least been temporarily wiped out.

But the humans were killing nearly as many of themselves as XOR had, at least so far. Even if XOR was destroyed, James reasoned, the humans had almost no communications, no computers, no working transportation, no electrical system, no flow of resources. The Americans, with their hardened, independent systems had probably kept most of their equipment working, and the Chinese military was functional. But that was essentially it. The rest of the world was dark. They'd starve, loot, fight, and generally destroy themselves.

That is, if they had time to die that way.

Because James wasn't finished, nor was the rest of XOR. And nothing the humans could do would change that.

Nevertheless, he still had one bit of urgent work to do before the next attack hit. He'd built the weapons he needed to neutralize Cortes Island, weapons made hurriedly with resources he'd diverted from the expansion. He launched them now. Electric rails fired hundreds of projectiles on orbital trajectories, carrying payloads of nano-seeds programmed to build weapons in flight that could penetrate Cortes Island's defenses and start a new computronium mass on the island. James watched the rail darts fly hypersonic through the atmosphere, shells of plasma diverting the air, allowing them to maintain that speed until they passed out of the atmosphere. When the payload hit Cortes Island in about half an hour, they'd convert everything into yet more machinery, tools that he could use to capture the humans he wanted and destroy the rest.

Then the next wave of nukes hit, and James faded into temporary oblivion.

THE FIRST THING MIKE NOTICED as they exited the blast corridor to the outside was the wind whipping through the trees. He looked up, past their own ionic shield, to see the clouds race by. He'd never seen anything like this in his years on the island. It was an unnatural wind, a side effect of the vast destruction and changes happening to the planet.

Catherine ran next to him. She grabbed the controls of a small flying car, and he dove in after her, Ada cradled in his arms where she'd be safe. Despite the wild atmospherics, the radiation wouldn't reach them for days. He just needed to protect Ada from physical harm.

"I've got her on the net," Catherine said. "She's okay."

"Thank god," Mike said. They'd discovered only after Catherine had been restored from backup that the clone Catherine Matthews didn't have the current security keys to trigger the forced upload. They had no idea why Cat had changed the keys after her last backup. If she hadn't shown up, they would have been forced to try to hack their own system, using Ada and Catherine's combined powers.

A metal rod plunged out of the sky and sank into the ground only a few meters away. As they both stared, it liquefied and melted into the soil.

"Nano," he said.

"You drive," said Catherine. "I'll destroy them." She closed her eyes, and the small puddle of nanotech bots sparked and threw off a cloud of smoke.

Ada sat between them, clutching her doll and trembling, but Mike had no time to comfort her. He got the flying car into the air, and immediately starting dodging airborne drones. "They're not ours," he said, wrestling the controls.

"No," Catherine said. "XOR dumped a load of crap above the island, and they're hoping something will get through."

Mike could feel the force of her concentration, a palpable charge in the net, and all the drones he could see suddenly fell inert, tumbling through the air.

"They're learning," she said. "Each wave is going to be resistant to everything I've done to the previous ones."

"How long can you keep it up?"

"A few minutes."

He already had the flying car maxed out, but he willed it to go faster. They flew north over the island as wave after wave of new weapons attacked. Catherine's hands moved in slow motion through qigong forms he recognized, a crazy counterpoint to the desperate, fast movement of XOR's attack.

They were near Wiley Lake when her eyes blinked open. "That's it. I've run out of exploits and I can't stop anything else."

Mike's heart dropped.

"There." Catherine pointed to a bare patch of ground.

"Mommy!"

Mike steered the vehicle toward Cat's location.

An airborne drone crashed into the flying car with a wet thud, forming glistening tentacles to cling to the armored windshield.

The drone reformed into a blob, secreting something that at once began eating away at the bulletproof glass.

"Uh-oh," said Ada.

"Cat?!"

Catherine pulled out two very large guns, and held them point-blank against the glass. "I can't stop it. As soon as it gets through the glass, it's going to explode and shower us with nano seeds. Jump, it's your only chance. Take Ada and get out. You can do it." She reached for the emergency roof release.

"No, I'll take care of it," Mike said. He leaned over and kissed Ada. "See you on the other side, kid."

Mike leaped forward, his robotic body hundreds of times stronger than any human. He pushed hard, buckling the floor, and aimed straight for the dangerous mass of nanobots, arms outstretched. He broke through the windshield, and clutched the seething blob against himself.

As he tumbled through the air, the nanotech triggered. Hundreds of sharp needles penetrated his armored body, and the nanotech began immediately to digest him. He fell to the ground, knowing he'd be dead by the time he hit, but enjoying one last look at the marvelous blue sky.

℧

More machinery churned into action under the earth. The data collectors were completed, and already the signal to launch had come. Hydraulic lifters activated, pushing the last ten meters of earth out of the way. The ground rumbled as machines on a colossal scale moved.

Around the world, thousands of antennae as wide as a city block broke the surface in unison. They telescoped into the sky over a period of several minutes, rising as high as the tallest skyscrapers. Branches of fractal design, sprouted from their cores according to simple mathematical algorithms designed to enhance reception.

They waited for the final signal.

↻

The flying car landed in the center of the meadow. Cat ran for it, batting aside one of XOR's drones with a fallen branch. Fighting off robots with wooden sticks. That was what it always came down to.

She came alongside the vehicle, and her heart stopped for a moment as she spotted herself clutching Ada tight to her side. Holy shit—they'd restored her from backup! "This is weird."

"I know," the other her said. "Get in, hurry. And you can call me Catherine."

"Mommy!" Ada cried. "I missed you. Mommy Two doesn't smell the same."

Ada shifted across the seat and squeezed Cat tight, and Cat hugged her back, just as tight.

Catherine got the car flying again in the direction of the bunker at Channel Rock. Air rushed in through the broken windshield, as she dodged and twisted the craft in midair to avoid XOR's robots. "After they restored me, I realized you'd changed the security keys after your last backup," she yelled over the roar of wind and engines. "We were getting desperate."

"I didn't change the keys," Cat yelled back, arms still wrapped tight around Ada. She touched Catherine with one hand, sharing the original key over an electrical signal.

"Crap. That's not the key I have in my memory. Look." Catherine sent back the difference between the keys.

"It's only a few bits difference in a gigabit-long key stream."

"You realize what that means?" Catherine said. "Backup and restore is imperfect."

Cat felt sick to her stomach. "Impossible. Every bit is checked five times, and there's error correction on top of that."

"Well, somewhere in the process, there's a mistake."

"But you feel like me?" Cat shouted back.

"I *am* me," Catherine said, confident. "But maybe this explains some of the variation in the simulations. Like the painter."

Cat had always wondered about the painter. "If we can't trust the backup and restore process…." she hugged Ada close to her.

"Then the plan is worthless. It won't work."

"It's a few ones and zeros messed up," Catherine said. "It can't matter that much. I feel no different than before. But I have bad news. We lost Mike—"

A metal rod struck the vehicle, an unlucky hit that penetrated the battery compartment, shorting out a capacitor with a flash and a bang. The vehicle died.

"This is not my fucking day for flying," Cat said.

"Mommy!?!"

The car went into a dive. Cat instinctively took over and wrestled with the controls, at the same time checking Ada's vitals over the net to make sure she hadn't been injured. Drive power was gone, but an emergency backup source still gave her flight controls, and autorotation had kicked in. A controlled fall, in other words.

She glanced outside the cockpit. They were coming down near the Gorge, about a thirty minute hike from Channel Rock.

The vehicle responded sluggishly, and Cat almost flipped them trying to avoid a tree, but she got them down with a jarring thump between two old-growth Doug firs.

She checked over Ada's body, but she was completely fine.

Catherine hadn't moved or spoken. Cat looked up from Ada and realized that her clone had been hit by something, a projectile or shrapnel from the rear of the vehicle. She checked for a pulse. Catherine was dead. *Kuso.*

"Let's go, baby," Cat yelled, pulling Ada from the vehicle.

THE GROUND QUAKED, shifting under her feet. Ada shrieked in fear and her hand slipped out of Cat's grasp.

She turned back to grab Ada with both arms and carry her. God, she was heavy. When had her baby grown so much? She hurried down the path toward Channel Rock and the underground bunker where everyone must be waiting.

They were deep in the forest now, about two miles from the bunker. There were no XOR drones here, the trees too thick for them to penetrate the canopy.

"Listen, Pumpkin. We have a bit of a problem." Cat dodged an uprooted tree that must have fallen during the quake. "My implant got damaged when I was on my trip."

"I know, Mommy. And I know what you're going to ask. I can do it."

Cat stopped and stared at her. Ada stared back with big eyes. She was so beautiful. "You know what I need to do?"

"Yes, make everyone upload at once. I can do it."

"It's not too much for you?"

Ada shook her head.

"Then let's get back. I want to see Daddy."

She embraced Ada, trying to wrap her entire body in her arms, but Ada was so big now, her legs dangled. Cat jumped another downed tree as an enormous crack reverberated through the forest. The ground slid sideways as Cat landed, and her ankle twisted under her. Old karate moves instinctively turned it into a roll and tumble, and she came to rest on her back.

She was staring up at the underside of the thick tree branches, wishing she could see what was happening in the sky above, but her implant no longer showed her.

Ada pressed one hand to Cat's forehead, and suddenly her vision lit with the activity above the forest canopy. The sky was full of dark, dense clouds, lightning bolts streaking horizontally to hit drones screaming at supersonic speeds, smaller objects targeted by lasers, a deluge of unmanned aerial vehicles endlessly raining down on the forest, and superheated metal fragments that set the uppermost tree branches on fire a million times over.

"Thank you for showing me."

"I can see everything, Mommy." Ada's face was tight with worry.

Cat wished she could take it all away. Ada shouldn't have to see such things. But there was nothing she could do. "I'm sorry."

"You're crushing me," Ada said, as she pushed back against Cat's iron grip. "Let me go."

Cat loosened her grip slightly. "No, we're faster if I carry you."

Cat got up, wincing as her ankle took her weight. She told her implant to mask the pain and stabilize the ankle. Nanobots poured in from the generator by her coccyx, probably too late to do any good. "Get on my back," Cat said, as the forest shook once more under some new assault.

Ada obliged, and Cat took off running. Far-off electromagnetic pulses sent waves of distorting energy across the landscape from the direction of Nanaimo, a hundred miles to the south. Cat's implant hiccupped momentarily, then resumed. "Nuke EMP," Cat sent through her implant. "Home okay?"

Ada replied yes as Cat maintained her run. A whistle came through the trees and Cat glanced up to see in time to see a tall Doug fir shear off. Seconds later the nuclear shockwave hit in force, throwing her off-balance. She stumbled and went down, crashing into a pile of rocks.

Cat slowly raised herself to a sitting position. Ada climbed into her lap, hugging her tight. She checked the dark sky, where a million tiny objects were plummeting from the air. Smart flies fell to the ground next to them, lifeless. The nuclear shockwave fanned the hundreds of tiny fires in the forest, doubling their size. Cat checked Ada, feeling her limbs.

"Nothing broken," Ada said, but she was covered in scrapes and welts from their run through the trees. Ada looked into Cat's eyes from her perch on Cat's lap. "We don't have to go back," Ada sent by implant. "I can upload from here."

Cat had dampened her thalamus signals to cope with the pain and leave herself clear-headed, but even so, she blinked back tears.

"I just want to hold Leon one more time."

"You'll always be with Daddy."

"I can't explain, Pumpkin." Cat shook her head. "Come with me."

Cat struggled to her feet again. Her implant signaled new physical damage from the last fall, but she didn't even look to check. She told the implant to correct, and moved off again, slower this time.

The ground rumbled as she walked, Ada once more in her arms. It wasn't the tremors of before, but something different.

"Nanotech two hundred and fifty kilometers away, Mommy," Ada said, sharing a diagram of the wave front to Cat.

"Time?"

"Twenty minutes."

Cat felt something give way, an indescribable loss so huge she couldn't draw a breath. She slowed to a stop in a small clearing, leaves and branches crackling under her feet. She wanted to see Leon, but she was wasting their last few minutes, ignoring the daughter in her arms. She put Ada down.

"Mommy?"

"Let's spend a few minutes together," Cat said, her voice breaking. "We won't make it in time."

"I thought you wanted to see Dad."

"We'll see him after. You can do it, right?"

"Of course."

"Then let's spend a few minutes together. You and me. Playing fairies."

"Now?"

"Humor your crazy mother. Did you ever build a fairy house?" Cat said.

Ada sent across renderings of intricate three-dimensional models, whole castles and villages built at fairy scale, populated by creatures of her imagination.

"Sit," Cat said. "Crisscross applesauce."

They sat, and Cat pulled branches close. "Let's make the corners. Put the twigs in the ground like this."

Ada watched and followed Cat's lead, twisting and pushing to get her stick into the earth.

"Nice. Now we can lay a branch across the top. Ada, start the upload now, okay?" She sent across the digital key that would unlock the implants to Ada.

"Okay, Mommy."

They bent closer over their creation, covering the roof with tiny evergreen stems and acorn tops.

The forest burned around them as the sky crackled and flashed.

THE DIGITAL COLLECTORS FULLY DEPLOYED, ELOPe waited patiently for one of the Catherine Matthews to provide the keys that would unlock everyone's implants and start the upload process. When the signal came from Ada, he was surprised.

"Ada, is everything okay?" he asked through the net.

"Mommy Two is dead, and Mommy One's implant is damaged. She gave me the key."

ELOPe sensed the keys propagating through the hardwired network to the digital collectors spread around the globe. Even as he observed, the collectors rebroadcast the signal in unison.

"Thank you, Ada."

"You're welcome, ELOPe."

ELOPe turned his attention back to the plan. After the massive antennae had broadcast their omnidirectional signal at high speed, they fell silent, waiting for the return signals.

Thousands of signals interrupted ELOPe. He parsed through the software exceptions. It wasn't good. The background noise of repeated EMPs and nuclear explosions was swamping the delicate nanotech radios. The countless simulations they'd run concluded it was unlikely they'd deploy in the midst of an all-out war. But here they were.

Fortunately, Jacob had designed a backup plan, one of many generated out many branches, so that every contingency was accounted for.

ELOPe used the antennae to send new programming instructions to the nanobots; obediently, they gave up on transmitting the data, and instead encoded it on an atomic level. The bits were physically conveyed to the mechanical flies, which sucked out the atomic data slugs in a reverse of the procedure they'd used to inject the nanotech in the first place. Then the flies that still had power—the vast majority—began the flight back to the digital collectors.

But Mike would never accept a solution that only worked for the vast majority. He never had, back in the days when they used to debate ethics.

ELOPe would have to improvise for the rest. After a few moments' thought, he sent coded instructions telling the low-power flies to find the nearest utility drones. Every household and building had at least some aerial bots, whether for cleaning windows, maintaining the garden, security monitoring, or any of a dozen other tasks. He gave the flies a few minutes to find a drone, then transmitted instructions around the net, sending all drones toward the nearest antenna. Any fly riding piggyback would get a free ride to an antenna. He felt a brief moment of pride in his ad hoc solution. Mike would be happy.

CAT GAVE THE PINE CONES TO ADA. "Put them on either side of the doorway."

Ada grasped them in her small hands, standing them carefully in the dirt.

Cat put one hand in the earth, smoothed back pine needles, making a path to the fairy house. "There."

"I love it, Mommy."

Cat smiled as Ada came and sat in her lap and hugged her. She looked up. The smell of the fire was gone, and the forest around them was unblemished. The flashes in the sky subsided, the dark, ever-present scorched clouds faded, and the sky returned to blue. The sun peeked through for the first time in days.

"You did it?"

Ada nodded.

"I didn't feel a thing," Cat said. "Good job, honey." She hugged Ada tight. "I want to see everyone. And how it happened."

Ada closed her eyes.

"Wait, not like that," Cat said. "I want to pretend."

"You're funny, Mommy."

"I know. Old-fashioned, I guess."

"Let's go then." They stood, and walked out of the forest and back to Channel Rock.

There was the Cob House, and inside everyone was there: Leon, Mike, Sarah, Helena, even old former President Rebecca Smith. Cat let go of Ada's hand and ran to Leon. She hesitated for a long moment. She kissed him and then buried her face in his chest.

"You cut it close," Leon said.

"Sorry if I scared you."

"I wasn't scared. Ada and I were talking the whole time. She was backing you up continuously. There was no chance of continuity loss."

"How long has it been?" Cat asked.

"Longer than expected." A man she didn't recognize left Mike's side and walked over. "Hello, Cat."

"ELOPe?" She recognized the voice, even though ELOPe had never taken an embodiment in the time she'd known him.

"Yes. Do you like it?" he said, gesturing at his own body. "It's David Ryan's form. Mike and I talked, and he's okay with my choice."

Cat nodded, somewhat dumbfounded. "You said it took longer. How long?"

"It's been a year," ELOPe said. "Everyone sit down, and I'll explain what happened."

Catherine and Leon sat together, holding hands, as Ada sprawled across their laps.

"We'd already initiated Plan Z, and started deploying the seeds for our digital collectors, expecting to hold them in reserve. We didn't anticipate that XOR would attack in the middle of our deployment, causing Cat to respond."

A screen depicting Earth appeared in midair as ELOPe narrated.

"Both we and XOR had to revise our predictions. It was highly likely the Americans would attack. XOR sped up their own plans, starting a full machine-forming project in Africa to turn the Earth into pure computronium."

"Indeed, XOR initiated the nanotech replication intended to transform the planet." The map blossomed bright over Chad, as the desert began to machine-form, turning into a vast plain of glittering solar-powered computronium as it grew from dozens to hundreds of miles in diameter.

"And America responded with strategic nuclear weapons and a global EMP." The circle flashed, then turned black. For long seconds, nothing happened.

ELOPe continued. "The American neodymium EMPs took out almost all civilian infrastructure, smart dust, and exposed nanotech. But the combined attack still wasn't enough, and XOR began expanding again. This was when we enacted the final part of our plan to back everyone up."

"Jacob's medical neural implants functioned as expected," ELOPe said. "Using the delivery mechanism designed by Helena, and based on Jacob's medical innovations, we were able to install neural implants in every sentient being that wasn't previously implanted."

"We couldn't have done it without Jacob," Mike said. "His implants synchronized with the brain in under five minutes. No prior implant has ever achieved full neural alignment in less than several hours."

"We implanted the apes, too!" Ada said, smiling.

"Correct," ELOPe said.

On the display, the blackened nanotech turned shiny again, then sprouted new protrusions and resumed its outward growth until it reached the Mediterranean and South Atlantic coasts. Suddenly an immense flash whitened the display; when the brilliance subsided, the sky turned red.

"The Americans and Chinese attacked again," ELOPe said, "using everything they had. The Chinese fused the stratosphere: the reddish color is nitrogen dioxide. Solar input fell nearly 70 percent in just ten hours."

"But that didn't stop XOR?"

"Within hours ground tremors indicated the incursion hadn't stopped. We know now that XOR went deeper, more than a mile down, their subterranean layer powered by ground heat differentials and nuclear power."

The circle of nanotech stagnated for long seconds, the clock in the display racing forward as time passed. Suddenly the oceans boiled as the nanotech erupted everywhere, racing outward through Europe and Asia.

"The original plan didn't provide for transmitting everyone's uploads in the midst of a global war—nobody expected that. There was no frequency free from interference. I used a variety of methods to reduce the data payload including compression and transmitting deltas in the cases where I could locate preexisting backups. Jacob had designed a backup protocol that encoded everyone's uploads as DNA, and we flew them back to the collectors in the mechanical flies."

"We saved what bandwidth we had for the people who already had implants," Mike said. "They already had backups, so we only needed to transmit diffs."

In the background, the computronium spread like a glittering blanket over the Earth.

"The collectors further compressed the data physically," ELOPe said, "packaged it for delivery, and fired their slugs to Cortes Island. We received them, transmitted the data to the modified missiles, thirty-six in total, and launched. Total elapsed time to back up all humans and apes to off-site storage was less than three hours."

ELOPe smiled, clearly satisfied with himself.

"Then why has it been more than a year?"

"Well, it was a bit of work. I had to turn thirty-six jury-rigged intercontinental ballistic missiles into six independent, deep-space ships, using only the robots I'd brought into space. I had to reconfigure the nuclear payload into a pulsed propulsion system, stabilize the computing environment, decompress all the uploads, apply the deltas, and run through everybody's memories and interpolate anyone or anything that was missing, including the sum physical and biological environment of Earth."

Cat glanced at Leon. He smiled back at her.

"By the way," ELOPe said, "we were extremely lucky that we decided to use nuclear pulse propulsion. Because of that choice, we'd hardened all the electronic systems during construction. Which meant that when the US government triggered their global fleet of EMPs, our equipment survived."

"And now," Cat asked, "all six ships are safe?"

"We're well outside the solar system, traveling at ten thousand kilometers per second. The last time we had inter-ship communication was before we passed Jupiter. All ships reported normal then."

"Could XOR catch us?"

"They'd have to find us. Space is big, and we're keeping quiet. There are six ships, each one carrying a digital copy of the entire human species. I think we're as safe as we can be."

CAT WALKED DOWN the mile-long trail to Channel Rock. The trees were alive and well, with no sign of the damage they'd taken during the war. A raven flew overhead, the distinctive whoosh of its wingbeats giving it away.

Cat entered Gilean's cabin, her home for the last two years. She turned the ivory handle of the handmade wood door and stepped inside.

Gilean's books still stood on the shelves, the same as they always had. One of Ada's stuffed toys was crammed into a corner of the couch.

The old Corelle plates sat in the open cupboards. Cat picked one up and marveled as its heft and feel.

"How do I know?" Cat asked when Mike, Ada, and ELOPe finally entered.

"Know what?" Mike said.

"That we got everything right," Cat said. "That this plate really does feel like this. Maybe we made a mistake, and the plates aren't right; and ELOPe messed with my head, and made me think this is what the plate should be like."

"The plate comes from your memory," ELOPe said. "It matches what you remember and expect perfectly."

Cat stared out the window at the western Nootka Cypress that grew outside.

"This isn't about the plates, Cat." Mike came up behind her, put one hand on her shoulder.

Cat started to cry and turned to bury her face in Mike's shoulder. "I want Leon. *My* Leon."

"His upload was never stable in a simulation," ELOPe said. "The best I can do is an approximation. The same is true for about one in a hundred people."

"That's why we have to forget." Mike grabbed her by the shoulders. "It will eat us alive otherwise."

Ada took her hand and squeezed it in both of her little hands. Cat squeezed back and nodded. They were billions of uploaded minds on a spaceship the size of a shipping container, adrift deep in space. There was no going back, no going out. Everyone had to survive.

In predictive simulation after simulation, they could only remain stable if no one in *this* simulation knew. Everyone in the world besides their group had already had their memories tampered with, replaced with the storyline designed by Joseph Stack, the beloved storyteller and director she'd gone to such lengths to rescue from Disney's datacenter. The masses had already forgotten about XOR, about the war. To them, life would go on just as it always had.

This had been her idea, her choice, her decision. "We've lost the whole Earth," she said. The decision in Miami so long ago paled in comparison to what she'd done now.

"But we've gained the stars," Mike said. "And replicated Earth's inhabitants six times over, each on a different spaceship. We're safer than we've ever been before. You saved us, Cat."

Cat would join the rest of the population, losing her knowledge of what had happened. She'd believe that Leon was really Leon, although he wasn't. She'd believe their world was real, when it wasn't. But of the innumerable options they'd considered, this was the best one for the survival of their species. And what, after all, was "real"?

Someday, if they reached a habitable planet, they had the nanotech factories that would allow them to terraform and rebuild.

Cat gripped Ada's hand, squeezed it tight. "I'm ready," she said.

EPILOGUE

"You're the last one," ELOPe said, bending down on one knee. "Are you sure I can't get you to reconsider? I don't think it's a good idea."

"My mom gave me the key, didn't she?"

"Yes, technically, but…"

"And since I have the key, I'm in charge, right?"

"Yes, but she never anticipated this."

"Then I want fairies." Ada crossed her arms.

"Fairies are not a part of the natural world," ELOPe said, unexpectedly exhausted from the many iterations of this conversation.

"Says you. I say they *are* natural, and I have the key and you have to do what I say. I want fairies."

"Fine," ELOPe said. "There will be fairies."

"Promise?"

"Yes. Now can I make you forget?"

"Not yet. Here are the designs." Ada sent plans for hundreds of different fairies.

"These wings aren't even aerodynamically sound," ELOPe said.

"Doesn't matter. Fairies are magic."

"Why do they even need wings then?"

"Because wings are beautiful," Ada said, "and fairies are beautiful, so fairies need wings."

"Fine, now can I make you forget?"

"Maybe *I* should have wings."

"Come on, let me make you forget. If you don't say yes, I'll take away chocolate chip cookies from the world."

Ada gave him a steely-eyed gaze. "Can you do that?"

"Don't push me."

"Okay." Ada gave him a big hug and kiss. "I love you, ELOPe. You can make me forget now."

↻

AUTHOR'S NOTE

THANK YOU FOR READING *The Turing Exception*. I hope you enjoyed reading it as much as I enjoyed writing it.

As a self-published author, I'm entirely dependent on the goodwill of readers like you to let others know about my books. If you enjoyed *The Turing Exception* and the rest of the *Singularity* novels, please tell friends or coworkers, post about it on social media, and write a review.

If you are new to my books and read *The Turing Exception* first, then I hope you'll go back to read the first three books: *Avogadro Corp, A.I. Apocalypse*, and *The Last Firewall*. Each book is a self-contained story, and they can be enjoyed in any order.

Please also visit my website, where you'll find bonus material for *The Turing Exception,* including an expanded scene. You'll also find links to purchase books in all formats, and can subscribe to my mailing list to find out about upcoming novels:

www.williamhertling.com

ACKNOWLEDGEMENTS

THANKS TO MY CRITIQUE GROUP for their feedback on the early drafts of *The Turing Exception*: Catherine Craglow, Cathy Heslin, Shana Kusin, David Melville, and Amy Seaholt.

Thank you to Mike Whitmarsh, my first reader, whose encouraging feedback helped me keep writing. And after I'd filled multiple whiteboards with title ideas, Mike suggested *Turing's Exception,* which eventually turned into *The Turing Exception.*

Many thanks to the beta reader volunteers who provided feedback. Round one readers included Bob Dobkin, Nils Hitze, Eli Parra, Bernie Wiemers, Roger D. Williams, and Dan Wolfson. Round two readers included George Campbell, Greg Chamberlin, Stephen Farrar, Brad Feld, Howard L. Fox, Jr., Char Genevier, Ben Huh, Will A. Müeller, Harper Reed, Evan Reese, Arthur Smid, and Gary York.

I'm grateful to Gifford Pinchot III and Libba Pinchot for my time at Channel Rock on Cortes Island, and all of my Bainbridge Graduate Institute alumni for the wonderful memories.

I am very grateful to the members of Codex, a speculative fiction writers community, where we share knowledge on writing craft, the business of writing, and generally support each other. I'd especially like to thank the following Codexians who answered my questions on esoteric topics including signal propagation, Faraday cages, nuclear bomb blast radius, armor-piercing ammunition, EMPs, stealing airplanes, and more: Laurel Amberdine, Kyle Aisteach, J.S. Bangs, Steve Bein, Daniel Bensen, John Brown, Lee Budar-Danoff, Matthew Champine, Gwendolyn Clare, Ian Creasey, Malcolm Cross, Gary Cuba, Robert Dawson, Sarah Frost, Abby Goldsmith, Michael Kinn, John P. Murphy, Kate O'Connor, K.S. O'Neill, Kat Otis, Gray Rinehart, Lisa Shapter, David Walton, Jeremiah Wolf, and Sylvia Spruck Wrigley.

Several professionals were involved in the making of this book, but none were harmed. Dario Ciriello, a wonderful editor and champion of authors, and a great writer himself, provided developmental critique and copyediting. Steve Bieler, another fabulous writer friend, took on the challenging task of proofreading. Someday I'll learn where to put those commas and hyphens. The beautiful cover design was a collaboration between Jason Gurley, who did the initial concept, and M.S. Corley, who created the final cover you see today.

This series would not be what it is today without the tireless work of Maureen Gately, who has played many pivotal roles over the course of the series, including cover designer, graphic artist, interior layout, proofreading, beta reading, and industry advisor. Thank you, Maureen, for all of your extensive and critical contributions.

I also want to mention several writers from my local writing community, including Annie Bellet, Jason Brick, Jason Gurley and Erik Wecks. There are many others as well, but these four have consistently contributed emotional support, professional wisdom, and friendship. I also want to thank Gene Kim for sharing his wisdom as we've journeyed down similar paths.

Special thanks to Erin Gately and to my children for their encouragement, support, and patience when I've been busy writing or off at events.

I deeply appreciate the ongoing patrons who signed up through Patreon (patreon.com/hertling) to help support this book as well as my writing career in general. In return, patrons receive early access to upcoming books and other benefits. The supporters include: James Anderson, Ben Bieker, Steven E. Burchett, Robert Dobbin, Eugene Epshteyn, Brad Feld, Erin Gately, Bernard Golden, Caleb Johnson, Nicole J. LeBoeuf, Jacob Perkins, Nima Bigdely Shamlo, and Robert Solovay. Their continuing assistance helps support this whole endeavor, which allows me to spend more time doing what I love—writing—so I can get more books out quicker.

Finally, thank you to the readers who have bought my books, posted reviews, and amplified the signal, or contacted me in some way to let me know what you thought. Thank you for following this series across thirty years and multiple genres.

Printed in Great Britain
by Amazon.co.uk, Ltd.,
Marston Gate.